JADEN

Tijan

DEDICATION

I always dedicate my books to my readers, but this one is dedicated to all the readers who loved *Jaded*, all the way back at Fictionpress. I also want to dedicate this book to two specific ladies. They both have breathed new life and love into this series, so thank you, Kerri and Lisa.

CHAPTER ONE

The day they arrested me everything happened in slow motion. They came for me outside of my classroom. It was the last day I had Miss Connors as my professor, and she had given me a hug. I stepped through the doorway, and two plainclothes detectives were there. Another uniformed officer stood beside them, and I saw the handcuffs next. Their eyes were dead. They didn't care who I was, who I loved, or as I looked over my shoulder at an old mentor—who I disappointed.

Miss Connors had a hand to her mouth, but there wasn't shock in her eyes. That's what stopped me. She wasn't surprised. She had counseled me after Marcus tried to kill me and when I had killed him instead. She'd given me advice and listened to my smart-ass comments.

She broke through my wall. Not many did that.

When they recited my Miranda rights, my head was bent. I knew the rest of my classroom had stopped to watch. I heard Carolina's voice in the distance, but it was faint. A buzzing sounded in my ear, and I couldn't shake it away. Then they pushed me forward. The uniformed cop took hold of my elbow, and I was led through the courtyard of the campus.

"Sheldon!"

I heard Corrigan's shout, and my heart skipped for a moment. There was disbelief in his voice.

He still believed.

As they drove me to the station, I concentrated on my breaths. One. Two. They were so shallow, but I kept going. My heart was racing, and I frowned at my lap. I didn't want to have a heart attack. Could a twenty-one year old have one? I couldn't stop a sadistic laugh breaking free as I thought about my life. If anyone would have one, it'd be me.

When I was brought through the station, I felt a burning in my stomach, and I lifted my head. Officer Patterson was in front of her desk. Her dirty blond hair was messed up, but when wasn't it? A cup of coffee was in her hand, and I wondered if that was her twentieth. She drank too many of those. I never cared before, but now I wondered if I should voice my concern.

Then I was in an interview room, and my handcuffs were clasped through a peg in the table.

They thought I was going to run. They couldn't have thought I was dangerous.

Another burst of laughter threatened to bubble up. They did think I was dangerous. Who was I? Not a spy. I was a college student. I had two friends, well—Denton had promised only friendship. So, I had three friends.

A file slammed on the table, and I jumped from the sound. Then a low baritone chuckle sounded out of a burly guy dressed in a blue-collared shirt and dress pants. His shirt had been loosened, and from the amount of wrinkles, it had been pulled out a long time ago.

"She jumps." He sat across from me and threw a leg up to rest on the opposite knee. He was the epitome of carefree.

I wanted to snarl at him. I wanted to frighten him back, but I didn't. He wanted that. Already I knew their game; it was what I'd do.

He flipped the file open and yawned.

My eye twitched. The ass yawned. This was my life and he yawned, but I closed my eyes and counted my breaths again. One. Two. Three—

"How'd you know Grace Barton?"

My arm jerked, and I drew in a breath. He sounded bored. He asked about my friend, and it sounded like he'd rather be taking a dump. He probably did.

"Hey. I'm talking to you." He leaned forward and snapped his fingers near my face.

I wanted to bite them off.

"Jeezus." He turned when the door opened. "She ain't talking."

A feminine voice spoke, "Yet."

She sounded arrogant.

I wanted to sink my teeth into both of them.

"She will." Laughter was evident in her voice as I heard another chair scrape against the floor. It squeaked under her weight. I wondered if she threw her leg up as well. They would've been a pair.

Then she leaned forward, and the amusement dropped. "Your purse was found in her car."

My heart pounded in my ears again. It was starting to thump so hard that my chest grew painful.

Breathe, Sheldon. One. Two. Three.

"She poured two glasses of wine. We know it was someone she knew. There was no forced entry. She had a movie playing on the television." The woman detective drew in a deep breath, and she gentled her tone, "Did you watch chick flicks together? Maybe the latest vampire teen movie, you know the one that's been so popular for a long time? A goddamn apple's on the cover of it. You know the one."

I drew in a shuddering breath. Grace had loved that movie. I loathed it after the one time she got me to watch it. I left after thirty minutes when Bryce called.

Pain stabbed me from regret. We'd been good friends then, and I had ditched her. Sex with my boyfriend seemed like a better way to spend the afternoon.

So much had changed.

And I swallowed again. Grace was dead.

"A lot of people are scared of you, Sheldon."

The urge to snicker threw me to the side. Why would I want to laugh at that? Then it clicked. Officer Patterson had told me one time, 'Use their first name. It starts to establish a connection. When they want to pee their pants and you're offering the one bit of sympathy their way, they'll start blabbering like you're best friends. We use it in interrogation tactics.'

The woman detective had started to tap a pen against the table, but she stopped now. And waited.

They would wait forever.

Then she sighed in disgust. "Come on, Sheldon! We're not the enemy. We just want to know what happened. We know you were there that night. We've got your purse, and there's some of your hair on the couch. We have your DNA. One of the wineglasses had a thumbprint, too. You were there, Sheldon!" She smacked a hand on the table. "Tell us what happened."

"Molls."

"What?" she snapped at him. Then, a moment later, she started again in a calmer voice. "You guys had been friends since high school, right? We have her confession on tape about what she did to you. That must've made you mad, huh? She was your friend. From what we've been told, you don't have a lot of friends, but that's because you intimidate people. Don't you, Sheldon? You scare them away before they can hurt you. Isn't that right? Or maybe I have it all wrong. You tell me."

My eyes were still clasped shut, but I envisioned her. She said her piece, threw her arms in the air, and folded them behind her head as she leaned back. She was in control again.

Something died in me.

They sounded so sure of whatever their accusation was. I tried to remember back to the classroom and what they had said when they put the handcuffs on . . . "Sheldon Jeneve, you are under arrest for the murder of Grace Barton . . ."

The rest faded from memory. It happened twenty minutes ago.

"Look . . ."

The guy detective must've gotten bored. A tone of impatience was clear.

He continued, "Let's cut the bullshit, okay? You and Grace were friends. We know that. You had a falling out. We know that, too. Then the night she admitted that she was the one who pushed you into a glass table, we found her dead. She died in her home, but I bet you knew that. Right? She was there because we think she was scared of her sorority, the sorority that wanted you to pledge. They wanted you, you bartered for her too, and then you backed out. They were stuck with her. They wanted you, not her.

Grace knew that. She was trying to fit in with them. She was desperate for friends—"

My voice cracked as I choked out, "How do you know that?"

He stopped for a second and then leaned forward. His voice was excited. "How do we know that she wanted friends? Or—"

"How do you know she was desperate?"

"She told us in her statement when she confessed about the hazing."

"Oh." And then I felt foolish. I knew that. I'd always known that.

"Witnesses told us that you had a confrontation with her. A sorority you were friendly with was caught pranking her sorority?"

His partner added, "Denton Steele was a witness as well." She sighed. "I'd like to get his witness testimony."

He chuckled. "Yeah, right. I'm sure his lawyers will open their doors for us."

I held my breath as they fell silent. I knew what they were doing. I was in a vulnerable state. They attacked me and gave me an olive branch. They gave me something I thought they wanted or I could provide for them. I was supposed to jump on that. I was supposed to look up, eager, and tell them that I could call Denton. He'd give his account of that night. I was supposed to think he'd come in with support for me, but they'd use that to question him about my relationship with him.

Denton was a celebrity. He used to be my neighbor. Our parents were best friends, and once upon a time, we'd had sex, twice. One of those times was when I cheated on Bryce. Not a stellar reputation for me, but they knew that. What they didn't know was that I wasn't stupid.

I knew how to play the game. I'd been doing it since I was a child.

People feared me, but it was because I spoke the truth, and I went for the jugular. I knew how to take anyone down, except for friends . . . well . . . I took Grace down that night. I lashed out at her and humiliated her in front of her sorority friends. I enjoyed it, and I had plans to do it again, but then she shook me. She apologized and seemed to mean it. Not many did that. It was always fake. Everyone lied to cover their bases, but no one really changed.

That night, I thought Grace had changed.

Why would I want to harm someone for that?

They were wrong. It was a matter of time before they found the real killer. I had to believe that. I had to hope for that, otherwise—I drew in another shuddering breath—what else could I hope for?

An awkward silence filled the room, and I waited until the lady detective started to tap her pen again. It would happen—and then it did.

Tap, tap.

It was more urgent this time. She was growing impatient. And I could sense the anger in her. I hadn't fallen into their trap. I held my breath and waited again. What was the next move?

"Okay, fine." She shoved forward, and I heard her voice grow in volume. She was closer to me now. "You're not stupid. We got it, but facts are facts. You were in Grace's house the night she was murdered. If you didn't do it, you saw who did. We both know you were there. We have video footage from the street."

I looked up now and held her gaze. I didn't blink.

She stopped for a second. She had brown eyes with bags underneath them. Her mascara was smudged. It looked like that had happened hours ago. And the tan complexion on her skin looked washed out. I asked in a quiet voice, "When'd you last sleep?"

She blinked.

"You look like you've been up for a couple of days now."

A startled expression flashed over her, but she blinked again and shook it away. Her jaw hardened when she clipped out, "You want to psychoanalyze me? I've been up for thirty-six hours now because I've got a dead girl that shouldn't be dead. And you know what really pisses me off? I'm pretty sure the girl who killed her did it out of spite and because her daddy is rich enough to get her off. This girl has some high-powered friends with lawyers that are already pounding our doors down. And I'm wondering which one of your rich boyfriends is paying their salary. So yeah, I've lost some sleep. Grace Barton was an innocent little girl who got caught up with the wrong, deadly group. She was playing a game with high stakes that she should've never been a part of, and I feel bad for her. I feel bad she ever considered you a friend."

She shot out of her chair and leaned across the table. Her face was against mine. Her breath was hot on my skin as she snapped, "So cut the bullshit and tell us what happened."

"I've got lawyers asking to see me?"

Her face twitched and her partner let loose curses under his breath.

"I want a lawyer," I said it so calmly, as if I always sat in that chair, on that side of the table, with my life held in question. I knew my eyes were flat. They always went flat when I was on the attack, but my insides were churning.

Someone killed Grace, and they thought it was me.

Everything happened after that in a blur. They shot out of there with stiff shoulders and anger in their eyes. Three lawyers entered after that, and I thought Denton had sent them. They never questioned me, but they instructed me. I wasn't supposed to say a word. I would be taken into holding, and I'd have to wait until bail was set. No matter the amount, I was reassured it would get paid.

I didn't care.

Denton. Bryce. They both had money. So did I. My father made sure my inheritance was substantial before he disappeared years ago.

Then the lawyers told me that my mother was at the police station. She wanted to see me, but I shook my head. I didn't want to deal with her. I hadn't for the last few years, why start now? The two, now three, people that I did want to see were advised against coming. Their names needed to be clear from this media frenzy.

My head popped up when they said that, and a lawyer told me as if he were a robot and I were a rock, that paparazzi were already outside. Grace Barton's death was linked back to Marcus' and since Bryce was connected, along with Denton, it was going to spread all over the country. A movie star and soccer's newest star, both in love with the same girl—I couldn't stop the cringe when I heard that—was gold for social media.

Everyone would know my name.

That was when I stopped listening. I didn't want anyone to know.

Corrigan's shout from earlier ripped through me. I never looked at him. I didn't dare. I would've bolted for him, and he would've fought for me. And then what would've happened? We would've both been in police custody. But then again, a small chuckle slipped out, it would've been like the old days. Except Corrigan was the one that always seemed to be calling us from the police station, and Bryce and I would come down to post his bail.

The humor left me then. It was me this time, but I wasn't in for a high school prank.

As I was led through booking and had my prints and my mugshot taken and then was told to wait in an overcrowded cell, I wanted to wake up. I wanted all this to be a dream, a nightmare, but then I found a corner in the back and sat down against the cold wall. I shivered and refrained from hugging myself.

A few girls were already sizing me up.

I wasn't weak. I wasn't about to start acting like it now.

I lifted my chin and gazed back. Everything in me was numb now.

I was being charged with Grace's murder. What worse could happen?

CHAPTER TWO

Lawyers posted my bail that afternoon, and instead of being led out the front, they took me out the back. We went down a flight of stairs and came out into the basement of a parking garage. A black limousine was parked in front, but two of the lawyers directed me to a car behind it. There were two other cars, all black, all nondescript.

We waited a moment, and I stood there while the lawyers bent their heads with a few of the police officers. They kept looking toward the wall and gestured with wide arm movements. It was then I realized I was hearing a buzz. I frowned as I tried to concentrate. That sound wasn't normal. Something was off, and then I heard a surge of shouts and a few flashes made their way into the basement.

Media.

I glanced up, taken aback. That's what this whole thing was about. They were creating a diversion for me. What they had said before had been true. But then one of the lawyers came toward me and gestured to one of the smaller cars. As I got in, he sat beside me, and we waited again.

I tried to see from my window. Two police motorcycles passed us. I assumed they took the front. Their lights flashed against the cement wall around us, and then I twisted around. There were two more behind us, along with a squad car. I could only imagine another squad car was in the front as well.

And then we inched forward. The police first, the limousine second, the third and fourth cars after them. We turned right when they inched to the left.

Paparazzi swarmed around them. I couldn't believe it. There were television camera crews and reporters everywhere. The limousine couldn't even move. A few men climbed on top of the limousine. Some tried to take pictures through the blackened sunroof.

My throat went dry at the sight. They were there for me, because I was linked to Bryce and Denton. And because they thought I killed my friend.

The lawyer beside me handed me a newspaper. He spoke in a bland voice, "You've been nicknamed already. You're 'The Queen Bee Killer.'"

I took the paper and saw the headlines. In bold capital letters was what he said. I saw a picture of myself from school, one of Bryce at one of his games, and one from the latest movie premiere Denton had attended. My stomach twisted, and I crumpled the newspaper into a ball. I glanced at him, disgust in my gut, and asked, "You think that's funny?"

He shrugged. "You'll get a lot of coverage from it. It's a good name."

"It's a lie." I lifted my mouth in a snarl.

The grin didn't leave, and he shrugged again. "There's no such thing as bad publicity."

My eyes went flat. "Or maybe it's true. Maybe I did kill her. You want to piss me off? I might gut you here and now."

His head whipped to mine, and the smirk vanished.

Finally. I relaxed against my seat. That was all I wanted.

He paled. "You wouldn't. I'm your lawyer."

I shrugged and smirked this time. "I'm sure there's more where you came from."

The other lawyer beside me shifted in his seat, but no other words were shared. After we drove for a while, I lost interest in where we were going. I wasn't stupid. I knew we wouldn't be going where I considered home, and I was right when we pulled up to a gate an hour later.

The gate was large, black, and imposing. It was a complete wall. The driver got out and pushed a button near it. A buzz was heard, but the driver bent down and spoke into the button. A moment later, he returned to the car, and the gate slid up. We rolled underneath it, and it went back down. It landed with a thud, and we had to drive another mile before the driveway curved to the right and a clearing opened for us. Everything was covered with a forest, but then we got a view of a mansion.

It looked like a castle, and my eyes couldn't help but go wide. Whose was this?

The front door opened, and I jerked forward in the seat. My seatbelt tightened, and I was shoved back, but I couldn't look away. I couldn't close my mouth. Everything stopped in that moment.

When we slid to a stop and the lawyers got out of the car, I was slower. My body had trouble moving, and my legs were stiff. My arms shook, and my heart raced as I pulled myself up outside the car. I had to hold onto it or I would've fallen. I heard my knees knocking against each other. I couldn't feel them, but I heard them.

"Hello, Sheldon."

The man before me was in his forties. He was dressed in a black business suit, which fit him like a glove, and he gazed back at me. He waited for my reaction. There were no words.

"Dad?"

He still had his thinning hair, but it was darker than I remembered. A rush of air left me. I lifted my hands and watched how they shook before me. I was detached from my body. Nothing made sense, but my dad was in front of me.

He had left for Europe. I never heard from him again and now . . . he was in front of me.

I stepped closer and studied him. There were crease lines at the ends of his eyes, like he had to squint a lot. There were worry lines on his forehead. His shoulders were the same, maybe thinner, but his eyes . . . I couldn't look away from them. They studied me as much as I studied him.

He blinked. A shine of tears was there, but he managed a small grin. "How are you, Sheldon?"

"Not good."

Then he laughed. The corner of his lips curved in. His two dimples flashed at me, but then he shook his head and wiped at the corners of his eyes. "No, you're not doing well right now, are you?"

"You bailed me out of jail. Those are your lawyers." Not Denton's. Not Bryce's. I twisted around and looked them over again. Another car pulled up behind us, and four more lawyers got out. All black business suits, all with bland features. And then I looked at the house, around the estate. "Who the hell are you?"

Neil chuckled and reached forward.

I cringed and ducked out of his way. "Don't. Don't touch me."

The grin fell away, and he sighed. He looked so tired then. "You've had a shock. I can see that."

"I want to talk to my friends."

"Your friends?" He frowned at one of the lawyers, the douche bag who had spoken to me in the car. "I thought you said her mother was at the police station?"

He clipped out a nod. "She was." His gaze slid to me. "She refused to see her."

Neil reared back an inch. His frown deepened, and he studied me again. "You didn't want to see your mother?"

I snorted. "Would you?"

A glimmer of a smile flirted across his face, but he ended on a solemn note. "No. I wouldn't."

I swallowed thickly. My mind still raced. "I want to see Bryce and Corrigan."

His shoulders sagged, and a sense of disappointment flared inside me when he murmured, "You're still friends with them."

"Yes." Though he hadn't said it as a question.

My father jerked his head in a nod and rubbed at his jaw. "It seems that some things have not changed in four and a half years."

"Except you." My shoulder twitched. What was that about? "What happened to you? I've had people ask where you were, but I didn't know."

"I left you money."

"That's not the question."

His eyes widened a slight inch, and he stepped back. He grew quiet, and his hand stopped rubbing his jaw. Then he laughed on a rueful note. "My god, you've grown up, Sheldon. You were confused and hurting the last time I saw you, but now . . . look at you. You're a woman. You're all grown up."

My jaw clenched, and my hands slammed against my sides. "I'm also accused of murder."

"Yes, I am aware. That's why I reached out to you."

Everything was wishy-washy for me. I knew I spoke how I always did, calm and strong, but my insides were twisting and churning. My stomach was doing constant somersaults, and I felt like a massive army of worms were slithering their way through my body. But at his words, everything stopped. A stone dropped in me. It all clicked into place.

My voice was hoarse. "You wouldn't have come forward, would you? If I hadn't been arrested, you never would've let me know where you were."

He didn't say anything. He didn't have to.

A wall went over me, and I turned away from him. This was a stranger in front of me. This wasn't my father anymore.

Then I looked around. "I'm right when I assume I'm going to be staying here?"

He nodded. His jaw clenched.

"Then I need a bag of my stuff. I need my clothes. And homework, I can't get behind."

"You won't. We've arranged for all of that, but you've been let go from the university. You can reapply after all of this is over. That's what their representative told my assistant, anyway." His voice was business-like now. He was the professional diplomat I always knew he'd been with his companies. "My assistant was able to get all your clothes, too."

"Well." I pressed a hand to my stomach. I would process all of that later. "Your assistant must've been very busy in the last five hours."

"She was. Beth is the best."

I felt a kick to my gut. I heard the admiration in his voice.

"I'll introduce you two, if you'd like to go inside." He shifted toward the castle.

I grabbed the backpack the police gave back to me and threw it over my shoulder. As we climbed the two levels of stairs and passed both tiers of plants and flowers, I felt like I was marching to my doom. And then my father stepped inside first, and I was transported to some English palace of royalty. Everything was gold and old. It might not have been a fair assessment, but I expected to see a butler emerge from the shadows along with two maids dressed in black dresses with white ruffles. When none emerged, I was relieved, a little bit.

And then we went farther inside, down the long hallway that extended from the foyer, and he turned into a large room. Windows were placed all around the wall. They extended from the ceiling to the floor, and white sheer curtains draped over them. They all had gold bordering on the ends, and I sighed again.

The place was cold and impersonal.

"Neil?" A soft feminine voice came from behind us.

He turned with a wide smile on his face. He held a hand out, and she came forward with a graceful smile. Her feet barely touched the floor as she glided toward us. As she took his hand in hers, she looked at me and stopped short. The lively mirth in her eyes fell away, and her smile vanished. She looked down to the floor.

I snorted.

Even her blond hair was pulled into a classy-looking bun. Fucking Mary Poppins had arrived as my father's glorified secretary. When his hand skimmed down her arm and fell away, I was pretty sure they were sleeping together, too.

"Sheldon." He didn't disguise the admiration in his tone. "This is Bethany Maller. You should be very nice to her. She's going to be your best friend here."

"Really?" My tone went flat.

She looked back up, but jerked her head to the side.

I sighed on the inside. She couldn't even meet my gaze. I held back my snarl, but this was going to be my best friend? This was going to be my jailor.

"Yes." His chest puffed up with pride. "She's a machine, Sheldon. She's the one who arranged everything for your stay with us. She has been in touch with the university, and she's the contact with the police as well. They know you'll be staying with us and have allowed it, but you mustn't leave the gate. You can explore within the gate, but you can't leave."

"Am I on house arrest?"

"Your bond was five million. I was able to post it so soon with the promise you wouldn't leave the estates. Don't make me lose five million, honey."

I folded my arms. "Don't call me that."

He drew upright. "I'm sorry. Sheldon."

I fixed Beth with a stare and stuck out my chin. "I want to see my friends. Denton Steele. Bryce Scout. And Corrigan Raimler. You got those names in your steel-encased brain?"

"Sheldon!" My father's voice whipped at me. "You will not be rude to her. I will not tolerate that attitude."

Then I turned my dead eyes to him. "What are you going to do, Pops? Send me back to jail?" I shrugged. "I'll get someone else to post my bail then. You're not the only 'Daddy' Warbucks I know."

"Sheldon. My god." He grasped my elbow. "Maybe you haven't grown up—"

"Excuse me? You show up out of nowhere, post my bail, and bring me to some reclusive hiding place you've got going on. Then you tell me what I'm allowed to do and not do? Pretty sure I can go back to jail, get bailed out by Denton or Bryce, and I'll still have a life. This isn't a life. This isn't a country where you can dictate my every move."

I spun on my heel and started to march away, but his words stopped me. "You're not safe."

I froze and remembered the paparazzi mob at the police station.

His voice was gentled. "You're a hit, Sheldon. My little girl got famous, but you're hated along with that. People think you killed your friend. They think you killed Marcus now. They think you're behind all of it."

I whirled around, pale. I couldn't believe what I was hearing. "I didn't kill Grace. And Marcus stalked me. He killed two of my friends."

Beth cleared her throat; it was dainty. "Uh, well, I talked with the detectives assigned to your case, and they're pulling all those cases back up. They re-examining everything, Sheldon."

My chest rose up and down. I had a hard time getting air. "You're saying they think I killed them? That I killed Leisha and Bailey?"

"You have a history of bullying people."

"I bully bullies. Never them, never people who can't protect themselves. That's despicable."

My father came forward. His eyes were sad. "You have a history of doing that very thing, Sheldon. You and Corrigan. Both of you were very hurtful to other students in high school. I received a lot of calls from the school's administration. I just never told you. I paid many of those parents to remain quiet, and they have been, but it's different now. The rules have changed."

My chest hurt. Something was pressing down on it.

"All your ghosts are going to come out. Everyone who's been hurt. Everyone any of you hurt—you, Corrigan, and Bryce included. All three of you ran your school harshly, and you know it, Sheldon."

"I protected myself." My voice was a whisper now. Something grabbed my heart and squeezed it. I felt it crumpling as I tried to breathe. "If they tried to hurt me, I hurt them back. That was it. That's all I did."

"That wasn't it and you know it. All three of you are to blame."

My mouth dropped. Who was he to judge? I snapped it shut. "I'm sorry. Are you my freaking God now? What place of holy hell are you at where you can judge me? You donated your sperm to Mom. Thanks for that. Did you raise me? Did she?" I narrowed my eyes and felt my blood start to boil. "No, I raised myself in spite of you two."

"Sheldon." He sighed and rubbed his hands together. They fell down against his suit next. "I'm not here for a family counseling session, though that might be helpful in the future. I'm here to help my daughter and to protect you. The estates are not a prison to you. You were brought here for your protection."

Beth edged forward. Her eyes glimmered with hope. "I have a room readied for you. You could wash up, if you'd like. I also have a phone for you to use. I guessed you'd wish to converse with your friends, and I sent them each a phone as well. They will be untraceable. There will be no records of the calls." She frowned. "Though I wasn't aware you were close with Denton Steele."

My dad snorted. "He grew up next door. His folks were best friends with Sharon and me." He shuddered. "That was a big mistake."

I thrust my hand out. "I want that phone."

Beth sucked in her breath, and her eyes went wide again.

CHAPTER THREE

"Are you okay?"

I had the phone pressed to my ear when Corrigan answered. Before answering, I turned and skimmed the hallway. I needed to make sure there were no lurkers. When I saw it was empty, I shut my bedroom door and sighed. "If you were to guess?"

"I'm sorry, Sheldon."

I sighed. A pounding headache was pressing against my temples, but fuck it. When I saw the room Beth had prepared for me, I laughed to myself in disbelief.

"What?"

"My dad's girlfriend must be really scared of me."

"What?"

I didn't pay attention to how his voice had sharpened. I was too busy scanning the living area, with a sectional in one corner, positioned toward a wall that had a large flat screen television mounted from it. Beside the sectional were two patio doors, and I could see a large table and chairs set up out there. An impressive view of the lawns was beneath the patio, and then I turned toward the rest of my room. Behind the sectional was a king-sized bed, located on top of a platform. Two closet doors were on one side, and there was a hallway—a freaking hallway—that led to a bathroom. "Shit," I muttered when I saw the tub. It was big enough for a three-person orgy to happen in there. Corrigan would crawl in with floaters and a snorkel. I had no doubt.

"What?"

I heard Corrigan's question and remembered I was on the phone. "Huh?"

"You said 'shit.' What's going on?"

"Oh. Nothing." I plopped down on one of the couches. I could still see the lawns from where I sat and even got a glimpse of a fountain. Toeing off my sandals, I sunk down on the cushions and wished I could sleep, but I knew I couldn't. I wasn't even going to try right now. I said into the phone, "I was saying that my dad's new girlfriend must be scared of me. The room she gave me is an apartment. For real." I scanned the room again. "The only thing I don't have is a kitchen, but hell, I bet she's got a mini fridge stuck somewhere in this room. I have a freaking hallway in my room. Can you believe that?"

"Okay. Back up. Your dad?"

I sighed. That's right. He had no idea so I told him everything. The surprise reappearance, how he posted my bail, the forest fortress, and the magical secretary/girlfriend that seemed too familiar around my dad for me to believe it was a new development. When I was done, Corrigan grunted. "Shit. I was going to brag that Denton, Bryce, and I all came together to storm the jail and demand your bail, but we got upstaged. I can't beat that."

All three of them were together? Right then? "Wait, you mean Bryce is there?" I suddenly felt a weight pressing down on my windpipe. A suffocating sensation was building within me.

"Yeah." His voice softened. "You want to talk to him?"

I did. "No." Later. I wasn't ready right then and there. "Listen, I'm going to demand for you guys to come here."

"I have a feeling your dad won't be on the Corrigan and Bryce bandwagon. I don't think it'll be a go, unless you can reenact the drive there and give us directions? Then we're all about that."

A low growl started from my throat. He was right. I cursed under my breath.

Corrigan chuckled. "I know he liked Bryce, but that was a long time ago. And him stepping in and getting bail before we could, that has to mean something."

And it did.

I found out an hour later when I was standing in his study and demanding my friends be given directions. I was met with a firm and final. "No."

"Why not?" My arms were crossed so tight over my chest, my breasts felt constricted, but I couldn't loosen them. I was holding myself back from lunging and putting him in a headlock, then trying to force the address out of him. It would've looked ridiculous, but it would've been fun at least.

My dad ran a hand down his face. The bags under his eyes seemed to have gotten bigger. "No, Sheldon. You're here for your protection, too. People hate you. They want to hurt you, and anyone knows the quickest way to you is through them. They'll follow them, and even though those boys love you, they'll be bringing some haters right to your doorstep. I can't allow that. I've been gone, but it was for your safety. I stepped in because I was forced to."

I snorted in disbelief. "Your absence was for my safety? Are you growing weed somewhere in this fortress? That'd make more sense. Clue in, Father dear. I had a stalker who tried to kill my friends and me, and then shit started happening again last year. I've never been safe."

"This is different."

"How?"

He shoved out of his chair and yelled, hitting the desk with his finger at the same time, "YOU'RE WANTED FOR MURDER!" He stopped, grimaced, and lowered his voice. "The entire nation hates you, Sheldon. Grace was a good girl. She was lost and hurting, and she wanted to be accepted—"

"She *was* accepted." By me.

He kept going as if I hadn't spoken, "—and the police have arrested you as the suspect. With your history, with everything you have done or has happened to you, it's all being brought up. The media has already painted you as a spoiled rich bully. That's what you are to them, and your attitude of *fuck off* is what they salivate over. You have dark hair. Grace had beautiful blond hair. Good and evil. That's what the nation understands, and the media is handing it to them on a silver platter."

"I need my family—"

"I am your family!"

"No, you're not. You're not. I don't ever remember a time when you were. Bryce and Corrigan are my family, and I want them here."

"They can't come here—"

All the crap he'd been dishing at me fell on deaf ears. I wasn't dumb. I knew how I was being painted, but he wasn't going to win this one. This time, I leaned forward and hit the desk with my finger. This time I was the one who yelled at him, "THEN GET

THEM HERE! You do it. You figure it out because if you don't, I'm finding a way out of here, and I'll hitchhike all the way back to the city, no matter what car picks me up."

I swept out of there.

My blood was pumping; the old Sheldon was tearing at me from inside. The old me would've trashed the house, then got obliterated and had sex. That wasn't me anymore, but damn, gritting my teeth, I wanted to do some damage. My fingers curled into my palms, and I sunk my nails into my skin. I pushed them farther in and stood there, trying to calm myself down.

"Oh my god," Beth gasped from behind me and then hurried around me. She disappeared down the hallway, but returned a moment later with towels. "Sheldon," her tone turned cautious, "you are bleeding all over the floor. I need to look at your hands."

I needed my family. Lifting haunted eyes to her, I said, "You're not my family."

"I know." Her hand clenched tighter around the towels. "Can I look at your hands?"

I clipped my head to the side. "A lot of bad shit has happened to me."

"I know."

She was speaking so softly to me, like a timid mouse, but for some reason I needed her to understand. I said, "I'm not crazy. I'm not horrible. I'm not a murderer. I can be a bitch, that's it. People have always wanted to take me down, and I don't let them. That's what I've done. That's my mistake, standing up for myself." An inner voice laughed in my ear. *Yeah, right. You've done your own damage.* I muttered, half to myself and half to Beth, "I need to find out who killed Grace. I can't stay here; I'm trapped."

As I was speaking, I was half aware of Beth kneeling at my feet. My hands were touched, then peeled back, and she pressed something into them. Pain sliced through, but I was barely mindful of it. It couldn't cut through the other pain that was already in me. Nothing could quiet the need to avenge what had happened to me.

I was led to a room. Water was turned on, and I felt Beth starting to clean my hands. I let her, and I told her at the same time, "I need my family."

She stopped and glanced up. "Your mother?"

"My family." I gave her a hard look. "You heard me in there. You know who I mean. I need them, not some guy who hasn't been around for years."

Turning off the water, she held my hands over the sink to let them dry. "Your father may not agree with me sharing this with you, but he's been away for a reason. He's had his own troubles over the years and staying away was for your safety, Sheldon, but trust me when I tell you that he never stopped thinking about you."

"He never cared before." The memory of when he came home one night flashed back to me. I told him someone had broken into the house, and he only wanted to talk to Bryce, to catch up and see how he was doing. It'd been a slap to my face, but that was the reality. Neil checked out long ago. Now he was demanding to be let back in? A snort came from me. Beth paused hearing it, and I pulled my hands away from her.

The storm had quieted inside me, a tiny bit, but I knew it would come back. I wasn't going to take this sitting back in a fortress. I knew that much.

Picking up some of the bandages she had laid out by the sink, I started to dress my own wounds. Beth moved back. I felt her gaze, watching me, and just kept doing it. I didn't stop until both of my hands had ointment applied to them and were wrapped up. When I was done, I glanced at her again.

There was a different look in her eyes. I didn't know it, and I didn't care to guess, but I murmured, "Please bring my family here."

With that said, I went to my room and a standoff commenced next.

A day went by. Nothing. They wanted me to meet with my lawyers so I refused. The longer he held back what I wanted, the longer I'd do the same to my father. My father would knock on my door with demands. I needed to be updated about my case. There were things going on, and I needed to know, but I refused everything. I didn't want to lash out like the old Sheldon. I'd been through too much crap to know better. I was more mature, dammit, but instead, I had to fight back in a different manner. I went the Gandhi route.

A second day went by. Still nothing, so I stopped going to meals with Neil and Beth. The few times I had sat with them had been tense anyway. It wasn't any great loss to me. The third day. Again, nothing. This time I just stopped talking to them. Again, no great loss. This was more beneficial to me. The fourth day. Same thing, so I stopped going anywhere within the fortress. I remained in my room.

This kept up for a week.

If this would last another week, I'd stop eating. I didn't want to do that, but I would. I wanted Bryce and Corrigan there, at least them. Denton would be a cherry on top at this point, but Neil remained steadfast. So after a second week of my silent protesting, I took the trays of food inside, but placed them back outside my room each night. No food was eaten.

Four more days went by.

I could withhold, but my dad pulled out all the stops. He even had pizza delivered and had the boxes set outside my room. I could smell that all day long. Then it was Chinese, then donuts, then the worst—coffee. I peeked out into the hallway once and was shocked. It resembled a school's cafeteria. Tables had been set up with buffet-style containers on top. Then I realized my dad had created a buffet line, but it was for everyone else to eat and for me to smell, and suffer over.

Bastard.

That was smart.

My stomach groaned and protested each morning, all day long. I thought I'd go numb from the hunger, that it might go away, but it never did. I just got hungrier and hungrier. And, seriously, the coffee aroma almost had me climaxing each morning.

I held firm, but it sucked.

Finally, after almost three weeks of this, the tables were taken away. I didn't know what that meant, but I just went back to bed. That was all I could do at this point. I was drained.

A soft knock woke me up that evening. I rolled over, but didn't get up. It would be Neil or Beth. She had started pleading with me to eat too, but instead I heard my dad say, "You won."

I sat up, but I couldn't talk. My throat hurt too much.

He sighed from the other side of the door. "They're coming."

My heart began to accelerate. I rasped out, "Are you lying to me?"

"No." He sounded defeated. "You won. Your boys are coming."

A rush of exhaustion overwhelmed me, and I lay back down. Finally.

*

I was sitting on the back terrace when the gates buzzed. I knew who it was. I'd been waiting all day. My body was riddled with knots, and when I heard the tires on the gravel, I couldn't sit still anymore. I stood, knocking the orange juice over. As it spilled across the table, Beth gasped. She dove forward with her napkin. "Sheldon!"

Two guards stood at the entrance. I paused for a moment. My father had said they were for my protection, but I wasn't sure. As I started for them, their hands went to their guns. I stopped. They stopped. My eyes narrowed, and my chin moved down. I asked, "Why can't I go out there?"

They glanced at each other, but didn't say a word.

She said from behind me, "Because they have to make sure it's them."

"I know it's them."

Beth came around with her hands full of wet napkins now. She was thin and frail looking, but I wasn't an idiot. My father's girlfriend had her own agenda. Disapproval was heavy in her gaze now as she raised her chin toward me. "You're here for your own safety—"

I shot her a dark look. I had waited for another week after my Gandhi protests were victorious and Neil kept reassuring me they were coming. He explained they needed to take precautions, to make sure they weren't followed, and to cover everything on their end, so they could stay awhile and not raise suspicion.

I didn't know if I could hold back anymore.

Beth started again, "You're not invincible—"

Fuck it. I started forward. I didn't hear the car doors open, but I didn't care. If they didn't come to me, I was going to them. They were only a few yards away now.

"Sheldon!"

The two guards moved together. They were a six-foot wall of muscle and machine guns. I rolled my eyes. It wasn't just my mother that tended to exaggerate. The amount of weaponry my father had was unnecessary. We weren't in a drug cartel.

"Move," I barked at them.

They waited for Beth's command. A disgusted sound came from her, and she muttered, "Yes, move. Let her go."

They parted, and I surged through them. Rounding the corner of the mansion, the doors on a black SUV opened. Even before the foot stepped onto the ground, I knew who it was. None of us had parted on good terms, but I didn't care. I felt them both in there. Then his black hair cleared the door, and I saw Bryce's startling blue eyes turn to me, and I launched myself. He took one step forward and caught me. His arms went around me, and my legs went around him. Shit. He was family. He was here.

It felt right. No matter the crap that happened, it was right.

"Sheldon."

At the sound of Corrigan's voice, I turned. My legs fell to the ground, and then he was hugging me, just as tightly as Bryce had been. Both of them were my family. He smoothed a hand down my hair and back and murmured, his head tucked against the side of mine, "Are you okay?"

I nodded. I couldn't talk, but I was okay at that moment.

Bryce said, "I was coming to bail you out. Denton, too, but when we got there, they said it'd already been posted." He gazed around, taking in the estate and mansion. "This is your dad's?"

Corrigan grunted. "Not so missing now, is he?"

I shook my head. "I don't want to talk about my dad." I paused. "Or my mom. Is there any news on the investigation?"

"Yeah." Corrigan's tone was somber.

"What?"

"That you did it."

I swatted at him. "That's not funny. I'm not laughing. I'm pissed."

He shrugged and stuffed his hands into his jean pockets. "That's all that's on the news. It's you, you alone who killed her."

"I didn't kill her."

Bryce said, "We know. I doubt they'd talk about anything else if it shed light on a different suspect. You're a known name now. The police's reputation is at stake if they find out someone else killed her."

I groaned. A headache was starting. "I can't handle this. I've been here for a month, and I'm already going nuts."

"Your dad's hardcore." Corrigan sounded frustrated.

I wasn't listening. The news was still all about me. What Bryce said was true. An anchor dropped to the pit of my stomach. They weren't going to look for a different killer. They were going to pin it on me one way or another. I closed my eyes as a helpless feeling came over me. I was drowning, and I was going to die if I didn't fight my way back to the surface.

I had to go back. I had to find who killed Grace.

Bryce had been watching me. He asked now, "Sheldon?" His eyes were narrowed.

I met them and shook my head. "We have to find who killed her. We have to, if they won't."

Corrigan let out a deep breath and raised a hand. "Can I make two suggestions?" He waited as we both looked at him. "One, we just got here, so can we wait a little bit? You don't know what we went through to get everything cleared so we could even get in that car to come to you. I'd like to chill for the night, at least. And the other thing, can we not bait the killer to your house, and can someone else get stabbed this time? That really sucked last time."

I grinned. A small chuckle escaped Bryce and me.

In that moment, that one split moment, it felt good. The three of us were back together. I took a little time to savor it, and then I decided, no matter what else happened, the three of us had to stay together. All the other shit was stupid.

CHAPTER FOUR

Once the excitement of having Bryce and Corrigan there had waned, the realization they were both there . . . at the same time . . . in the same room, filtered in and awkwardness ensued. Holy crap. The last few months had been tense anyway, but the last real communication with them had been when Bryce kissed me, and I left to cuddle with Corrigan in his hospital bed. I'd been on lockdown from almost everyone, and the times when I talked to Bryce or Corrigan hadn't been about us. Grace. Corrigan's health. Bryce's soccer training. Those had been the conversation topics, and now, well, everyone knew the new turn in Grace's murder investigation. Call me foolish, but I didn't want to talk about it the first night they got there. What that left was what was going on among all of us and glancing at each of them, seeing the clenched jaw, fisted hands, tight shoulders, I knew they weren't eager either.

"Well." This was lovely. "Guys, want to get drunk and watch a movie?"

"Yes."

"God yes." Bryce groaned.

We headed for the basement. When I showed them the movie theater, Corrigan's eyebrows went up. "Sheldon, this is a real theater."

I nodded. "My dad's rich." I paused. "Really rich."

The screen was mounted on one entire wall with leather couches set up in eight rows. Each end of the couch had a chair that lounged back and placeholders between the couches for drinks and snacks. Opening a cupboard, blankets were folded and piled high. I gestured to them. "If you guys get cold." Then I indicated a set of closed closet doors in the back of the room. Opening them, a bar was exposed with glasses hanging on the wall, and a good selection of beer and alcohol stored below in the refrigerator. Blue lights displayed the bar, so if the room was dark, we could still see what alcohol we were grabbing and pouring.

Corrigan laughed. "I've never been a huge fan of your dad's, but I think I now have a Neil Crush. Shit, Sheldon. I see where you get your love for booze."

Bryce chuckled. "We've always known. Half the time we got drunk, it was from her dad's liquor cabinet."

Um. I looked down. Half the time Bryce and I had gotten drunk, it was from my dad's liquor cabinet . . . not Corrigan. Those had also been the times we ended the night in bed and some of the times during the afternoon, too. I kept quiet. I wasn't going to clarify that for them.

Corrigan did, though. He barked out an abrupt laugh. "Right. That must've been your time together, the two of you. I know I usually brought my own alcohol over." He turned to me, pinning me in place with his gaze. "Or we got booze from The Café Diner. That was our tradition, apparently."

Bryce was quiet, and I had to admit I was relieved. Clapping my hands together, I looked around for the remote. "Well, then. How about a horror film?" I laughed. "It'd be appropriate for us."

I said it, and then I waited. My heart dropped. The joke wasn't a good one, and when I only heard silence from them, I knew they agreed. I shrugged. "What? Not even a pity laugh?"

Corrigan pressed his lips together and turned away.

Bryce shook his head, sighing. "Are you serious?"

"Come on. It's fucking awkward right now."

Corrigan looked back. "Yeah, guess whose fault that is? Not him or me. I know that much."

Bryce jerked his head up and down, and as the two were now standing next to each other, both turned toward me, waiting for my response, I didn't like this image. They were gorgeous. Bryce's jet-black hair had grown out, but not much. He had it spiked up, while Corrigan's hair had a little curl in it. Bryce was wearing a black shirt and jeans, and Corrigan had on a white polo over jeans. Both of them were lean with an athletic build, but Bryce had more definition. His soccer training had built his body into a machine that was for speed and strength, but he was so damn alert. His eyes were clear and focused solely on me, while Corrigan had a hurtful glint in his. However, they were still waiting for my response as I continued to stand and admire them.

In that moment, I felt like it was them versus me. Fuck me. I'd lose if that were the case. Rolling my shoulders back, I lifted my chin. "What?"

A wall slid over Corrigan's face, and Bryce rolled his eyes. He muttered, "Are you kidding me?"

"Look," I started, "I don't want to talk about it." I gestured around the room. "You're here. I hate my dad, but his place is kick-ass. Can we put on a movie and forget about real life for two hours?"

"No."

Corrigan muttered, "That'll make it more awkward."

"I'm not enjoying this conversation."

"Are you supposed to?" Bryce shot back at me.

I was startled by the fierceness in his tone and saw that Corrigan seemed to agree with him. Both were staring back at me with heated expressions.

"No." I took a breath, readying myself. This conversation was going to happen. "Okay. Fine. I don't know what to say. Nothing's changed."

They glanced at each other, and Corrigan said, "I think we just want to know what page we're all on."

I loved them both. That was the page, but I said, "You never shared your page with me, so I have no idea."

Bryce backed up a step.

Corrigan frowned. "And I said I didn't want to say anything until you—"

"Just fucking tell her," Bryce cut in. His shoulders were so rigid. "He loves you. I love you. And you haven't picked one yet."

Oh god. A sick sensation shot through me, all the way down to my feet. We were back to this, but who was I fooling? I needed to choose, but I couldn't lose the other one.

They were both waiting, watching me.

I pressed a hand to my stomach. "I can't, you guys. I can't pick, especially now. I need both of you."

"Sheldon," Bryce's voice softened, and he glanced sideways to Corrigan, "I think we'll both agree that the other one won't leave. We love you, and we wouldn't want to be anywhere else during this thing. We need you as much as you need us."

I shook my head. I couldn't. I didn't even know myself. "Guys . . . please . . ."

"You need to pick." Corrigan stepped forward. "It's not fair to us. You know that."

"No."

Bryce cast Corrigan a look. "I think we can wait, at least during this time. I know I won't be able to go anywhere anyway."

Corrigan turned back to him. "Are you serious? You're okay with just waiting and not knowing?"

"What's the alternative?" Bryce gestured to me. "She doesn't know. Look at her. You can see the panic in her eyes."

I frowned. He was right.

He continued, "She needs both of us, Cor. If she picks me, would you really stick around? I would, but damn, it would hurt. This isn't about us anyway. It's about what Sheldon needs."

Corrigan bit out, "Easy for you to say. You're the one she'll probably be screwing while she sneaks into my bed to be held." A nerve on the side of his jaw clenched outward. "I don't know about you, but that's a different torture all on its own."

"You'd rather have her pick? During this time? She'll feel cut off from the other one, and I'm sorry, but if she's found guilty, this might be our last time to spend with her. I don't want it defined and not be able to hold her."

My eyes got big. A new surge of panic drenched my insides with ice water. "Guilty?"

He swiftly turned to me. "I didn't mean that, but." He paused, looking down at the ground. "Someone set you up, Sheldon. What if we can't find out who did that? What then? I'm just . . . if you pick Corrigan, I can't spend this time with you and not be able to hold you." An anguished tone came to him. "Maybe that's me being selfish, but I can't do that. Even if you pick Corrigan, I still won't be able to stay away."

He held my gaze. Even though a few feet separated us, I felt like I was in the palm of his hand. He was holding me, stroking me, making me feel safe. Making me feel loved. My chest tightened. Then it exploded inside me. I loved Bryce. I never stopped, but it had been shoved down and numbed. With that, memories of our past came at me, and I was right back there on the day Marcus was in my home. I closed my eyes, but images of Corrigan stabbed and bleeding on the floor wouldn't go away. That sickening feeling. Fearing for his life, wondering if my best friend was going to die, knowing the guy responsible was still in my home, and he was going to get away.

I wanted to hunt him down, like he had hunted me down. The need for revenge, to take his life, had overwhelmed me. Bryce, too. He turned the tape off when I found Marcus and provoked him. It looked like self-defense, but the truth was, that I had killed him.

Oh god. I didn't want to remember that day, what we had done, what I had done. I turned away.

"Sheldon." Bryce started for me.

I shot a hand up, stopping him. "Don't. Please. Don't."

My shoulders lifted up and down, as I tried not to dry-heave. We killed him. Together. I'd been trying to forget that day for years, but I couldn't. I loved Bryce, but I couldn't forget what we had done, and the two were intertwined. That's why I put so much distance between us. If loving Bryce meant remembering that day, I had chosen to forget one if it meant forgetting the other, but my god, I couldn't forget how much I loved Bryce. It had never gone away, and just now, just this look from him, had unlocked the box again.

I took gasping breaths, trying to get ahold of myself and the storm that had been unleashed inside me. As I did, I glanced up. They were both waiting. Differing levels of concern were on their faces, but they had no idea what I was enduring.

"Please," I rasped out. "I want to forget." Marcus' death.

They nodded, thinking I was asking to forget about Grace.

I didn't clarify that. I didn't want to.

Corrigan went to grab some blankets as Bryce got some alcohol. Both of them went to the middle couch and waited for me. I settled down, and they sat on either side of me. I was stiff at first, wave after wave of blind terror was crashing down on me, but then Bryce pulled one of my legs over his lap and he started rubbing my thigh. It wasn't in a sexual manner, but a comforting one. He was trying to reassure me, and after a moment, it started to work. Some of my tension smoothed out. Then I felt Corrigan lift his arm, and he pulled my head into the crook of his shoulder, underneath his arm. I closed my eyes, feeling both of them there, both of them trying to take care of me.

It was true. I needed both of them. I loved them both, but I couldn't think about choosing. They were both my best friends, and that's what I needed most in that moment.

*

"Sheldon."

I grew aware of Corrigan saying my name. His shoulder nudged my head gently. He said, "Hey."

Bryce spoke over me, "She needs to sleep."

I'd fallen asleep, and as they kept talking, a lull was settling back over me. It was like a large blanket, enfolding all around me, making me feel warm and peaceful. I was falling back asleep, but I heard Corrigan murmur, "I know. You want to carry her?"

"You're still hurting from the accident?" As Bryce asked that, I felt myself lifted in the air. I was pulled tightly against a warm chest, a very solid, warm chest, and I could hear his heart under my head.

He stood and Corrigan said quietly from beside us, "Yeah. My ribs still ache at times, and my shoulder blade feels weird, too."

"All the time?"

"Nah. It comes and goes." His voice sounded a little clearer. "It'll get better. I don't know why it still hurts. The doctors said I'm healed."

Bryce tightened his hold on me, securing me even closer against him. "Do you know where we're going?"

Corrigan laughed softly. "No clue. This place is huge. I don't remember how to get back to her room or even ours."

"Our rooms are right next to hers." But Bryce paused, standing still. "Maybe we should just sleep in the theater?"

"And if she snuggles up to one of us?"

"Then she snuggles up to one of us. It's whoever she needs." Bryce's tone dipped down. "What's your problem? I thought we agreed on that."

"I know. I just," Corrigan hesitated, "she's going to pick you. I can see it. She loves you so much she's scared of it."

"You don't know that." Bryce stiffened underneath me. "Trust me, you don't know that. She might like to get fucked by me, but she goes to you for the emotional stuff. You don't think that kills me?"

"Bryce," Corrigan started, wariness in his tone.

"Stop, Corrigan. She loves both of us. You might only see how she feels about me, but I see how she feels about you. Whoever she chooses is the one she can't be without, but she loves both of us."

The heaviness from sleep was fading. The more they talked, the more awake I became, but I didn't want to wake up. I just wanted to sleep, to remain where I felt sheltered. Safe.

"Knowing Sheldon, she'll toss a fucking coin."

Bryce laughed. "That would suck, but yeah, I could see that."

"Denton called me earlier. I hope she doesn't pick him because she can't pick between us."

A low groan came from his chest, right where my head was resting. "He called me too, and fuck that, but I could see her doing that." He paused and murmured, "I hope not." He said that so quietly, with so much emotion, that it jolted me wide-awake. I knew without a doubt I would be haunted by his tone of voice just now.

"Hey." Bryce shifted and looked down at me. "You awake?"

I didn't open my eyes, but grumbled, "Your lack of faith in me is pissing me off."

Corrigan laughed from the side. "Yeah, well, we didn't want you think you could just use us to help you fall asleep every night."

I squirmed in Bryce's arm, getting more comfortable. My eyes were still closed. "Fuck that. Isn't that why you two are here? To help me sleep?" I grinned, teasing them, but I didn't want to look. I still didn't want to deal with the truth of what they were talking about.

"Ha-ha, Sheldon."

Bryce asked, "Where do you want to sleep?"

"In my bed." And with that said, I knew I'd have to open my eyes. After directing them to my room, I sent both of them away. No matter what was said, I knew it wasn't fair to use one for comfort and not the other. They were right. I did need to choose, but fuck, at the same time, I couldn't.

Both Bryce and Corrigan frowned at me from the hallway. I stood in my bedroom. The door was open between us, but we were all in a standoff. I lifted an eyebrow. "What?" My hand gripped the door, but I wasn't sure if it was to shut it or to hold me up.

"You're sure about this?"

I nodded. "You both are right. It feels weird to sleep with both of you, and I shouldn't lean on one and not the other. It's not right so I'm going to be sleeping alone from now on." I had been since Grace's murder, but knowing they were so close and saying those words aloud solidified it for me. I would've been tempted to crawl into one of their beds. It wasn't right. I needed them right now, but I needed to think about them, too.

I tried to smirk at them, but it failed. "I'll see you both in the morning then." That was meant as a joke, but there was nothing teasing about the statement or about how I said it. A knot was in my stomach, and as I stared back at them, it tightened. "Okay. Well. Goodnight."

They both continued to frown at me.

Feeling just all sorts of weirdness about this situation, I didn't know what else to do so I did the logical next thing.

I shut the door in their faces. Then I crawled into bed and didn't sleep for the rest of the night.

CHAPTER FIVE

I was tired the next day. I was tired the day after and the day after that. In fact, I was tired the entire week and the week after that, too. The thing that pissed me off was that I was the only one. I swear. Bryce and Corrigan seemed to have renewed their friendship. They were all about the hugging, laughing, slugging each other's shoulders, and they even started to have their own inside jokes.

Gag me.

Their cheerful attitudes wore off on Neil and Beth. My dad always adored Bryce so he seemed in heaven having him here. I could tell he got over whatever issue he had before allowing my friends to the house, and Beth, I didn't think she could prance any more around the house before it turned into a skip. She was giddy with Corrigan. It took me another week before I finally got it.

I was sitting outside on the patio lounger, watching both of them in deep conversation with Neil and Beth. Bryce was sitting under the shade, nodding at whatever my dad was saying and using his arms to make gestures. I heard the word 'soccer' a couple of times and 'football' the rest of the time so it didn't take a genius to figure out what they were talking about, but then I turned to the grilling area. Beth and Corrigan had their heads bent over a mixing bowl. He was wearing the apron she handed him, both in matching pink frilly aprons, and when she pointed to a garnish, he picked it up and broke it into pieces into the large bowl. After giving him an approving grin, she handed it over, and he resumed whisking it, smirking a little to himself. He glanced up, caught my gaze, and his eyes widened. He looked like he got caught at something.

I frowned.

They'd both been up their asses the whole month—then it hit me, smack in the forehead, and I felt like an idiot.

Bryce and Corrigan were working Neil and Beth. I didn't know why, but I knew they were. It made more sense. Bryce was always polite to my dad, but never this congenial, and Corrigan, well, he loved his mother so much that baking wasn't too far of a stretch, but his banter with Beth was flirtatious, not adoringly like he was with his mom.

Things made more sense. The world was right again. I could relax, not worried I woke up in an alternate universe.

I didn't get a chance to ask them their plan until after dinner. Beth made meatloaf—yes, meatloaf—but she topped it off with three glasses of Moscato wine. Neil joined in, and the two were as drunk as skunks. It didn't take long for the adults to giggle their way down the hallway and up to their room. That was when I shoved back from the table and stood up.

Both Bryce and Corrigan looked up.

I jerked my head toward the back door. "Outside. Now."

Each wore a guilty expression.

I snorted. I wasn't mad. I was just out of 'the know,' and that didn't sit well with me. As I sat in one of the loungers and they took the other two seats, I folded my arms over my chest. "I know you're doing something. Fill me in. Now."

They shared a look.

Bryce shook his head. "Fine."

Corrigan nodded. "Okay." He leaned forward, resting his elbows onto the table. "We've been out here too long. It's been three weeks and nothing. We need to get you into the city, and we need to do what you always do."

My eyes narrowed. "That doesn't sound like a compliment."

Corrigan's mouth flattened, and Bryce sighed. "Cut it out, Sheldon. You wreak havoc. It's what you do. We need that again. We need to figure out who's framing you." He glanced to Corrigan and seemed to hesitate for a moment. "I can't speak for Corrigan, but I've tried calling Officer Patterson. She won't return my calls, and she's never done that. I know Denton's tried, too."

"You're in contact with Denton?"

Bryce nodded. "Yeah. He tried to send his lawyers in, but your dad beat him to it."

I shook my head. "I thought it was his too, but they were my dad's lawyers."

"Yeah." Bryce scratched at his head. "I think he said something about that. He wasn't given a choice, just told to back off or something."

Corrigan's arms dropped and landed on the table with a thud. His eyebrows furrowed together. "Can we skip these pleasantries? Sheldon, Bryce is buttering up to your dad, and I'm kissing your new stepmom's arse."

I winced. "Please don't say that word."

He waved that off. "Whatever. We're doing what we have to do."

I pursed my lips together.

He rolled his eyes at that. "You can be annoyed all you want, but we didn't tell you because you couldn't act any different. If we'd told you, you would've been a lot nicer."

He had a point. Bryce finished for him, "And if you're nice, they would've been suspicious."

"I'm not that bad."

Nothing. Total silence. They both gave me pointed looks.

"Fine," I relinquished. "I'm nice to you guys."

They shared another look, but this time both wore small grins. Bryce turned, including me in on that look. "And we love you for it."

"So, what's the plan? Kiss their ass and hope they'll let you take me to the city?"

"No. Kiss their ass in the hopes they'll trust us."

I lifted an eyebrow. "That's it?"

Corrigan answered, "Hope they trust us . . . enough so they might leave . . ."

"Your plan sucks." Bryce held up a hand. "Just wait. There's more." I waited. He tilted his head to the side, searching for more. Then his head jerked back, and he slapped a hand to the table. "Like for a date night. We all saw how they were tonight. Maybe they'd go to a hotel for a weekend alone. You know. To get away from all of this?" He turned to both of us. "It's worth a shot? Right?"

I snorted, shaking my head. "That plan sucks. My dad's been on lockdown for years. He's not going to be talked into leaving for an orgy. No. We need to make them leave." I frowned, thinking over the possibilities. "I don't think he'd leave if the lawyers made him go. He'd demand for them to come here. No, the only people he'd leave for would be the police." I shuddered. "And let's not re-enact that scenario. The less I step foot into a police station, the better off I am." No, no, no. Wait. I snapped my fingers. "Explosives."

"Uh," Corrigan started, jerking forward in his seat.

Bryce's eyes narrowed to slits, but both were quiet.

They were thinking it over. Finally, after another moment of silence, Bryce glanced to Corrigan and their gazes locked for a few seconds. Then he started, "Sheldon, I don't think letting you near explosives is a good idea."

"Yeah." Corrigan laughed abruptly. "Imagine if the police caught you. Talk about making yourself look even guiltier."

I scowled. "Not me. You two would have to do it or one of you would have to sneak out to do it."

"Wait." Bryce held up a hand.

Corrigan looked ready to argue, but he silenced and leaned back in his chair again.

Bryce added, "What are you talking about, exactly?"

"My dad won't leave, not unless the police order him. The only other way he'd leave is if he's forced, like if we're under attack."

"Meaning?"

"'Meaning.'" I held my hands out. It wasn't that hard to figure out. Was it? "Get some big ass fireworks and set them off next to the house. It'll be awesome. They'll think we're under attack, and off we go, being carted right back to the city." I loved the plan. It would work. I knew it. I was getting buzzed just thinking about it.

Gazing at the other two, still silent, and showing no reactions, I asked, "What do you think?" They looked at each other for the fourth time. "Come on, you guys. It's a good plan." I was pleading here. Almost. "No one gets hurt. There's nothing illegal about it. Just . . . make sure to get the biggest fireworks that go *kaboom*. That's it." I waited another second, then added, "It'll work."

It'd be awesome. I knew it.

The corner of Bryce's mouth curved up into a half-grin. He said to Corrigan, "You or me?"

Corrigan's eyes got big. "Me. Definitely me."

"What are you guys talking about?" I looked between them.

"Who's getting the fireworks?"

Corrigan placed his elbows onto the table and nodded, one firm movement. "Me. I'll get 'em. I'll make it be awesome."

I wanted to purr like a cat being petted. I was loving this. "Good. Then we get back into the city and figure out who killed Grace." I had my own explosive plan for when we figured out who that was. "This is going to be amazing."

Corrigan was excited. I could tell, but Bryce still seemed hesitant. He shot Corrigan a warning look. "Just don't get something that'll actually leave a crater-sized hole in the ground."

Corrigan nodded. "Got it. No crater-forming fireworks. I can do that."

Bryce said further, "And don't set fire to anything."

"No fire-starting fireworks. Got that, too."

"I suppose we can't test it out?" Corrigan and I shared a look. What was he talking about?

I snorted. "Right. He can go to a gun range and set one off . . ." I trailed off. "You could do that."

"Sounds like a plan." Corrigan was all business now. I saw the anticipation and excitement building. He grinned. "It's been a long time since we caused havoc. It feels good."

"Good?" I shook my head. "It feels right." We were both grinning at each other.

Bryce groaned. He said, "Why do I have a feeling this isn't going to go how it's planned?"

I frowned at him. "Hush it, Superstar. Let us deviants do what we do best."

Corrigan added, his grin now stretched from ear to ear, "Causing chaos and kicking a little ass." He gestured to me and back to him. "That's what we do best."

I nodded. This would work. I knew it.

*

The plan started without a hitch.

Corrigan feigned he needed to go to town the next day at lunch. He said a professor was arguing his online courses so he needed to go in to deal with it.

Neil hadn't been happy. He said, "Do you realize the trouble it took to get you here? There are people who are going to be following you. They know you're close to my daughter, and a lot of people want to kill her."

I grimaced. "Don't sugarcoat it or anything."

Neil turned on me with a scowl.

That was how I must've looked whenever I glared. He looked scary and ominous. I made a mental note to try not to scowl so much. I'd have to figure out something else, maybe a half-glare?

He snapped at me, "Why? Isn't that how you are with everyone else? And no, I'm not going to sugarcoat it. People want to kill you, Sheldon. They hate you. When are you going to start figuring this out?"

I shrugged. "People have hated me since high school. It's because of my sweet disposition. I'm so damn cheery."

"You're joking?" His scowl kicked up another notch. He was becoming even more intimidating. He asked again, "You're joking?"

"What else can I do? Welcome to my life, Daddy Dearest. I've been stalked long before this. I killed a guy. He tried to kill Corrigan. I've been shoved into a glass table. This. Is. My. Life. I should've been expecting this, to be honest."

He started laughing, shaking his head. "My daughter." He shoved a hand at me, pointing. "So beloved. Yeah, right. You've had this *fuck-you* attitude since you were born."

I felt a burning at the corners of my eyes. I flinched, refusing to let anything he said get to me.

He continued, "Your mother and I tried to be there for you. We did. In the beginning. Then you started sneaking out, skipping school, doing only God knows what. Drinking. Did you ever do drugs? I'd be surprised if you hadn't. You were having sex—I don't even want to know when." He turned to Bryce. "I know it was you. You were the main guy with her, and I don't want to think about all the others that must've been between her legs—"

Bryce punched him. It happened so fast.

Neil was spilling those hateful words, each one of them was a blow to me, and I was struggling to keep my composure and then *BAM!*—he was down. Bryce stood above him. His hand still in a fist, and he was shaking, staring down. A vein bulged out from the side of his neck.

My dad looked bewildered. He cradled a hand to the side of his face and looked up. "Bryce?" It was like his best friend had stabbed him in the back.

I started laughing. This whole thing was hilarious.

Everyone looked at me. Beth had paled when my dad started talking, and she yelped when Bryce hit him, but now she moaned and moved farther into the background. That's when I knew she was made of weak sauce. She wasn't going to hack it, whatever was going to happen with all of this.

"You're laughing?" My dad pushed himself back up until he was standing.

Bryce moved back, now just a few inches in front of me. A set expression filtered over his face. Cold. Stony face. He was showing his alliance to me. Corrigan had a similar expression, and he moved to the other side of me. All three of us were in line now. As I registered their show of loyalty, their strength surged through me, mixing with mine, and I was comforted again with just having them there. That's what I needed to be able to take the fight back to whoever was trying to destroy my life.

"Sheldon?"

I shook my head, sending a scathing glance at Beth. She swallowed nervously before looking away. Then I said, quietly, "Do you have any idea what's going to happen?" I was talking to both of them, Beth and Neil.

My dad frowned. He was still cradling the side of his face and cast a wary glance to Bryce. "Yes, Sheldon. I am very aware of what's going to happen. You might go to prison. That's what. And you're laughing."

I shook my head. "No, Dad."

He quieted instantly.

I couldn't remember the last time I called him that term. My nostrils flared. It'd be the last time, too. I wanted his attention, and I got it. "No, Neil. This isn't going to end with me going to prison. You're a fool if you think that. No. This is going to end bloody. I'll never get to that part because whoever framed me wants to torture me. Hell, they already have been. My car's brakes were cut. They still don't know who did that, then Grace's death. It's all connected. I've already endured one stalker. He killed two of my friends, but this is worse. This person, whoever it is, wants to hurt me. They're taunting me, making me go on the defensive. No." I clipped my head to the side. "This person wants me to die, slowly and painfully."

"How do you know this?"

A hollow sensation filled my chest. It was burying deeper and deeper, making a void as it went. I jerked a shoulder up. "Because it's what I would've done. If I wanted to mess with someone and really mess with their mind, I'd frame them, too." It was genius, in a way.

Neil scoffed, "Don't tell me you're impressed with them?"

"No, no." But I was, in a sick way. "It just confirms I have to find out who's doing this to me." I glanced at Corrigan. He still needed permission to leave. "Do whatever you need to do to make sure Corrigan can get leave and come back safely. Please."

Neil sighed. He sounded defeated. "Sheldon, I don't—"

"Let him, Neil." I was putting my foot down. "This is my life, my future. He's my best friend. Let him go and do what he needs. It's the least you can do."

His jaw clenched. I knew he didn't want to, but then he looked away, and I also knew we had won. This was a small battle, one of so many to come, but a relieved sensation covered that void in my chest. It wouldn't last, but it was small and fleeting.

I grinned at Corrigan, who nodded at me.

Our plan was a go.

Corrigan left that afternoon.

CHAPTER SIX

Corrigan was gone all day, and Neil and Beth had retired to bed after supper that night or dinner as Beth called it. She liked to sound more sophisticated than the rest of us. Because I could be sophisticated, too, I took a bunch of her wine outside. Bryce joined me on the patio with two large glasses, and without a word being spoken between the two of us, I filled them both to the top. Leaning back, we clicked our glasses together and sipped, still not talking.

I enjoyed this.

Having him here. Drinking wine with him. Feeling the old comfortable silence between us. It was like this with Corrigan too, but when they were together, even though they both were playing nice, an underlying tension was always there.

"What's wrong?"

I glanced at him. "Huh?" God, he was beautiful in the moonlight. I'd forgotten how much at times.

"You sighed."

"I did?"

He nodded, sipping his wine and narrowing his eyes briefly at me. "Are you worried about Corrigan or whoever's framing you?"

Both. "Corrigan. Duh." I grinned and lifted one shoulder in a shrug.

He continued to watch me, then the corner of his mouth curved up into a slight grin. "Liar." He sounded sad.

I started to shrug, but no. I couldn't even lie to myself. Instead, I reached for the wine glass again and drank the rest of the contents. "I don't want to talk about the other stuff, not right now."

He dipped his head forward. "You're going to have to, you know?"

"I know." My hand tightened around the stem of the glass. "Let's get back to the city and go from there."

"I talked to Denton today."

"Yeah?"

He took another sip of his wine. "Yeah, whenever Corrigan gets back and does his thing, Denton's ready to go. We can stay with him."

"At his house?" My mouth was suddenly dry. The idea of staying at my old neighbor's house, so close to my old home had my stomach churning. "Bryce," I stopped. My hand went to the table, and my fingers curled around, holding onto it tightly. Marcus had been in that house. He stabbed Corrigan there; I closed my eyes as I remembered that night. Bryce turned the video off, and I raised my gun. I'd been ready. "Bryce, god."

"Hey." He leaned forward. One of his hands rested over mine. "Look at me."

I did, but it didn't help. Seeing the mirrored anguish and haunted expression in his eyes had my stomach churning at a faster rate.

He said, his hand tightening over mine, "It's time we faced it and faced him. I know. Sheldon, I know." The haunted look doubled, overtaking everything in his gaze. "Trust me. I remember that night too, but it happened and we did it together."

I shook my head, pulling my hand away. "No, you didn't. You—"

"You provoked him, but I told you, too. I turned the video off."

"You didn't pull the trigger," I whispered, letting my other hand fall from the table and to my lap. My hands wrapped around each other. "I did. I killed him. You didn't."

"That's bullshit. I'm a part of it. You weren't going to do it. You only did because I told you. I gave you permission to do it."

I shook my head. I was going to anyway. I went down there for that purpose, but saying those words aloud felt like I was confessing to the real murder I committed. I hadn't killed Grace, but I had murdered someone else. "No, Bryce. All you did was turn off the monitor. That's all. You weren't in that room with us." It would've been different if he had been. I knew that with certainty. Bryce would've tackled him, maybe punched him so he was unconscious. Marcus wouldn't have been dead now, but I couldn't do any of that. I had one weapon. It was the only way I could've fought back, and I chose to use it in a lethal way.

Marcus' death was on my hands, not his.

"Fuck that. His blood is on my hands, too."

I looked up, shocked. It was like he read my thoughts, but he hadn't. His hand was clenched around his glass, and he was looking out into the backyard. His jaw clenched as he whispered again, "We've both been running from that. It's time we stopped." He swung those piercing eyes my way again. "Being away from you, watching you cling to Corrigan when we were in Spain, I know all of it was because of what we both did. You didn't want to talk about Marcus, about how we're both to blame for killing him, but it's here now. You're going to be on trial for a different murder. We can't run anymore."

I shook my head. "I'm not." With those two words, my stomach stopped churning. All the emotions that were racing inside me calmed and settled to the bottom again. He was right. No more running. No more lying.

We shared a look.

It was time to deal with everything.

That was when the first explosion went off.

"What the—"

It was a loud boom, and within seconds, the ground shook. Bryce jumped out of his chair, but I grabbed hold of the table. I wasn't going to fall over, but it was surprising. "Holy shit."

Bryce held a hand out to me, not to help me up, just to check on me. "You okay?"

"Yeah."

He headed farther off the patio and was gazing into the forest. "It came from out there."

Was it . . . "Corrigan?"

He turned back to me and shook his head. "Who knows? If it was, he should be running here soon."

The second explosion went off then, and this time the table started to slide over the floor. It didn't go far, just a few inches, but I lurched forward anyway. Stopping it, I stood up from my chair and started for the door. No matter who it was, I wanted to grab our bags.

"Where are you going?"

I threw open the door. "I packed bags for us."

"No, Sheldon." Bryce raced for me and grabbed my arm. "Think about it. If this is anything serious, we need to get out of here."

"Yes, but—"

Then all hell broke loose.

"SHELDON!"

It was my dad, and turning, I saw him race from the hallway, holding onto Beth's hand. They were both in robes, but while Neil's was tied with pajama pants sticking out underneath, Beth was trying to hold hers closed with her free hand. It wasn't working. She had a silk nightgown on underneath, and she stumbled, crying out. Neil stopped, grabbed her arm, and hoisted her up in one movement. It happened so fast, if I hadn't been watching, I wouldn't have caught it. Her slipper fell off, and muttering a quick curse, Neil stooped down and swept it up, shoving it into his robe's pocket. He was to the door by then.

As he shoved us outside, a lot of things happened all at once.

I took in his harried expression, Beth's pale and trembling features, and then realized I could see my dad and his girlfriend so much clearer because there were bright lights coming from behind us.

"Sheldon." Bryce moved close to me, holding my arm.

They were large flashlights, and there were more than a pair of them. Six flashlights were coming from the left, another four from the right, and I whirled back to my dad and saw there were another two coming from inside the house.

"What's going on?" Beth clutched her robe shut, looking all around us.

Neil tucked her close. "It's just the security teams. They're sweeping the grounds." He skimmed over me. "You look fine."

I wasn't sure if that was a question or accusation. I shrugged, but my insides were still feeling the surprise from those bombs or whatever they'd been. "I've been through worse."

Bryce caught my gaze and shook his head, one side of his mouth lifting to show his amusement. He knew I was scared shitless, though, I was still holding out hope the explosions had been fireworks-gone-wrong sort of thing, and Corrigan would come running around the corner. I wouldn't have cared if he had burned half his hair off, just so I knew everyone would be okay.

A third explosion went off then, and like the others, the ground shook. This one was closer and stronger. Beth cried out again, stumbling to the side. My dad yelled. He threw an arm out, reaching for balance while trying to hold her from falling to the ground. Bryce's hand squeezed tightly on my arm, and I knew what he was going to do. We both leapt for them. Bryce reached and took hold of my dad while I caught Beth. Grabbing onto her arm, I clambered for a quick hold on her shoulder and somehow yanked her forward so she wasn't falling.

She reached for me and clutched onto me, breathing deeply, for a moment. When the last of the tremors were over, she lifted her head. I saw the terror in her eyes, and she seemed scared to even breathe. She bit down on her lip, then turned back for my dad.

"Neil," she whimpered.

He folded her back into his chest, thanking Bryce and me over her shoulder while patting the back of her head.

Bryce lifted his eyebrows at me. We were all shaken and he frowned. "What now?"

"Mr. Jeneve." A security guard stepped through the door onto the patio. He was releasing his radio, and he pointed his flashlight out to the backyard. A ton of security guards were approaching us. They were no longer just flashlights, but we could see their figures now. "We have a car waiting. They'll take you to a secure location."

"Thank god," Beth continued to whimper.

I frowned.

Neil ran a brisk hand over his head. "Do you know what caused those explosions?"

"We haven't found any intruders, but we'll do a more thorough search once you and your guests are off the perimeter and safely away."

"Yeah. Okay." My dad started forward. "Sheldon, Bryce." He stopped and searched the patio again. "Is Corrigan not back yet? I thought a car had come through—"

"I'm here." A voice spoke up from behind me and my heart leapt into my chest as I whirled around.

He flashed me a grin, raking a hand through his curls, as he straightened from the wall in the shadows. He materialized to the side of one of the security guards as if he'd been there the whole time. The guard closest to him jumped back and reached for his gun reflexively.

Corrigan held up a hand. "Sorry. No, no. Friend, not foe." He held both of his hands up in surrender. "I'll announce I'm here better next time. I swear."

Relief swept over me. It was overwhelming, and for a moment, my knees buckled under the abruptness of it. Then I shot him a dark and pointed look.

He shrugged, his smirk deepening to show off a dimple in his one cheek.

Bryce muttered, "My god."

Corrigan laughed, his eyebrows wagging up and down now.

Beth frowned, taking on the exchanges. Then she shook her head and followed behind my dad, who was being led by one of the guards. When the three of us didn't follow right away, he barked over his shoulder, "Get going. Now's not the time for jokes. Let's go."

Corrigan saluted him, but my dad had already turned back around.

The three of us formed a close huddle as we started to follow the guards.

Bryce whispered, leaning close, "That was close, Cor."

"I know. I'm sorry." He flashed an apologetic grin. "I, uh, think I got the wrong *presents*. Too strong, you know."

"Yeah," I hissed. "You don't say."

"Sheldon! Boys!"

"Whatever. Let's talk later. We have to make sure to go to Denton's house now." Bryce broke in front and hurried behind my father, who was climbing into the back of a car.

"You okay?" I brushed the back of Corrigan's hand. I wanted to hug him. I would've, if we had time. Once we were in the car . . . no, not even then. It would be too suspicious.

"Yeah. I'm good." Warmth filled his eyes as he studied me. "You okay?"

"I'm better." Then to hell with it. I grabbed his hand and squeezed it hard. He was my best friend. I needed to know he was okay. "Thank you."

He nodded and held back so I could get into the car first. There were guards all around us, shielding us. Before I ducked down and climbed to my seat, I turned and slid my arms around him. I didn't give a damn. I needed to hug my friend.

After a second's hesitation, Corrigan hugged me back.

"Any time, you two."

I pulled back and got inside. Avoiding Bryce's gaze, I ducked my head down and reached for Corrigan's hand as he slid next to me. My dad's impatience didn't even piss me off. That's how grateful I was to have them both there again.

My dad rapped on the window. "It's time to go."

Finally. We were going back to the city, back to find out who was trying to frame me.

One of the security guards had slid into the back with us. There were three rows of seats, and he had taken one of the first seats. His hand went to his radio, and he spoke into it, "All clear. Go ahead."

The car started to roll forward.

The guard asked, "Mr. Jeneve, to the safe house?"

My dad opened his mouth to answer. Bryce leaned forward, cutting him off. "We can go to Denton Steele's home."

The guard looked to my father.

"What?"

Bryce said again, "Denton Steele. He still lives near your old home, but I've been in contact with him. He said we could go to his home at any moment, if we needed."

My dad narrowed his eyes and tilted his head to the side.

Not good. I spoke up, "He has security, too, Dad." Fuck. I'd called him that a second time. Cringing, gritting my teeth, I saw how his eyes widened and added, "My relationship with him isn't that known. No one will look for us there."

I was lying. People did know I was friendly with Denton, but I was hoping my dad didn't know that fact. Corrigan and Bryce turned to me. They were thinking the same thing. People did know. I shook my head at them, the slightest of movements. I wanted it known. I wanted people to look for me there. No, I wanted Grace's murderer to know exactly where I was going to be, then maybe they'd come to me.

Maybe I could find out who was trying to make my life hell and exact some of my own revenge.

"Denton Steele, huh?" My dad was mulling it over. He sighed, shaking his head. "We were good friends with his parents. It'll be nice to catch up with him, see how they're doing."

"They divorced."

My dad gave me a regretful look, pinching the top of his nose. "I'm aware, Sheldon, but I'm sure their son keeps in contact with his own parents."

A retort was at the tip of my tongue. Corrigan squeezed my hand, and I knew he was telling me to shut up. *Don't rock the boat, Jeneve. Let us count this one a win.* Hearing my own thoughts, I swallowed it and gave Neil a smile instead.

"You're right." I tried to deliver that with a cherry on top, all the while holding off from rolling my eyes at myself. *Be fake.* I told myself. *Be fake and let's catch this fucker.* I took a breath. That was more like it.

"Fine. Let's head to the Steele household."

The security guard nodded and reached for his radio again to relay his instructions.

Beth looked over herself and grimaced. "My. I'm going to meet a superstar like this. Neil, we'll need to send for clothes."

My dad lifted his arm and placed it around her shoulders. She snuggled into him as he murmured, rubbing a hand up and down her arm, "I'm sure that can be arranged. We'll get everything sorted out."

As those two got comfortable for the long drive to the city, I was anything but. The closer we got, the closer we were getting to Grace's killer. Ignoring Bryce, ignoring Corrigan, and even ignoring that same-old tension that's always there between the two, I needed to keep thinking. I would find this fucker, and I would make them pay.

The closer we got to the city, the more focused I became.

CHAPTER SEVEN

We had to be flagged through a gate for the community and then again when we got to Denton's house. I was impressed. There'd been no security measures like that when we lived in the neighborhood, but I was even more impressed because Denton had his own private one installed. A lot of the other houses didn't. When we were flagged through and drove up the driveway to Denton's house, the car in front of us and the car behind us stopped. Security guards swept out and immediately began canvassing the area.

I asked my dad, "How many staff members do you have?"

He didn't bat an eyelid. "As many as it takes."

Oh-kay then. "Good to know."

Denton opened the door and leaned against his porch's railing as he waited for us to come up. Crossing his arms over his chest, he tilted his head back with a smirk appearing on his face.

I shook my head. Only Denton could get away with wearing red khaki pants, loafers, and a buttoned-down white and red striped shirt with sunglasses on top of his head. As I went up the stairs to him, I said, "You know it's one in the morning. You got paparazzi skulking around in your bushes? You need to look *cool* at all times?"

"Didn't you hear from the tabloids? I'm so vain that I have mirrors on the backs of every door? I constantly have to reassure myself that I'm still good-looking enough." He laughed, raking a hand through his dark hair and dislodging his sunglasses. Taking them in his hand, he held his arm out and gestured for me to come closer. I did and he wrapped his arms around me in a tight hug. "Damn. It's good to see you, Jeneve. I thought the next time I saw you would be with you behind bars."

I laughed, but stepped back and delivered a strong punch to his chest. "Not funny, douche bag."

"Oh, come on." He made a show of looking me up and down. "Orange could be your color. It brings out those precious lips of yours." He flicked a hand to my lips and shot me a grin. "And really. You should be thanking me. I normally have a butler open the door. Good for you that I figured out how to let you through the gates or you would've been sitting in those very securely-looking and heavily guarded cars of yours." He frowned over my shoulder. "Do they have guns?"

"Don't worry about them. I think they're more for show than actual harm. They won't murder any of the paparazzi you pay to take your pictures."

Denton barked out another laugh. "Damn, Sheldon. Just like always, you got cutting remarks."

"I try." A slow grin was forming the longer we traded jokes and jabs. I agreed with him. It was good to see him, too. It felt like too long. Then the reminder of why it'd been so long since we last saw each other filtered in—nope, not going to the last night I saw him. It was too serious. I needed to bring the light-hearted banter back so I made a show of looking around.

"And are you serious?" Not only had he added a security gate, but skimming over his house, I saw he had added almost an entire house onto his. It was a mansion now. I waved a hand at the renovations. "Did your house birth another home?"

He burst out laughing. "No, I'm not serious about the butler. I have no staff except a chef that comes in, and yeah, my house got pregnant." He turned to look at the outside of his home. "Once the community put up the gate out there, I decided to add my own. I figured it was time to expand. I didn't want to move and find a new home so there you have it. I did my own expansion. It was a bitch to plan, though. Some of the pictures were sold to a celebrity gossip website. They didn't run the story. Nothing there, but still pissed me off. I had to fire half the construction crew to weed out the freeloader."

I was still grinning that his house got pregnant. Feeling the rest waiting behind us, being polite, I allowed myself one more joke. "Your house got pregnant? All your orgies do that? Too much sperm flying all around?"

"Yes." More laughter came from him. "What can I say? I'm fertile enough to infect my wood structure."

Oh no. There was so much I could do with that, but Neil came up the stairs. He held a hand out. "Please stop, you two. Seeing you two joke like this is bringing back a lot of memories right now. Let's keep the traumatic events to one thing right now." He held his hand out, and the lines around his mouth softened into a small smile. "How are you, Denton? It's been a long time."

Denton withdrew completely from me and reached to shake my dad's hand. He glanced sideways to me, but said, "Likewise, Mr. Jeneve. It's been a long time."

"Yeah." My dad stood there a moment, just looking at Denton. A sad look appeared in my dad's eyes, and his mouth twitched before he turned away. "Your parents are well?"

"They are." Denton snuck another look to me. "I've heard about your recent . . ."

My dad had gone missing, but he'd never been declared missing. Just wanting to bite any future awkwardness in the butt, I clarified, "Yeah. He disappeared. The details are still fuzzy, but my bet is that he owed money to the mob. Did you, Neil? How much do you owe them?"

"Sheldon!" Beth gasped from below.

"What?"

"It's fine, Beth." Neil lifted a hand to appease her. "And yes, Denton, I did move away for a while, but it's not what my daughter is insinuating."

I frowned. "No insinuation. I stated it for the record."

He ignored me, a forced mask of politeness coming over his face. "I'm sure we'll have plenty of time to catch up. Thank you again for letting us into your home."

"Ah. Yeah." Denton stepped inside and held the door open. "Come on in, everyone. Do you guys have any bags with you?"

As he asked, Neil held a hand out to Beth, and she was the first inside. My dad rested a hand at the small of her back. Bryce and Corrigan came next, both meeting my gaze with their own mirroring smirks.

Bryce laughed softly. "Same old Sheldon."

"Yeah." Corrigan indicated for me to go ahead of him. "It's nice to know that even being framed for murder doesn't slow her down."

They were talking to each other, but watching me. I pointed to my chest. "Yeah. Right here. Address all statements with the appropriate pronoun, me, not her. Wait. You, not her. Right here. Stating it again. No insinuations here."

We had stepped inside, and Denton shut the door. Overhearing our conversation, he piped in, sliding his hands into his pockets, "Oh, we all know." He glanced at Bryce. "I heard Sheldon's in the house? Is that true?"

Bryce's grin grew. "I heard that, too. You think she's around? Corrigan?"

"Nah." Corrigan clipped his head to the side. "I don't think she's here. I think the mob came after her instead of her dad. She's gone. That ship has sailed."

"You guys are annoying."

Bryce ignored me. "You're right. We should make up now, for real. No reason for this distance."

"You're right." Corrigan held his arms out. "Come here, you big Super Soccer Stud. Let's be best friends again."

Bryce stepped forward, and the two hugged each other, their arms patting each other on the backs.

"Yep. Annoying. That's what all three of you are being."

"Wait." Bryce lifted his head. He turned to Denton. "We're not including Denton. Come here. He's the big star. He's an A-list movie actor. That's what Oprah told me. I watched her Master's Class last night."

Denton burst out laughing.

Corrigan tugged him over. "You're right. How selfish of us. Come here. You're so handsome, Denton. You make my lady parts throb."

"Oh my god." Denton was shaking his head, but he hugged both of them back. "I forgot how the three of you could be." He glanced at me. "Sheldon—"

I flicked him off, then held my hand up and waved my middle finger at all of them. "Screw you, guys."

"Come on." Corrigan lifted an arm to me. "We're just having fun. Get in here, too."

I didn't move and continued to glare at them. My middle finger was still in front of me. I wanted that gesture showcased and dipped in bronze.

Corrigan waved my hand away and grabbed my wrist. He tugged me in. Bryce and Denton both moved and all three of them tugged me so I was in the middle of the love fest.

This was just wonderful.

I stood there, rigid, as the three of them moved closer.

"Oh, Sheldon. You're the glue in our friendship lockets."

"Screw off, Corrigan."

His head rested on my left shoulder.

Bryce's head went to my right shoulder. "She's the stick in our kebab."

Corrigan barked out a laugh. "That was good, Bryce."

"Thanks. I've been working on being funnier."

"It's paying off."

"You guys," I growled in warning.

Denton added, squeezing closer and his forehead rested on the back of my skull. "My turn."

"Oh god." I groaned.

"Sheldon, you're the hotdog in our bun."

"That's a good one," Corrigan murmured in my ear.

"Without you, it's just bread."

Bryce said, "Yeah. No taste. We'd go dry. Cracked."

"Pure carbs. No enjoyment." Corrigan was laughing in my ear.

"We'd all get fat then." I could feel Denton's silent laughter, as he pressed closer into the back of me. "Denton and I can't. Our careers depend on our lean beautifulness."

"Ha. Our beautifulness."

"Oh my god." I'd had enough. I tried to break away from them, but all three tightened their hold on me so I ducked down and crawled out through their feet. "You guys are too annoying now."

Corrigan started for me. "Come on, Sheldon. We're having fun."

I rolled my eyes and darted out of his reach. "Forget the murderer. Take me away now." Wait. "Never mind." I asked Denton, "Where's your wine? Can we please all get drunk tonight?"

"Yep. Same old Sheldon." Bryce and Corrigan shared a look; both were trying to hold back their grins now.

Denton nodded and headed down the hallway. "Yeah, that sounds like a perfect plan. Let me get your dad and his . . ." He halted and lifted an eyebrow.

I answered, "Girlfriend."

"Ah. Got it. Let me get your father and his girlfriend settled for the night. I need to ask if I should find bedding for all those guards too or not." He kept going down the hallway and turned in the same direction Neil and Beth had gone.

I turned to see Bryce and Corrigan laughing. They were whispering more jokes to each other, and I shook my head. "Screw waiting. I'm going to find his liquor stash all on my own."

"Where are you going?" Corrigan called out as I took off.

"Away from you two. It's like I stepped into an alternate universe or something." They weren't faking like I thought they had been. As that realization settled in my gut, I stopped in my tracks. I thought they had been faking it, putting on a good front for my sake, but they weren't. They actually were getting along. Turning back around to them, I just stared for a moment.

Giggles were coming from them. Giggles. From grown men. Only true friends laughed like that.

I waved a finger between them. "When did this happen?"

They stopped and drew to their fullest height. Bryce frowned. "What are you talking about?"

"I thought you guys were faking before. I thought . . ." I thought I had destroyed their friendship? They were acting like they had in high school. It was—I felt a kick in my gut—nice. Then hope started to grow. Did I dare hope . . . the old trio was back?

"Oh no." Corrigan clipped his head in a fierce motion.

"What?" My arms jerked, and I spread my fingers out, pressing my palm to my side.

"We're friends despite you." He gestured to Bryce. "I still love this guy, and he loves me. No matter who you pick, we're not losing a damn good friend. This is *despite* you," he repeated and stressed that word.

My mouth went dry. "What do you mean?"

"The two of us are going to remain friends, but once you pick, the person you don't choose steps away from you."

"Me?"

Bryce nodded.

They were serious, dead serious. I didn't know how I felt about this.

Bryce's tone sounded harsh. "We've discussed it. Whoever you don't choose steps back from you, but not each other. We'll still be friends."

"But—" My mind was racing. I was going to lose one of them. "You told me this wouldn't happen. I would still have both of you." I needed them. They were my family.

"You'll still have us."

"But." I pressed my fingers to my temples. A headache was coming on. "You're not making sense."

"We'll both care about you. That won't go away, and yes, we'll both still be here for you, but not in the way you want. Not in the daily way. If you need us, like really truly need us, we'll be here for you," Corrigan said.

Bryce finished for him softly, "But it's not going to be how you want it. We're still family. We'll be here for you if you need us, but not every day. It's like we're a family member that moved away. Every now and then maybe we can see you, but not every day. It can't be like that, Sheldon."

Corrigan added, "It's the fairest way to do it."

I was going to lose one of them. No matter how they were saying it, I would lose one of my family members.

Bryce was studying me, and he pressed his lips together. "Stop whatever you're thinking. Stop it. This is the right way to do it, and you can't deny this. You fell in love with both of us, and that's not fair."

"But—"

"Stop, Sheldon." Corrigan was scowling now. "We don't lose both of you this way. It would happen anyway. Once you picked, that other person would have to go away anyway."

"But—"

"Just stop, Sheldon." Bryce and Corrigan were right next to each other. They were looking at me with the same determined expressions, and they had decided. I had no decision in the matter. The lump got a shot of testosterone and grew to a goliath size in my throat.

They were right. No matter what, I would lose one of them.

I jerked my head in a nod. "Okay." I took a shuddering breath in. "Okay." Then I let it out.

"All right." Denton's cheerful voice was like a knife breaking the tension in the room. It was jarring and almost brought me to tears. Feeling them coming, I pressed a hand to my eye and turned away.

Denton didn't notice. He was heading back for us. He clapped his hands together. "Papa Neil and Step-Girlfriend-Mama are all settled. I don't need to worry about their staff. I guess they have their own protocols or whatever, but I put a bunch of wine and champagne on ice. Everything's set up downstairs and waiting for us to party the night away." He was grinning from ear to ear. "What do you guys say? Are we good to get our booze on?"

I didn't answer. I couldn't. My throat was burning.

"Yes." Corrigan stepped forward. "We're ready."

There was a moment of silence.

Denton asked, "Sheldon?"

Bryce said over him, "Sheldon, you ready?"

No.

My throat wouldn't stop burning.

He stepped closer and put an arm around my shoulders. Turning me forward, he nodded at Denton. "She's good to go. Let's forget about the shitstorm going on for the night and have fun."

"Oh . . . sure . . ." I felt Denton's gaze on me.

The decision was made. It was final. They made it without me, and they were letting me know I had to accept it. It was how it was going to be, but fuck— it hurt to swallow that. Then I jerked my head in another nod. "Yeah." It was the right thing to do. "I'm good to go. Let's get shitfaced tonight."

I had to say goodbye to one of them.

"All right then." The cheerful tone had waned from Denton. His grin faded as well, and he started back down the hallway. "I suppose follow me then?"

CHAPTER EIGHT

The police were notified of everything that happened; that my dad's security team found evidence of fireworks-gone-wrong. When Neil got the news, he was sitting across from me at the breakfast table and immediately looked at me, then Corrigan, and Bryce. His eyes went flat. His lips pressed together in a firm line, and he let out a loud disapproving sigh before murmuring into the phone, "Fine. Yes, canvass any neighbors to see if they could've gotten onto the property." His gaze came back to me and stayed. "But I have a feeling you won't find much."

Bryce was at the coffee machine. Corrigan had just sat down with toast on his plate, and I had lifted my own coffee cup to my lips for a sip. Everyone stopped what they were doing. Denton came into the room then and halted abruptly, looking around at everyone. A quick frown appeared, and then he shrugged, sliding into one of the empty chairs. He swung his head around the room with an easy grin. "How's everyone doing this morning?"

No one answered.

My dad ended his call. The disapproval seemed to have doubled, and he looked among all three of us again, Denton excluded because, hello—puppy dog smile and innocent eyes. No. My dad knew who had been behind the explosions now.

He sighed a second time. "I hope it was worth it... whatever you three did to get here."

My jaw firmed. "It will be."

He shook his head and stood up from the table. Taking his coffee and the newspaper, he saluted Denton with his cup. "No offense to your presence, but because of my daughter and her two friends, I've found that I've lost my appetite."

"Oh." Denton frowned. "Okay." After he left the room, Denton asked, "What was that about?"

"Nothing." I gripped my coffee cup tighter. "Just . . . he wants me to hide. I have a different opinion."

"Oh." He glanced to Corrigan and Bryce, who were still frozen in their state, waiting. And just like that, both finished what they were doing. Bryce poured himself some coffee, and Corrigan bit into his toast. Bringing his coffee and a cup for Denton, Bryce took my dad's empty seat, and for a moment, all four of us were quiet around the table.

Corrigan finished his first slice of toast and picked up his second. Before he bit into it, he said, "All right. Quiet time is over, folks. What's the plan?"

Everyone looked at the other. No one said a word. Then I laughed and shook my head. "No one has a clue."

"Well, screw that. Let's figure something out."

Denton was still swinging his head from one end of the table to the other. He leaned forward now. "Wait. You guys are going to figure out who framed Sheldon?"

"You got any ideas?" Corrigan asked.

"No, but—" he stopped, a quick frown appeared.

"But what?" I leaned forward, resting my elbows on the table. My coffee cup was suspended in front of me.

"I heard a rumor." He looked to Bryce.

"About me?"

"No, about that model you were dating." Denton cast me an apologetic look.

I rolled my eyes, but the mere mention of her brought a nice little stabbing pain to me. Lovely.

Bryce looked at me, too. "I swear, Sheldon, I slept with her once. The rest of the time was just making sure she never went off the deep end. That's all over now. She's got nothing on me anymore."

"No." Denton cut in, stopping anything I might've said. "That's the rumor I heard, not about you or Sheldon, well, not really. I heard her assistant was the one who cut Sheldon's brakes. The reason why," he looked at Corrigan, "you had that accident."

"Wait. What?" Corrigan jerked forward in his seat.

"Where'd you hear that?"

Denton turned to me. "My agent told me. She heard it from one of her clients. You know how that stuff gets around."

Her assistant cut my brakes? I glanced at Corrigan. She'd been the reason he got in an accident? His gaze was clouded. I couldn't decipher the emotion, but when he met my gaze and looked away with a cringe, it left a sour taste in my mouth. It also set our next step in stone.

I wanted public. I wanted a confrontation. I wanted to ruffle some feathers, and maybe the real killer would make a mistake.

"What are you thinking?" Bryce had been waiting. He leaned forward. "I recognize that look."

Denton frowned. "Is it sad I recognize it, too?"

Corrigan turned back, a half grin on his face. He shook his head, a sad laugh coming softly from him. "It's that look that always gets us in trouble."

They were right.

We'd probably get in trouble.

I didn't care, and thirty minutes later after I relayed the plan, they didn't care either.

"Right." Denton clapped his hands together. "Now for the best thing. Disguises."

*

Sneaking out of the house was the first part of the plan. Bryce announced his excuse first. He was going to call his agent and then take a nap. Corrigan was second. His excuse was a movie. He would be in the theater watching a movie. Then Denton, who had the real excuse. He let everyone know he was going to have dinner with a movie producer. That much was true, but he didn't give the details that the dinner was at the same hotel where Bryce's ex Guada-whore was staying at too. And me—I gave no excuse. At this point, Beth and Neil seemed relieved if I wasn't in a room with them. There was no tension, so when they went to the pool for a relaxing afternoon, I snuck into the garage first. I climbed into the trunk, leaving it open, and a moment later, Corrigan crawled in with me. Then we waited, but it wasn't long before a driver came over and got behind the wheel. We could hear him saying to someone else, "Yeah, boss needs a ride to the city. No, Car One. It's what he wants. Yeah. Yeah."

After that, everything worked like clockwork.

The car started and pulled around to the front. The back door opened, and we heard Denton say, "Mr. Scout needs a ride as well. He has to meet with his agent."

I felt Corrigan laughing behind me, and I elbowed him in the gut. "Hush."

He wrapped his arm farther around me, pressing behind me. He whispered back to me, "Stop worrying. I'm just thinking of your dad and Beth, what they'll think having the entire house in peace for the whole afternoon. I bet they won't even know until we get home."

"Or until the paparazzi finds us. I'm sure my dad will get a call right away. He'll be pissed."

Corrigan's laughter was comforting next to my ear. "Same old Sheldon. That's what he'll think. It's nice to have you back, have all three of us back together."

I laughed, but the chuckle died in my throat a second later. It was nice, but it wouldn't last. The three of us were done after this, after I picked. Suddenly, I couldn't see one reason why he was laughing now. "Shut up, okay? Get ready. It won't take long."

"Got it."

The car ride was bumpy. I knew when we arrived at the hotel, as the car slowed, voices and shouts sounded right above us. It was a constant murmur of noise, but then Bryce's name was shouted, and everything went up three notches.

"BRYCE!"

"Where's Sheldon?"

"Are you here to get back together with Guadalupe? How does Sheldon feel about this?"

"Is it true you've been hiding out with Sheldon? What about Corrigan? He's been missing, too."

"If you're here with Denton, does this mean the rumors that the two of you hate each other are false?"

"Bryce! Tell us something?"

They were all shouting at him, right above where we were in the trunk. Some touched the car, then we heard a different shout, right before the car sped up a hill. "Back away from the car. I said, GET BACK!"

Then it was silent. The car came to a complete stop, and the trunk opened, blinding both of us from the sudden light. Bryce smirked down at us, holding the top of the trunk so it wouldn't fall back onto us. "Come on. Hurry up. The hotel security's been alerted we're here so they're expecting us around the front. They'll get curious and come looking if we don't show up in the next thirty seconds."

Corrigan rolled out first. I started right after him, but hands picked me up under my arms. Bryce lifted me clear from the trunk, and murmured in my ear, "Be safe. I mean it." Then he let me go and shut the trunk.

"Sheldon," Corrigan hissed from the side. He had dashed behind some foliage, and I took off after him the same instant Bryce hurried back to his seat. As I reached Corrigan and he pulled me down, the car sped forward and went around to the front of the hotel.

That was when I poked my head out and surveyed where we were. It wasn't the same hotel as before, where his ex had been staying while I was at the same hotel. This was a different hotel.

Corrigan told me, "It's the Palloy."

That made sense. The hotel was known for its privacy for celebrities. It was almost a fortress. A thirty-foot wall surrounded the hotel, and the only way in and out was a gate, which was situated around the back of the hotel. Guests arrived and drove around to the front. They could unload and enter the hotel, knowing no one was taking their pictures. I looked up to the top of the wall. There were no trees for paparazzi to climb. It was completely bare.

Corrigan added, "If they touch the wall and climb, they're trespassing. The wall is property of the hotel."

I frowned.

"What's wrong?"

I sighed. "This isn't going to be the shitstorm that I wanted it to be."

"What do you mean?"

"I wanted attention. I wanted the media to know we were here."

"They will. Trust me." Corrigan stood up, but was still crouching over so his head couldn't be seen from the top of the foliage. He motioned for me as he started heading toward a back door. As I followed him, he whispered back to me, "I know some guys from school that used to work here. They aren't supposed to keep phones on them, but they do anyway. Catching a photo and selling it to the tabloids helped buy one guy a car."

"They never caught him?"

"They did, but they just fired him. He went somewhere else and did the same thing. Tabloids spend a lot of money for those pictures, some of them anyway."

Pressing my lips into a flat line, I didn't want pictures taken and sold. Whatever was added could be made up or twisted into a lie. I wanted cameras. I wanted actual paparazzi in the lobby. I wanted all of it caught, then blasted on some show. This wouldn't do. Corrigan tried the door handle, but it was locked.

"I thought you were going to go in and sneak an ID card from someone?" That had been the plan.

"I will. I just wanted to try this way first." He glanced at me. "You going to be okay waiting out here?"

I gestured to the bushes next to the door. "It's a stalker's wet dream." Giving him a smile, I patted his arm. "I'll be fine. Go ahead. Give this girl her fairytale and break her into this ritzy hotel."

He laughed. "I will. I'll be back in a few, okay?" As he slipped past me, his hand brushed against mine. Acting on impulse, I grabbed for it. Sudden tears threatened to spill out, and I wasn't sure why I was feeling this way, but when he paused and looked back, I just squeezed his hand and whispered, "Be safe."

"You okay?"

I nodded. I would be. That's what I reminded myself. I would be, at the end of all this.

Corrigan left, disappearing around the corner silently. He was supposed to sneak in through a side door, that either Bryce or Denton was going to open for him. Bryce and Denton had talked about the hotel layout. I hadn't paid much attention. I'd been too busy plotting what I was going to say to Guadalupe and her assistant, but I wished now that I had paid more attention.

Then the back door opened. I slunk farther down behind the bush, hoping they couldn't see me as one employee stepped outside and lit a cigarette. He leaned back against the wall, inhaling and seeming to savor the taste of it before letting it back out. I frowned. This could take a while, but then a name was called from inside the building.

"Aron."

He opened the door and stuck his head inside. "Here?"

A woman dressed in a housekeeper's uniform came to the door. She saw the cigarette and heavy disapproval flashed to her face. She shook her head, her hands resting on her hips. "What are you doing? Those things will kill you."

"Yeah, yeah." He took another drag before asking, "What do you need?"

She gestured inside, over her shoulder. "Security's saying a door was left open by the west stairs. I'm supposed to send you over to check it out."

He made an impatient sound. "What? Can't they check the security cameras?"

"Glen said he was in the process of wiping the footage from yesterday. He messed up though and accidentally deleted the footage of today, too. He said to have you check it out, just post there and make sure no one's trying to slip in."

"Come on." He held his cigarette up. "I'm taking a break."

"Take a break over there, but no smoking." She batted at his arm as he lifted it for another drag. "Too many people can see you over there. Too many big people are here today."

He groaned, but snuffed out his cigarette and made a motion for the door. "Okay. Come on. I'm going. Move out of the way, woman."

She shook her head again, her eyebrows bunching forward. "I know your mother. Watch your tone with me, or I'll tell on you."

"Yeah, yeah." His tone was still smart, but it had softened. His head went down as he followed her inside.

This was my chance. Before the door could completely close, I dashed for it and stuck my hand inside, catching it before it completely closed. It slammed on my hand, and I realized how heavy these doors were made. They were designed to slam shut with force.

"What the—?"

He was coming back. I had to think quickly. Looking around, I grabbed his discarded cigarette and held it between the door. Pulling my hand out, at just the right moment, the guy came back and reached for the door. He pulled it shut the rest of the way, and this time it did shut. I heard from the other side, "Goddamn doors. This is the fourth time they haven't shut, just this week."

"Let's go!" the woman called after him.

"I'm coming! Jeez, woman."

I held my breath, standing frozen until I was sure they had gone far enough away where I could dare to try to sneak inside. I tried the handle. It was still locked, but I pulled at the door.

It swung open.

"Thank you, Mr. Cigarette Man," I murmured under my breath and pulled out the cigarette. It had jammed the door so the lock hadn't clicked into place, even though the door had shut all the way. Then I moved inside, but a thought struck me.

I pulled out my phone and sent a text to Denton. **The back door can be opened. Can you have someone let this info** 'slip' to a trusted media source? I need them inside the hotel for this showdown.

A second later, my phone buzzed. **Done. Be safe. They almost caught Bryce opening a door. They're on the lookout. The media has doubled outside the gate since we arrived.**

Thanks. Then I moved forward, muttering to myself, "That's exactly what I want to hear."

CHAPTER NINE

I didn't know where Corrigan had gone, and I wasn't going to wait. I sent him a text. **Inside. I'm heading for her room.**

He replied instantly. **Don't. Wait.**

No. Wherever you are, stay there. I'm going to get in trouble, but it'll just be me then. Besides, you can be backup if I need help.

You'll need help. Wait for me.

Bryce is with her. He'll help.

Sheldon! Stop. I'm almost to your door.

Sit tight and wait it out. I'm going to head up and bring them to the lobby somehow. I'm not at the door. Already gone.

Sheldon.

I didn't reply, and instead, headed farther down the back hallway. I was in the employee section. As I went past a room, I reversed and backtracked. It was a locker room. Slipping inside, I grabbed a housekeeper's uniform. I felt a little ridiculous in the gray skirt and top with a black vest, but whatever it took to blend in. Then I started trying the lockers. The first three were locked, but the fourth sprung open and a nice, shiny, ID badge was inside. I snatched it up and clipped it so the picture was facing against me. If someone saw, they'd see the ID badge, and I hoped that was enough for them to keep moving. I didn't want that extra attention, not until I got to where I needed to go anyway.

Once I got to the stairs, I sent Bryce a text. **What room?**

10th floor, room 1014. I'm inside already.

Should I knock to get in there? We didn't plan this part.

I'll stand next to the door and let you in. She's here.

He didn't mean Guadalupe. He meant the assistant, but I wanted both of them. I sent one last text, **Good**, and headed up. I bypassed the elevator and went up the stairs.

As I ascended each floor, memories came flooding back. First, hearing from an entertainment channel that there were rumors Bryce had been with her. That'd been a nice gut punch. Bryce hadn't wanted to talk about it then.

Another floor. Another memory. *A reporter stuck her microphone in my face and asked, with a polite* fuck you *smile as she was hoping for blood from me, "Is this because Guadalupe arrived at LAX two hours ago? I heard rumors that she's going to attend Bryce's first Suns game. Does that concern you at all? Is that why you left Spain, because of her?"*

My jaw was clenched firmly now, and I circled to head up the next set of stairs.

With that, another image came back to me. *I opened the door to the Public Relations room, hoping to surprise Bryce, and instead, I'd been the one surprised. He was holding her in his arms. His. Mother. Fucking. Arms.*

The fourth floor. A fourth memory. *"He's close to Guadalupe. I know you don't want to hear that, but they're close. They're friends, Sheldon. I know Bryce would be upset if she were upset."* My hand gripped the rail harder, hearing Bryce's agent's warning.

I wasn't supposed to upset her. *Her.* Upset. He had been warning me away.

That fucker.

I rounded for the fifth floor. I remembered when I found her at the hotel and had booked myself a room. *I followed her down to the lobby, only to hear her praises by the front desk staff. He'd been so eager to gush. "She's beautiful, isn't she? I have a friend of a friend to her makeup girl. They're going to have dinner with Bryce Scout right now. Have you heard of him? He's a big soccer star. They both just moved here. She came for a movie, and he followed her here. She could do so much better."*

Oh yes. I had a good steady boil going as I trekked the sixth set of stairs.

Images of Bryce and her on television. He'd gone to a movie premiere with her. He wore a tuxedo, and she had been beaming on his arm. She had been his date, when I was in the same city. He could've asked me, but he didn't.

He had taken *her.*

Then at the hospital. I sucked in a breath. The fury raised another notch.

That had been my time, my territory. Corrigan had been in a car accident. Bryce was there with me. It was our family time, not hers. She had come, trying to take him away from me. Like always. I remembered the look in her eyes when I told her to leave. She had sucked in her breath and she had wanted to fight me. I could tell. I always recognized that look in others, then that assistant. She had come forward, casting her disapproval over Bryce and me.

He told them to go. I'd felt so much relief, but then that assistant snapped at him, making sure he would call them later.

Like he needed to check in with her, make sure she was okay. Like she was his girlfriend. He caved, saying he would.

The betrayal had been solidified in me with that one.

They left, but he might as well have gone with them. Now, remembering all of it, that had been the time when he could've cemented the separation. He said he ended things later, once his little brother's trust fund was safe and his mother couldn't hurt Luca. I remembered the whole explanation. Guadalupe had been a mistake, but he tried to end things right after she had teamed up with his mother, the same mother who hated me with a passion. Holding Luca's trust fund hostage, Bryce's mother forced Bryce into a relationship with Guadalupe.

He went along with it, working to find a way where his mother couldn't hurt his little brother. Somehow he worked everything out. Luca's inheritance wasn't held hostage by their mom anymore and that meant Guadalupe had no leverage. He ended things with Guadalupe, but the damage was done. Now, remembering all of it again, hearing his excuses, envisioning her smug look of triumph, how that assistant acted like Guadalupe should've been reassured, not me, not Corrigan, not the ones who had really been hurt.

All of it was coming at me in waves as I covered the last three floors. By the time I reached for the door handle for the tenth floor, the flames had formed a nice fiery rage in me.

I almost felt sorry for them.

Rolling my shoulders back, I went to room 1014 and knocked. There was a slight pause, then it swept open and Bryce stood on the other side.

His eyes narrowed, seeing the mask on my face, and he nodded. He knew. He understood what was going to go down, and with that movement, I knew he would stand by my side. No wishy-washy bullshit this time.

"Bryce?"

I heard her voice from farther inside the room. Bryce and I were standing in a small hallway. He said to me, "You ready? It's just the two of them."

I nodded and started for where the bedroom was.

He was right behind me.

As we passed the bathroom, the door opened and a different voice asked, this one sharper, "What the hell is going on?"

It was her assistant. What was her name? I stopped and turned my icy stare on her instead. She was the one rumored to have cut the brakes. I couldn't remember her name.

I sneered at her, looking her up and down. "I can see how you were able to slip under the car."

For a moment, I saw the guilt there. It appeared for a split second, then it was replaced with her own icy look back at me. She asked, with gritted teeth, "What are you talking about?"

I stepped toward her. Her straight, black hair had been pulled into a tight bun at the base of her neck and head. She was thinner and shorter than I was. Funny. I didn't remember her being this tiny. Then I continued sneering at her. It was probably because her crazy overcompensated for her height.

"You're nice and tiny. You must've fit under my car just fine, you know, when you cut my brakes."

I watched her. I wanted to know if she'd react, show anything, but she didn't. Her face was a porcelain mask of nothingness.

There wasn't even a flicker of her eyelids. The only reaction she gave was a smug grin, but that formed as she delivered, with acid dripping from her voice, "Sorry, but no. My condolences to your friend that drove it instead of you. I'm sure you pissed off whoever had cut the brakes."

There was nothing wrong with her statement, but there was everything wrong with it. The undertones were screaming at me loud and clear. Too bad it was your friend, not you. That's what she meant.

I hissed and went for her.

"Hey." Bryce intercepted me, stepping in front of me.

I pushed forward, pressing against him, but he held firm and his hand reached behind, resting on my hip to keep me firmly in check.

I growled. "Let me at her," I snapped at her. "You put my friend in the hospital."

Her eyes narrowed to slits at my words. I wanted her to hear those words. I wanted her to hear the violence there.

"That's too bad." She lifted her lip in a sneer. "Really."

Too bad for Corrigan, too bad he ended up in the hospital. I could hear her taunting tone on repeat in my head—that was her message. Yes, too bad. Too bad for her when I would lunge for her and claim that I was only reaching for the phone behind her. Oops. My hand slipped and punched her in the face, but I was really only trying to call the front desk.

Oh yes. My own thoughts were sarcastic. Somehow, that made perfect sense in my mind, but I was seeing red. I wanted at her. "I'm going to hurt you."

"Bring it." She never faltered or reared back. Her gaze held mine steadily, and I knew it was her. If there'd been any doubt, there was none now. This bitch put Corrigan in the hospital.

I was going to return the favor.

A new wave of fury surged in me, and I tried to slip around Bryce, but he checked me again.

Then I saw her reaction.

Bryce turned so he was facing me. Both of his hands were on my hips, holding me back, and the same disapproving look she had given me at the hospital appeared again. Her eyes flickered, showing some anger, and her lips pressed together, then curved down at the corners. The lines in her forehead strained as well.

I grinned. She hated that I was touching Bryce. "You don't like this, huh?"

If she had a knife, I wondered if she would've used it right then and there. That was how she was looking at me now.

Oh, honey, you just made this so much easier for me, I thought before my entire attitude switched. I forced myself to relax. A new heat formed in me, and I welcomed it, letting it fill my body. I almost sighed. This was Bryce and me. This was our old connection, the attraction I'd always felt for him. I had kept it locked inside me for so long. It was overpowering, and because of that, it was too overwhelming for me.

I did bad things when I let my need go free, but that's what she didn't want. So that's what was coming out.

Bryce felt the shift, and he gazed at me, confused, then I let him see the hunger. His eyes darkened in lust. The response was like throwing gasoline onto burning coals. The flames leapt high in me, filling every inch of me and I wanted him. My blood was humming, the rush building and building, stretching my need for him until I was taking quick and shallow breaths.

The room started to melt away.

There were people there, people I hated. I felt a dark sensation in the room and knew that was the assistant. She was saying something behind her, but I didn't care. I lifted a hand and placed it onto Bryce's chest. He caught it, pressed it more firmly onto his chest, and I felt his heart racing.

God.

I wet my lips. Images of us together were on a constant loop playing in my head. As he kissed up my throat in our school's closet, as he slid inside me when we skipped class, when we had fought and he shoved me against the wall and kissed down between my breasts, so many times when he was above me, moving inside me, as he pinned my hands above my head. He'd watch me. I'd watch him.

I felt that primal connection coming back to me.

I wanted to feel that. I wanted to feel him again.

"Bryce," I murmured. It'd been so long.

"Stop," a voice snapped, and I was pulled away. Rough hands gripped my arms, tightening their hold. I felt nails against my skin, and I was shoved backward. Then a face was in front of me, and she snarled, "Get out. Get out of this room," she said over her shoulder. "Call security, Lupe."

Wait. I blinked. My chest was rising up and down, almost gasping for air. What was going on? I'd been trying to do something. My focus came back, and I saw the assistant glaring at me. Her hands were still on me, holding me back against the door. Her entire tiny body was writhing now. I could feel the suppressed anger from her, then my own came back, shoving whatever else had been going on with me out of the way.

I swallowed over a lump in my throat and shoved everything down.

Fuck. I'd been messing with Bryce to piss her off. It worked. Too well.

I gritted my teeth. All of that clicked in my head in one heartbeat, then I wrenched my arms up and around, unlocking her hold from me. I snarled, "Get off me." As her hands fell away, I shoved her back. One good push. She hit the wall by the bathroom.

"Hey!" Bryce shouted from behind me.

I tuned him out, tuned out all those other feelings about him too, and zeroed in on my target. I came in there for a fight—this was it. I wasn't going to let it get away now.

"Bryce!"

That voice. My anger went up as I recognized his ex-lover calling to him. She sounded panicked, stricken.

She was weak. But she wasn't my target. The assistant lifted her hand in the air, her fingers were spread out, and I knew a resounding slap was coming next.

I ducked her arm. As she swung through, hitting only arm, I twisted my arm up and around her. Pulling her head down, I cemented my hold, wrapping my other arm around her neck and latching onto my arm. I had her in a headlock.

Her feet, though. She was going to kick at me.

"STOP!"

Guadalupe was next to Bryce, her mouth hanging open. Her hair was up in some up do, and a brief thought to pull it out popped up in the back of my mind. I skimmed a hard look over her and saw the green dress she wore. The cleavage was loose, hanging low so there was a good eyeful of her breasts. Only the nipples remained covered. A string of pearls swung down in the cleavage as well. She held a phone in one hand and her purse in the other.

I wanted to rip those pearls from her neck, then I wanted to grab her phone.

Think, Sheldon! I barked at myself, struggling as Guadalupe's assistant was trying to break free from my hold. She kicked out, landing a good whack at my leg, and I almost buckled. She got the side of my knee. If she hurt my knee, she could really do damage to me, but I wanted Guadalupe's phone, too.

"Sheldon, what are you doing?" Bryce started toward me.

"Get back!" I maneuvered us so that I was against the wall, still holding the assistant in my headlock. While she kept trying to kick me, I applied pressure and lowered her to the ground. She couldn't kick as much now.

"STOP!" Guadalupe shouted, both of her hands, phone, and purse included, flew into the air. "What are you doing? This is insane."

It was. And it'd result in a restraining order. I hadn't thought everything through, but I needed that phone, and I needed this to go to the hotel lobby. I wanted the showdown to happen there, where people could hear.

My eyes darted to Bryce's, and I nodded at Guadalupe. He frowned. "What?" he mouthed at me.

I jerked my head in sporadic motions, widening my eyes dramatically. *The phone. The effin-loving phone. Get the phone.*

His eyes narrowed. He scratched behind his ear.

I rolled my eyes from frustration, then I felt teeth sink into my arm. I felt blinding pain first, then heard a scream rip out of my throat. The assistant bit me. I glanced down, and she was still biting me. Her teeth were fully embedded into my skin.

"Get off!" I rasped out, the scream had left me hoarse. "OFF!"

"Let her go!" Guadalupe rushed to my side and started to pull at my arm.

Her assistant's teeth sunk farther in, and my skin ripped from being pulled by Guadalupe. Batting her away, I clambered out, the pain slicing me, "You're making it worse."

"Let her go. She'll stop biting."

Fuck, fuck, fuck.

The pain was too much. I was starting not to be able to think clearly around it, then Guadalupe started clawing where my hand was locked onto my arm. Let go. That command sounded in my head and I obeyed, knowing it was the only way to get the assistant off me. As soon as I did, I started to fall sideways. Bryce scooped me up against him, held an arm around my waist, and pressed a towel to my arm. He murmured into my ear, "I got it."

I nodded, not remembering what we needed to get. I said anyway, "Good."

Guadalupe clasped a hand onto her assistant's arm, who stood to her feet. She wavered unsteadily, scowling at me, but she was sweating. The anger was still there, but she was weakened from the physical confrontation.

KNOCK, KNOCK!

"This is hotel security. Open the door," a deep voice commanded from the other side of the door.

The phone. It could have information or evidence we needed. We still needed to get it, but Guadalupe moved around me. She opened the door, allowing three security guards to come inside. They took one look at us, the blood on my arm, how haphazard the assistant looked, and immediately a guard grabbed my arm while another seized her arm. The leader lifted a hand radio to his mouth and pressed the side of it. "Two subjects. We're moving them to the security office."

"I want to press charges." Guadalupe pointed at me. "She attacked Maria."

Maria. That was her name. I'd been trying to remember. I sent *Maria* another scowl.

"I want to press charges, too," I announced.

Guadalupe cast me a dumbfounded look. "You came in here. You attacked *my* assistant."

Maria opened her mouth, but Guadalupe silenced her with a look. "Don't. I'll do the talking for you."

Where was Guadalupe's phone? I wondered that, but remarked, "She touched me first."

"What? That's ridiculous." As she held her hands up in frustration, I saw it was empty. I started to look around. Where could she have put it?

"All of this will be handled in my office." The head security guard gestured down the hallway. "Rick, Nelson, take them down to my office. Do not leave them alone." He stepped to the side.

As we started forward, I twisted around. The head security guard lifted a hand, stopping Bryce and Guadalupe from coming with us.

I called back, "I want Bryce with me."

Bryce looked at me and gave me the smallest headshake possible.

I shook my head back. "Yes. I want you with me."

"Rick, don't let her go. This will be handled with the hotel only."

Wait—what? The elevator doors opened, and we were led inside. As they slid closed, the guard holding onto me, Rick, pushed the lobby button. The office was on the main floor. I tucked that information to the back of my mind and asked, "You guys aren't going to call the cops?"

He stared at me, but didn't respond.

The other guard, Nelson, ignored me. He was staring straight ahead. Maria was on the other side of him, leaning against the wall. She was staring right at me.

I rolled my eyes. "Stuff your hostility. This had been coming for a while, and you know it."

She shot back to her feet. "Stay away from Bryce! That's what I know. He broke Lupe's heart when he tossed her away for you."

I frowned, confused for a moment. That's right. She was angry with me because of him. This was about Corrigan to me. "Fast forward. That's completely over between them. There's no shot for her."

As I said that, some of the flames from before awoke again. I remembered the press of his body against mine. The warmth, how he felt with his hands on my hips. His touch had been intimate. A tingle started again, remembering the hunger I always used to feel for him.

My throat became dry. Before I caught myself, I wet my lips, envisioning that almost-feral look in Bryce's eyes again. It was there, but it had been banked for so long, but the stoic, no-nonsense Bryce was still there.

A sick laugh drew my attention from my thoughts. Maria was shaking her head as she smirked. "You're the one with no shot. Lupe and him. It's been destined. They're supposed to be together."

The guard's hand tightened on my arm. "Enough! Stop talking, both of you."

"No."

Maria shot him a withering look as well.

Then the elevator doors slid open, and we were led into a hallway. I could hear sounds from the lobby growing clearer so I knew we were heading toward it, then our hallway intercepted another hallway and there it was. But my guard kept going forward. We were going past the main lobby.

That couldn't happen.

I started to go for the lobby. Rick stopped and pulled me back. Maria looked confused, too.

I strained against his hold, but again, he jerked me back. "The office is this way." He started forward, but I dug my heels in. My thoughts were swirling. I needed to break free from his hold.

"What are you doing?"

I still didn't move.

"Look." Rick shook his head at me. "We'll handle this internally. I know both of you want to press charges against each other, but our boss is back there and will talk sense into both of your parties. This hotel does not allow scandals to happen." As he was speaking, he was studying me, weighing the impact of his words. "I'm sure you don't really want the police to be called."

"He's right," Maria called out. Her guard and she were waiting for us farther down the hallway. "Think about this. You're being an idiot. I'm heated too, but you're wanted for murder. This can be dealt with quietly. You can press charges later, if you really want to."

She was scared.

Her eyes were more focused. She was thinking clearly again, but so was I. I heard what she was saying. I heard what the guard was saying, too. They wanted this to go away, both parties. Maria and the hotel. This would hurt Guadalupe. That was Maria's main concern now.

I needed the press. She did not.

I'd have to make a run for it, an abrupt break from his hold. I needed to do it, surprising him, or he wouldn't let me go.

Maria saw my intention and shook her head. "What are you thinking? Think about your murder case."

"I am."

Then, with a quick prayer thought in my mind because I had no idea what consequences might come from this, I burst forward at a sprint. I tore from the guard's hold and the chase was on.

CHAPTER TEN

There were two reporters by the front door. They were just inside the lobby and hiding in a back corner. A fountain and a row of trees were helping to cover them so the staff wouldn't kick them out. There wasn't much to identify them. One was dressed in business pants and a professional looking silk shirt, while the other had on a business skirt, a similar shirt as the other one. It was in how they were made up. Their makeup was flawless, but heavy enough to be noticed in person. Not on camera. On camera, they would've looked perfect. Their hair was also styled to frame their faces, but there was enough volume added to their hair to make it known it wasn't holding up by itself. There were also two guys behind each of them, dressed in other clothes, clothes that weren't meant to be seen on camera, but to be comfortable off camera. I didn't know where their cameras were, but the fountain and row of trees were probably hiding those as well.

I made sure to sprint right past them, and as I did, I heard their gasps. One said, "That's Sheldon Jeneve!" I heard them scrambling, but I went to the front desk. I got their attention; that's all I wanted. Once at the front desk, I stopped. One moment. One breath. I had no idea what would happen after this, but I held onto the front desk as my knees buckled, whatever would happen—was going to happen.

I raised my head up. I was going to make this count.

"Miss?" The front desk clerk looked stunned.

"Sheldon!"

I turned. One of the reporters was coming right for me, and there was no hiding on her part. Her microphone was extended toward me, and the camera was perched on the guy's shoulder behind her.

The front desk staff went into action then as well. "No press allowed." The front desk clerk had gotten over her stunned spell. She pressed a button, then lifted her phone.

"Sheldon Jeneve, why are you here in this hotel?"

The second reporter asked, "Did you come with Bryce Scout or Denton Steele? Are you dating either of them?"

The front door slid open, and two more reporters ran inside. That was when the security guard, who'd been after me, cursed and veered for the front door instead. He grabbed one reporter and physically carried her back out. More guards were streaming into the lobby by then, along with other hotel staff.

Crap. They were going to snuff this before it even began. I had to talk quickly. I leaned into the closest microphone and looked straight at the camera.

A hush went through the room then. They were all waiting for me to speak. Not even the reporters dared make a sound.

A tickle started at the back of my neck, and I turned, pulled by some invisible force, and I saw Corrigan standing in a side hallway, just off the main walking ways in the hotel. He caught my gaze and a small, so tiny and ever so slight smirk formed as he nodded to me. That was his approval. He was giving me a nod of encouragement. I felt it, warming all of me, filling me up and tears threatened to spill. I blinked rapidly, holding them back, but then I saw Bryce appear beside Corrigan. They were both waiting in the shadows for me.

That was enough for me. Both of them there together.

I turned back around and spoke, closing my eyes and not giving a shit how ridiculous I looked. I was speaking from my heart.

I said, "I came here today for one reason, to confront the woman who cut my car's brakes last spring. That incident was buried by the police department and ignored. It resulted in one of my best friends, who was driving the car, being put in the hospital—"

Light bulbs started flashing as I talked and someone asked from the side, "Can you give us a name?"

"Who cut your brake line?"

"Do you have proof the police covered it up?"

More and more people were filling up the lobby. After the first person spoke up, questions were thrown at me.

"Are you saying the police department isn't looking at all the evidence? Is this a cover-up?"

"Are you being framed? Is that what you're saying?"

I ignored all of them, needing to say what I had come to deliver. I opened my mouth again and started, "I was at his bedside when I was notified that another friend had been murdered."

There was a sudden pause, but I knew it wouldn't last. I could only imagine what they were thinking. This is when I opened my eyes. They were stunned, but there were others whose eyes were lit up from excitement.

This was my statement. Grace's murder had never been addressed by anyone in my camp. I shouldn't do this, but I was. I took a breath.

Here goes.

Clearing my throat, I said softly at first, "I've always been known for being mean, for being a bully, for pushing others down—"

A female pushed closer, jostling the crowd. "Are you saying you're not?"

Another hushed her. "Let her finish, Annie."

I started again, ignoring the interruption, "The truth is that I don't push people down to hurt them. I do it to protect myself. I'm sure you are all very aware of my mother. Using me has become her ticket for attention. I do not endorse that, nor do I have a relationship with my mother, but I'm aware that I will never be able to stop her from this behavior. I bring her up as one example of who I grew up with. She's my mother, but she's someone who uses me."

"You're saying you're the misunderstood victim now?"

Another person laughed. "That's quite a defense, there."

I shook my head. They were going to spin it into something else, but I had to try. I just had to try. "Grace Barton was one of those people I was cruel to. I thought she was a fake person. I was wrong. I learned she was a genuine person. She was one of the strongest people I have ever known." I drew in a shuddering breath as suppressed sobs choked me. As my emotion was heard, the room quieted again. "Grace became one of my best friends, along with two others." I glanced to the side. So did everyone else.

Cameras started flashing again, and I heard whispers. "Bryce Scout."

"That's Corrigan Raimler."

"All three of them are here. That can't be coincidental."

Someone called out to me, "What about Denton Steele? Are the two of you still good friends? He drove here an hour ago. Is that how you got on the premises?"

I ignored everything; I had to get this out. My heart was pounding. "I need to be very clear about one thing. The headlines are saying that Grace was my enemy. She was not. Our friendship hit a bump in the road. She was taken in by a sorority in the hopes they could draw me in as well. I believe they wanted to use my relationships with certain people to help further their own house. I am not a sorority girl. In my experience, most girls have always stabbed me in the back so I shy away from large groups of females especially." I paused, then chuckled. "Well, shy isn't the right word. That's not my way, but Grace didn't believe me when I told her she was being used. She was blinded by the power of being accepted and being popular. She's the one who pushed me into a glass table. She also helped vandalize my home and the night she was murdered, she confessed to all of it. Grace Barton was not my enemy. She had hurt me, but she was trying to make amends."

This was the hard part. Even thinking about that night, I felt tears welling up.

Screw it.

I let them fall. This was my heartfelt speech. I had to make it heartfelt all the way through. I couldn't hold anything back now. "I was stubborn that night when Grace apologized to me. I told her it wasn't enough, but the truth is that it was. It would've been. I really believe that Grace and I would've made things better. We might not have had the closeness we had before, but I would've tried. Grace was a genuine person who had lost her way. She realized that fact and she took responsibility for it. I don't know who killed her. I know the police think I did, but I didn't." My voice trembled. "I loved Grace and to whoever *did* kill her." I turned so I was looking directly into the camera. I hardened myself. I made sure my voice didn't wobble. "To whoever killed her, I'm coming for you. I don't know who you are, but I will find you. I. Will. Make. You. Pay. That's my promise to you."

As soon as I finished, a surge of adrenaline filled the frenzy. People started pushing to get closer, knowing I was leaving soon. I could feel their desperation.

"Sheldon," someone murmured my name. It wasn't a reporter. There wasn't a hidden agenda attached to that voice. I looked up, reacting to the intimate concern I heard. It was Denton. The flashes were blinding, and he held a hand up to shield his eyes. He said to me as he tugged at my hand, "Come on. You said what you needed to say. We have to go."

"Denton! Denton!"

"Sheldon, are you threatening the real killer? Are you going to get revenge for your friend's murder?"

"Denton, are the two of you a romantic couple now?"

"What about Guadalupe? Is she still with Bryce Scout? Sheldon, what do you think of their relationship?"

"You said you were here to confront who cut your brake lines?"

Hearing that last question, I stopped. Denton stopped as well. We were halfway to where Bryce and Corrigan were. Seeing that I had paused, they started for us. They were going to flank me and pull me from the growing mob.

I saw the determination on both of their faces.

Turning, I looked in the direction of who asked that question. Realizing they had my attention, they called out again, "Did you? Who cut your brakes?"

Everyone held still, waiting for my answer.

I had no idea where Maria was, or Guadalupe. I knew they were furious with me, but I was just as furious with them. Guadalupe took Bryce from me. Her assistant tried to take me away, hurting Corrigan in the process.

Maria was obsessed with Guadalupe, but Guadalupe was obsessed with Bryce.

So I said, speaking my first lie in this whole twisted tragedy, "Guadalupe Ramirez cut the brake lines on my car. She did it because Bryce Scout was going to leave her to renew our relationship. She wanted to hurt me. She wanted me out of the way."

Then I turned and ducked my head. Bryce froze beside me, but as I moved past him, he and Corrigan formed a wall around me. With Denton, all three of them hustled me from the main lobby. Security staff was waiting for us, and one guy clipped out, "What the hell was that?"

Denton shot back, "Just get us out here. She could be in danger."

He jerked his head forward and began to lead the way. We were shown down a hallway, through the kitchen, and down into a basement hallway. I had no idea where we were going, but then we climbed stairs, and a set of doors were thrown open. The sun was harsh, and I squinted against it, trying to see where we were.

I had no idea.

We were behind a different building, one that I didn't recognize from the hotel. A car was waiting for us, and we climbed inside. Before Denton closed the door, the head security stuck his head inside. He looked stern as he said, "I'm warning you. The hotel is not happy with the stunt you pulled in there."

Denton reached for the door. "Shut it, Deacon. My team will deal with any ramifications your hotel might drum up."

"So, that's how it's going to be?"

"She did nothing wrong. I doubt Maria will press charges and Sheldon only spoke her side."

"She lied."

Denton stopped, glared up at him, and said, "Prove it." Then he shut the door. The guard jerked up out of the way. Once it was closed, Denton pressed a button and ordered, "Let's go home."

Corrigan asked, after we had traveled a few blocks in silence, "So, to recap this last venture, was it successful?"

I laughed, emotionally drained. "I put the assistant in a headlock."

"You did?"

Bryce chuckled. "She did. It was ridiculous to watch."

I grinned at him. "I was trying to distract her and Guadalupe so you could get her phone."

Corrigan glanced over. "Did you?"

Bryce held my gaze for a moment. More had happened up there, but I didn't want to talk about it. He nodded, understanding me even though I had no idea how he could know. He said, "Yes." He pulled out a phone, but it wasn't Guadalupe's.

"I wanted you to get Guadalupe's phone."

"It wouldn't have mattered. She doesn't keep anything on it worthwhile to us. Maria's, however, is a whole other story." He pressed the screen and started to scroll through it. Then he handed it over to me. Right there, on the screen, in black and bold letters was a text from her to Guadalupe. I smiled. I couldn't hold it back, and it stretched from ear to ear.

I looked at Corrigan. "You asked if this venture had been worth it?" I passed the screen to him. "It was more worth it than you can imagine."

Right there, on the screen, Maria wrote, **I cut the brakes. Now that bitch won't be in the way.**

Guadalupe responded, **Good. Bryce is mine.**

"Whoa." Corrigan's eyebrows went up. "It's right there." He pressed a few more buttons and handed it back to Bryce.

"What'd you do?"

"I sent that shit to the cops. Now let's watch 'em squirm."

My sentiments exactly.

CHAPTER ELEVEN

We were met in the front entrance by my dad and Beth. I had one second to take in the fury and balled fists before my dad started yelling. He was throwing questions at me, and I felt déjà vu from the reporters again.

I checked out. I'd been through the wringer just now. I wasn't going to sign up for another one. Bryce and Corrigan took over, though. I went to the back and rested while I let all of them duke it out.

Somewhere, in between my dad's constant yelling and Bryce swearing back at him, I heard my dad yell, "Then what the hell were you thinking? This doesn't help her case at all! It's all over the news! Our personal phones are being flooded with calls."

Corrigan flung his hands up in the air. "Fuck her case then."

My dad went rigid. His eyeballs almost popped out. "Excuse me?"

"I said, 'Fuck her case.'" Corrigan folded his arms back over his chest and leaned back against the wall. He glanced to Bryce, the two shared a look, and Corrigan seemed even firmer in his statement. "I said what I said."

"You said what you said?" My dad shook his head in disbelief. "Are you kidding me? Are you KIDDING me?"

Corrigan frowned.

Bryce moved to stand next to him.

My dad burst out again, "Her case is everything! They only have circumstantial evidence on her, but with this stunt—this is actually something. The media has this now. They can see her yelling and cursing. You think people are going to like that? Public opinion matters. If the public hates her, that doesn't help her case."

Yelling and cursing. I started to laugh to myself. Of course that was all he had heard. He hadn't looked past the volume of my voice. He didn't actually hear the message I was sending. For some reason, this struck me as hilarious, and the laughter kept pealing out of me. I couldn't stop it. The tension in the room was thick, and I knew this was inappropriate, but fuck it, how Corrigan said, just fuck it. This was hilarity gold. My own father had no clue the message I was sending to the real killer.

"You think this is funny?"

It wasn't my dad who expressed judgment. I had expected it from him, but I glanced up, wiping tears from my eyes, as I couldn't contain myself. It was Beth who stood with her hands formed into fists, resting on both hips. Her feet were spread out and a firm look of disapproval was on her face, it was worse than my father's. A glaze of dislike mixed with it. That helped contain my laughter, and I stood, rolling my shoulders back, and I tilted my head to the side.

"Oh boy," Denton muttered behind me.

I stepped toward her, but caught another look shared between Corrigan and Bryce. All three of them knew the shift that had just happened, but they didn't say anything. They knew. They had learned. No one judged me, not unless they earned that right to judge me, and this time, this girlfriend of my father's, had just made a huge mistake.

I asked coolly, "You disapprove of me?"

A flattened look entered her gaze, and her hands fell from her hips, but she didn't move back. She held her ground.

That was a point for her, for now. I moved even closer, so it was just her and me, staring at each other. Face to face. On the same eye level, I asked, so softly now, "Do you think I'm not acting appropriately?"

"Sheldon—" My dad started toward us, but I caught movement from the corner of my eye. Both Bryce and Corrigan blocked him with their heads slightly down. They were going to let me finish what Beth had started.

"Do you?" I prompted again. She hadn't said a word since her first outburst. I was waiting. I was hoping for it.

"I think—" she stammered, then stopped to regroup. Then her tone came out firmer, clearer, "I think your father has done nothing except try to help you, but you have only met his actions with a level of ungratefulness that I've never witnessed before."

"You think that?"

"Yes." Her gaze was firm. "I do. It would be in your best interest to listen to him. He's only trying to help."

Then I laughed. It was soft, almost tentative at first, and then grew to a harsher, mocking sound. As I kept going, Beth pressed her lips together.

"Do you think I was acting inappropriately when I was stalked in high school?"

Just a slight flicker of confusion appeared before it was masked. Her chest rose and dropped as she made a sound of annoyance.

I nodded. "Do you think it was appropriate for my father to leave me during that time?"

Another small flicker of question. Did she not know the history? I cocked my head to the side and scratched at my chin. Maybe she didn't? So I asked, "How was I supposed to act when two girls that I liked and wanted to call friends were killed?"

She wasn't holding back the confusion now. She glanced to my father, but I blocked her view. I wanted her to deal with me, not him, not whatever he would say to make my questions irrelevant. I knew he would somehow, it was his way and his idea of how to handle this, but I was the one with experience. Not him. Beth needed to get this reality check.

"Beth?"

"Huh?" She looked down to the ground and expelled another sigh.

I frowned. Why all the sighing? She hadn't been stalked. "Am I bothering you?"

"No—"

I interrupted, with a chilling smile, "Good, because I haven't even gotten started."

"Sheldon, this is enough—" My dad tried to push through Bryce and Corrigan. They closed ranks again, forcing him back. When he started to go around, Denton straightened from the wall, a third in the line now. Bryce and Corrigan were facing me, their backs to my father, but Denton was staring right at my dad. He said quietly, "Let your daughter finish."

"Denton!" My dad bristled.

"I'm sorry, Neil, but I think it's something you both need to hear."

I felt the change from my dad. He backed up and took another inventory of the situation. I considered it from his point of view. Here I was, a daughter that he hadn't seen in years, but who came across like a bitch. She drank too much and was way too highly sexualized as a kid. That was me. Jaded, but real. Now fast forward where he's in his own world, with his shiny new girlfriend, and he's forced to bring in his abandoned daughter. She's wanted for murder. She's got an attitude and she won't sit still and just be thankful for the help he's providing. Now he's been put in his place, the movie star had spoken, the one that had been separate from all my bad behaviors growing up.

I got the distinct impression that my father would shut up and start thinking differently. Maybe. I hoped.

"Go ahead," Bryce prompted me.

I nodded and met Beth's gaze again. The bite had left me so my tone wasn't as clipped as earlier. "I've been stalked. I've been hunted. I've had two and now three friends murdered. I almost lost one of my family twice," I gestured to Corrigan, "and I've killed someone too, but it wasn't the murder I'm being framed for. The cops didn't help catch Marcus. We did that. They didn't catch who shoved me into a glass table or who cut my brakes. Grace confessed to the first, and we finally got a confession for who put Corrigan in the hospital a second time. So, if you're asking me to be quiet and sit back because it looks bad for my case? I won't do that."

"Sheldon," she murmured.

I lifted a hand, stopping her. I needed to finish, for her and my father. "I won't sit back and hope things get better. Life doesn't get better if I do nothing. I've learned that the hard way, but it's my life now. It's my freedom. My future." I whipped around, the need for my dad to hear this was urgent in me. I went to him, and Corrigan and Bryce parted for me. I was right in front of him. "If you think I was yelling and cursing in that hotel lobby and that's all I was doing, you're an idiot. I was saying 'fuck you' to Grace's murderer. I wanted him to know that I'm not scared and I'm not quaking in my boots. I'm ready to fight and if he won't come to me, I'm more than ready to go hunt him down instead." I stopped, my chest was heaving.

Neil held my gaze, studying me intently, and then he let out a soft breath. His head hung down, and he said, "I'm sorry, Sheldon."

I closed my eyes. Those words hit me like a blast of cold air. I never knew I needed to hear them, but as soon as he uttered those words, a hole inside my chest shrunk a tiny bit. I felt raw. I was dying of thirst, and I had been starving for that message from him for so long. I blinked and stumbled back a step. Someone caught my arm and held me upright.

I had no idea I'd been yearning for those words.

Then I stopped myself, stopped any crumbling I might've done. I wasn't Daddy's little girl. I never had been, and those two words weren't about to bring that change for me. My fairytale was the neglected princess who fought for her own survival.

I'd keep surviving. I'd keep fighting. I never needed my dad before, and I sure as hell didn't need him now.

I turned away and left.

As I passed the hallway leading to the front door, I heard a quiet voice. "Sheldon?"

My feet stopped before I registered a new presence, and I turned, stricken, horrified, and for some reason, glad at the same time.

"Mena?" That couldn't be right. I blinked, rubbed at my eyes, but it was her.

She held a hand up in a small wave. "Hey . . ." Her tiny smile turned timid and she tucked her hand back to her side, slipping inside a sweatshirt she was wearing. The jet-black hair was gone. She had dyed it blond, but it looked natural. She was still petite. She'd been wearing a tank top, trendy miniskirt, and black boots the first time I met her. Dressed in jeans, a sweatshirt, and sneakers, she barely looked like the same person. "I'm guessing my brother didn't tell you I was coming?"

"Sheldon?" Corrigan was coming, followed by Bryce, and Denton. The first two slammed to a halt right behind me, riveted by Mena as well.

I waited, holding my breath. Then I heard Corrigan exclaim, "What the hell, Denton?"

"Fuck," Bryce grunted, raking his hand through his hair. "FUCK!"

Mena frowned at her brother. "You didn't tell them?"

"Uh . . ." Denton went to her side, facing us, and held his hands out. "Sorry, guys. It . . . this," he gestured to his sister, "completely slipped my mind with everything going on."

Mena turned, facing him squarely. She moved her head to the side and her hand came back out from her sweatshirt to land on her hip. "You remembered to tell me."

He shot her a pointed look. "I know. Thank you." He looked right at me. "I'm sorry. I really am. She's going to college here."

"My college?" Corrigan cursed, starting to pace back and forth behind me. "This fucking sucks!"

Denton ignored him, talking over him, "She's only here for a while, until she gets on her feet with school. The plan is for her to wait a few months and then find a friend, someone we both trust for her to room with."

"So, she's here? For the duration?" Bryce's tone was sharp. He was sending her a dark look. "How long have you known we'd be here?"

She opened her mouth, but Denton moved in front of her, blocking her from Bryce's interrogation. He folded his arms over his chest and clipped out, back to him, "You need to back down. Mena's my sister, and she has more right to be in this house than you do—"

"Exactly my point," Bryce ground out. He didn't back down. "Did you know about this before we came here?"

"Yes, but—"

"We shouldn't have come here." Bryce reached for my arm and started to push me back to the hallway. "We're leaving. We're not safe with her here."

"Hey! Whoa. Whoa," Denton called us back. "She's my sister. I can't turn her out."

"No." Bryce shook his head. "You should've turned us out. That's the whole point. You know how we feel about your sister—"

Mena stepped toward us. "I'm right here."

Bryce kept going, "—even if you trust her, I don't. Corrigan doesn't. I highly doubt Sheldon does."

As he said those last three words, I felt Mena's gaze come toward me, resting on me. A weird sensation of guilt filled me, and I stepped to the side, away from Bryce and Denton. I didn't know what this feeling was about. Mena had burned her bridges. I had taken her under my wing, befriended her, but she hadn't stood up to Bryce and Corrigan. She didn't earn their trust, even when I told them to give her a shot, but I couldn't do it for her. They did. They shut up, gave her an opening to stand up to them, but she hadn't.

They broke her instead, and she started to sleep with one of our enemies. She became one of our enemies after that and had a full meltdown at one of our parties where she was found by Denton and then shipped off to a psychiatric place. She'd been there for a long time, and the last I heard was that she had gone to a residential program somewhere else.

It was Grace.

That was the guilt I was feeling.

Grace had been our common link at the end. She went to visit Mena, and according to Grace, Mena always asked how I was doing. *". . . you feel guilty because you couldn't help Mena. I was a better friend to Mena so you befriending me is almost like you're supporting Mena in a way."* Grace's voice came back to me, and I reached out for the wall. Her words washed over me, mingling with so many other emotions—grief, pain, being haunted, all of those and more. I shook my head, needing to clear my thoughts. I couldn't . . . Grace's voice drifted back, I couldn't shake her words, *"Mena didn't want you to know how far she'd fallen."*

How far she had fallen. I lifted pained eyes. Mena was watching me intently. Searching her gaze, I didn't see the embarrassment that Grace had mentioned when I asked about their visits.

She looked strong. She looked content. She looked at peace.

Not like Grace, my own thought laughed at me, taunting me. Grace was dead. Grace wasn't strong. Grace wasn't content.

Grace was dead.

I felt her, right then and there, like she was in the room with me. I felt rage from her. She was definitely not at peace.

"When are you going to avenge me? When are you going to deal with my murderer?" I winced, feeling her laughing at me.

"Grace," I whispered under my breath, folding over. My head bent forward and I slumped down against the wall closest to me. I hadn't done a thing, not yet, but I was trying.

"You're just focused on yourself. Yourself, Sheldon. It's always about you. What about me? I'm dead. DEAD! You're alive. Stop crying over that fact."

I shook my head. This wasn't real. Grace really wasn't there. She wasn't haunting me.

"STOP!"

Everything was too much. I couldn't lift my head. I couldn't focus on what they were saying, whoever they were. Mena's shrill voice broke through, but I kept my eyes closed. A part of me, the irrational side of me, was scared that if I looked up, Grace would be sitting next to me. Angry. Hateful. Disappointed.

It wasn't about me. It was about Grace. This was all about her now. She was right, whether she'd been real or not. I had to suck it up and find her murderer, not for me. For her.

"Grace," I whispered again. I am so sorry. I am so sorry.

"Sheldon?" Corrigan was kneeling in front of me. His hand cupped the bottom of my face and he lifted my head.

I kept my eyes closed. I couldn't look. She'd be there.

"Sheldon?" Bryce's voice was close; he was next to Corrigan. "What's wrong?"

"No." I tried to pull from Corrigan's hand, but he kept it firm. He didn't let me go. Instead, he murmured, "Hey. Hey."

"No." I tried again.

"Hey, come on. It's me." He moved closer, and I felt his arms sliding underneath me. Then he picked me up and stood, cradling me against his chest.

I tucked my head into his shoulder and burrowed there. My hands clutched onto his shoulders. I didn't want him to let me go.

He readjusted his hold to free one hand. Then he smoothed it down the side of my face, tucking my hair behind my ear. I heard him say, his voice coming through his chest to me, "She needs rest. I'm thinking this breakdown was bound to happen."

Then, with a soft murmur for my ears only, he whispered, "I won't leave you." He turned and left. He headed to my room and laid me down on the bed. When he straightened and started to leave, I acted on impulse. I wasn't thinking.

I reached for his hand.

He stopped, looked down. "Sheldon," he started, the struggle obvious on his face.

I tugged on his hand again. "I don't care." I should've. But I didn't. "Stay with me. I don't want to be alone."

I didn't want to be alone with Grace. As he gave in and crawled to lay behind me, I held onto him as he rested an arm over me. Corrigan was my shelter. He always had been. A part of me knew this was wrong. I shouldn't be using him this way, but I needed someone with me. I had to.

"Grace," I whispered, closing my eyes, and settling farther down in the bed.

"Mmm?" Corrigan lifted his head.

"Nothing." I cleared my throat. "Nothing."

But I felt her.

I had a feeling she wasn't going anywhere.

CHAPTER TWELVE

When I awoke, Corrigan wasn't beside me. I frowned. The bed felt vacant, but I had slept with him for so many nights before, when I only wanted to be held and comforted.

Knock, knock.

I lifted my head at the door. That's what had awoken me.

Knock, knock.

It came again. Sitting up in bed, I gazed around, saw the darkness outside the window and wondered how long I had been sleeping.

"Sheldon?"

It was Bryce. Hurrying to the door, I opened it, but looked around behind me. Was Corrigan in the bathroom? Should it matter? But it did. Bryce had lifted his hand for another knock. He lowered it, his eyes penetrating mine as he asked, so soft and so damn tenderly, "You okay?"

Normally I would lie. "No." I didn't this time.

He nodded, his face clouded with concern and wariness. He cleared his throat. "Is Corrigan with you?"

My eyes flung back to him. He knew. I swallowed back a small amount of guilt, raking my fingers through my hair. "He was. I—" How did I put this? How could I explain it? "I needed someone and—"

Bryce nodded, finishing for me, "I know."

I hadn't asked for him. That unspoken message seemed to hang between us, and I felt how heavy the atmosphere turned. Shit. I caught the hurt in his eyes. I reached out, again not thinking, and touched his arm. He didn't move back, but he didn't take my hand in his. I hadn't wanted him to. I just wanted to reassure him. So I said, "Corrigan's been there for me. You know this. After Marcus—" I stumbled on my words. My cheeks flushed. What was wrong with me?

"Sheldon," Bryce squeezed my hand, lifting it from his arm, but he let it go. It fell back to my side. "I understand. I really do."

Did he? He didn't think he was needed. I read that thought and surged across the space between us, or I started to. I stopped. Fear slammed me back.

I was scared of reaching out to Bryce. I was scared of comforting him, of telling him . . . what? I had no idea. I finally just admitted, "I want to come to you. I do, but my feelings are locked inside me. Corrigan's always been there for me. I'm not saying you haven't, except about Guadalupe, but that's partly me. I pushed you away. I left you for him. Screwing another girl, I can't really get mad at you for that, but . . ."

"Sheldon," he started again, pointing down the hallway.

"I'm sorry." I needed to feel vulnerable. I needed to peel open my doors and let whatever happened happen, but that's what I was fighting against. Not Bryce. Just whatever would happen when I did that.

I didn't want to feel vulnerable. That's *all* I was now.

"Hey." He stepped closer. His tone turned soothing and he cupped the side of my face. His thumb rested on my cheek, and a tender smile looked back down at me.

God. My chest filled. The tenderness there was loving. My pulse started to pick up, and I was struggling to stand still. I felt my knees starting to knock against each other. His hand was holding me in place. My entire body snapped to attention at that small touch from him. Without thinking or realizing, I lifted a hand to rest over his own, but his words were a slap to me.

"The police are here."

"Oh." My hand thumped back to my side, and I retreated back to my room, moving from his shelter. I looked, as if they would be coming up the hallway, coming to arrest me once again. "Where?"

"At the front door. The hotel thing. They're pissed."

"Why? I didn't violate anything."

He lifted a shoulder, frowning darkly. "Who knows, but they're here, and they're pissed. I guess your dad was supposed to have informed them when we left his house and came here, but he didn't."

Police were a pain in my ass on a normal day. Pissed police were going to be a fucking hangover that could never be nursed away.

I groaned, my faculties quickly coming back to me. I needed to fight. *Get it together, Sheldon.* I needed to be clear, calm, and rational when I went down there. They were the enemy now. I'd have to fight. I always had to fight.

"Okay. I'm ready."

"You sure?"

I nodded. "Let's go." I gritted my teeth. Bryce started forward, and I followed, shutting my door. As we went downstairs and back to the front entrance, déjà vu came over me. I'd just been there. The same group had been there, with the same concerned and angry expressions. Skimming a quick eye over them, there was no Mena this time. The two detectives who had interrogated me had hostile looks on their faces.

Okay.

I stopped and turned toward them. "De*fec*tives." It was game on.

The woman rolled her eyes, then rested her hands on her hips. The ends of her suit jacket were pushed back from the motion, her badge and gun were clipped to her hip. She wore a buttoned-down shirt, tucked inside her jeans that showed off her trim figure. She didn't look the hostile mess she'd been at the police station. Her hair had been in a messy bun, the ends loose, but this time her hair was swept into a pristine-looking bun, clipped at the base of her skull. She looked the epitome of a professional, then I caught the sideways glance at Denton, and her lips pressed together for a split second.

"Denton Steele was a witness as well." She sighed. "I'd like to get his witness testimony."

Her words came back to me from the interrogation room. I had thought it was a manipulation to get me to talk, but maybe not. As her gaze lingered on the movie star, she pressed her hand against the side of her head, making sure her hair was in place.

I grunted. A smart-ass comment was on the tip of my tongue, but I caught Bryce's look. His eyebrows shot up and the message was received. He had caught the look too and he was right, I swallowed my comment.

Her eyes narrowed, then when I kept my mouth shut, she said, "We're not here for a fight, but we are here for some extra measures."

"Extra measures?" My dad materialized from behind me. As he moved in front of me, he held Beth's hand in his behind his back. She paused next to me and glanced sideways at me. My dad cleared his throat. "What are you talking about?"

Officer Molls shifted so she was facing my dad squarely. "Your daughter was supposed to notify of us of her whereabouts."

"She did." My dad amended, "My lawyers did when they posted her bail, and we notified you about why we moved to this home."

"Yeah. They did." The female detective shifted so she could see me around him. "But Sheldon's not a normal suspect. She's out, but pending house arrest."

"This is ridiculous. She's not been found guilty ye—" Neil bit back what he'd been about to say.

Yet.

She's not been found guilty yet. That's what he'd been about to say. At that understanding, I moved back a step. My dad thought I was guilty. I crossed my arms over my chest. That meant he thought I had done it—I had killed Grace.

My throat burned.

My own father didn't believe in me.

Bryce stepped close to me. He didn't reach out and touch me, but the back of my elbow rested against his chest. It was his way of being there for me and I closed my eyes, feeling him move in even more. I drew in his strength.

Corrigan came to my other side. They were both flanking me, showing their support for me, then we heard Denton speak. All three of us looked at the same time.

Denton said, "What do you mean 'pending house arrest,' officer?" He moved closer, cutting off my dad as he'd been about to speak again, and as I watched him, Denton transformed into his movie star persona. His eyes squinted slightly, becoming darker and beckoning. His head lifted so it was at a seductive slant, and the corners of his mouth curved up in an alluring grin.

In that one second, he had gone from my childhood neighbor to the guy who graced billboards all across the nation.

And it worked.

Detective Molls' chest rose and held still. Her eyes widened and her lips parted. Then her cheeks reddened and her hand lifted back up to flatten her hair against her head. It stayed there, as if holding the side of her head and she seemed paralyzed, gazing into Denton's eyes for a moment.

"Molls," her partner rasped out. He snapped his fingers, drawing his partner's attention back to the room.

"What?" She jerked backward, breaking her gaze from Denton to look around the group. Her voice was hoarse. "Huh?"

Denton's grin grew, becoming even more mesmerizing.

Her gaze skirted back to him and she swallowed. "Um." Her hand fell back to her side, flattening over her badge.

I narrowed my eyes, wondering if that was a nervous tick. She touched her badge when she was nervous? No. She was still looking at Denton, like she couldn't turn away. She was off-balance. She was star struck; that's what she was. He had stripped away her control.

"Get ahold of yourself, Molls." Her partner moved so he was standing in front of her, addressing the group. The same no-nonsense attitude he had at the police station was with him again. His eyes snapped to mine and he narrowed them, lifting a package that he'd been holding in his hand. "You get an ankle monitor, Princess."

I started to surge forward. To be honest, I wasn't sure which pissed me off first. The babysitting bracelet or the fact he called me *Princess*. I snarled. I'd show him a princess, and my hand formed into a fist, lifting to swing.

"Oh whoa." Bryce grabbed me by the hip and pulled me backward.

"Shit." Corrigan saw it, too.

Both of them came together in front of me, like two ends of a curtain closing in one brisk movement.

"What?"

Bryce spoke loudly, "How does that work?"

"This?"

"The ankle monitor, yes." Bryce's elbow nudged Corrigan.

"Yeah," Corrigan added. "Like does she only have so many feet to go or what? You said she's under house arrest. Is that legal? She's not been convicted. Isn't that when that punishment happens?"

The male detective's voice was strained, tense. "Not that I have to explain the actions of our judicial system, but she's not technically under house arrest. She will," his voice grew clearer, and I could tell he was moving toward me, "need to wear this so we know where she is at all times."

Bryce and Corrigan held firm.

The guy stopped right in front of them, then he said in a low warning, "Move aside, gentlemen."

"It's fine, you guys." I touched both of them on the back. They moved aside, but only after another moment of standing guard for me.

As they did, the male detective raked a hard eye over me before he knelt at my feet. I lifted my pant leg, and he put the ankle monitor on me. Just like that, no big fuss, and I was tagged like an animal. I glanced down, lifting my ankle so I could see it better.

I was a walking GPS alert now. This was awesome. I groaned. "Can I shower with this thing?"

"Nope." He hoisted himself back up. There was no sympathy on his face at all. "Stick the leg out and wrap it with a bag if you don't want to get electrocuted or have the police department at your house. There are no alerts set if you wander out of the house. You can go about as much as you want, which I doubt is much since everyone and their long-lost aunt knows you're The Queen Bee Killer, but whatever rocks your boat. Just know we can always find you now." He smiled a very nice fuck-off sort of smile, and he winked. "Have a good day, now."

Sliding past Bryce and Corrigan, he gave them both a once-over, then looked to Denton. He was thinking something. I could see it on his face, but all he did was grunt and shake his head. Then he murmured, back at the door, "Come on, Molls. I've got a handkerchief in the car for your drool."

She sucked her breath in, it was such a slight sound that it was barely heard, and she hurried after him. Her voice carried back to us as she said, "I wasn't—"

Corrigan burst out, "Who the fuck cares?" And took two steps to close the door, letting it slam shut by itself. He gave it a mock salute and then flipped his hand around so his middle finger was extended. "Good day to you, police dicks."

"Well." My dad looked around, his eyebrows raised high. "That was . . . unexpected."

My scowl deepened. "I can't shower. 'Unexpected' is not a term I would use to describe this visit."

"Fuckheads." Corrigan slid his hands into his pockets, hunching his shoulders. "That's the term I would use."

My dad sighed. "Well, I can't say that I'm not a little grateful. Sheldon, with that monitor, if there are any more murders, they'll know where you were or where you weren't. This could help in the case."

"That's lovely." I gave him two thumbs-up. "Here's hoping someone else will die now."

"Sheldon," he said quietly.

Beth spoke over him, resting her hand on his arm, "Your father's just worried. That's all." Giving his arm a squeeze, she held her chin high, and left for the kitchen. As she did, the back of her silk robe swayed back and forth behind her. Then I noticed the rest. They were all in their pajamas, somewhat.

Corrigan was wearing grey sweats and a plain white shirt. Bryce had on black sport pants and a grey shirt, while the movie star had on oversized blue scrub pants . . . and no shirt. I wolf-whistled. "I must be really out of it not to notice that."

His eyebrows bunched together. "Notice what?"

I waved a hand up and down. "It's a Monet of muscles, the six-pack, pectorals, it's just . . ." I pretended to kiss the air. "A masterpiece."

He rolled his eyes. "Nothing you haven't seen." He smirked. "Twice."

I shot back, "I don't remember any clothing being taken off for the second round." Then I winced and realized the stoic expressions on both Bryce and Corrigan's face. "Uh . . ."

"Shut it." Bryce smirked. "You've seen me naked the most here—" He halted as Corrigan abruptly swung around and left, heading down a hallway. "Uh. Never mind. Enjoy Denton's masterpiece all you want."

I pressed my lips together. There was another comeback there, a crude joke just asking to be told, but I kept quiet. There'd been a time when Corrigan would've said it for me. He would've winked, and delivered a better joke than I could ever think of, and he'd follow it up with pinching my ass.

Not this Corrigan.

I watched as he kept walking away. This Corrigan was tense, quiet, moody, and dark. His shoulders were rigid and his head was bent forward. As he turned to go to the bedroom, I caught his side profile. His dark blond hair fell over his forehead. His jaw was hard, and his anger emanated from him.

I felt a little tingle inside me.

"Sheldon?"

Bryce distracted me. "Huh?"

He frowned, rubbing at the side of his face. "Do you want someone upstairs with you? I know Corrigan was there earlier?"

"No." That word ripped from me quicker than I could stop it. "I mean, no. Thank you, though. I'm awake. I'll probably go watch a movie alone or something."

"You sure?"

I nodded. "Yeah." That damn tingle was bothering me, more than I wanted to admit. "Yeah. I'll be fine."

"Okay."

He lifted a hand and headed toward where Corrigan had gone. As he did, Denton swung his head to me. "Wanna get drunk by the pool?"

I groaned. "God, yes."

"See you out there. I'll go get the good stuff."

"That's why we're friends." I laughed.

Denton started for the basement, but looked back. "For my wine?"

"That and this." I waved my hand up and down at him. "If I'm Princess, then I'm just going to call you Superstar. How's that? Or maybe Super Stud? Celebrity? What about Movie Stud? I like that one."

"Har-har, Sheldon." His voice trailed off as he descended the stairs. "Mock me if you want to, but I can tell when you're still hot and bothered. Don't deny it . . ."

He had moved farther inside the basement so it was just me left in the front entrance. Me, myself, and I. Denton's words echoed in my head. 'Don't deny it.' I groaned again. I wanted to deny it. I wanted to deny it so damn much.

That tingle was still with me, and an image of Bryce holding the side of my head at my door kept flashing in my mind at the same time.

Hell. Getting drunk wasn't going to do it. I'd have to be drinking all night long, and with that thought, I headed to my room for a sweatshirt. I'd need it if we were going to be drinking until sun-up.

When I got back downstairs, Denton was sitting on one of the loungers by the pool. Stepping outside, the cool air hit me first. It was a fresh wave of oxygen and for a moment, I just stopped, closed my eyes, and breathed it in. It was dark out, but the moon was high above. Its reflection was mirrored in the pool. When I went over to sit in the lounger next to Denton, there was a wine bottle on the floor between them.

Chuckling softly, I sat and grabbed that thing. Hello. It was the good stuff. Denton always had the best of the best. When I finished taking a drink, Denton was watching me with an amused grin. I asked, still clutching the bottle, "What?"

He shook his head, still grinning. "Nothing."

I held the bottle to him. "I see wine, and I grab. It's as simple as that." Waving it at him, I smirked back. "You should know this by now."

"I do." He reached down on the other side of his lounger and pulled up another bottle. "I brought red out for you. The white stuff is for me."

"Oh." Then I laughed. "You do know me."

"Very well, Sheldon." His tone turned soft, and he gazed back out over the pool.

We were alone in the backyard. I couldn't say we were alone in privacy, I had a feeling someone was watching us from the house, but for right now, it was just the two of us by the pool. Speaking of that, I murmured, leaning back in the lounger and getting comfortable with the bottle, "What is your sister doing back here?"

I didn't want to talk about the ankle monitor, or anything else regarding my current legal predicament. As I said that, a shiver went down my spine. I had a feeling one of those prying eyes was hers, watching from some window above us.

Denton let out a loud sigh. "I have no idea." He looked down into the bottle, frowning. "She wants to start new, and she's doing well. What kind of brother am I to turn her away?"

I straightened in my seat, sitting forward. This was a different Denton. Years earlier, he would've barked at me for asking that question. He was protective, too protective at times, but there'd been a reason. Mena was mental. True blue crazy. She needed meds. She needed supervision. She'd been in a residential program for a long time.

"Do I need to worry about Corrigan and Bryce?" He glanced up to me. Still frowning. I had a feeling Denton would be frowning from here on out. Mena had that effect on people.

"You know they don't like her. I don't think they ever will, and now that we're all under the same roof . . ." I let that sentence hang between us for a minute. Truth be told, I had no idea what either of them would do. Bryce hated Mena with a passion in high school, and Corrigan seemed to feel the same now. I lifted a shoulder up, but I didn't let it drop. I didn't know if I should shrug this off or not. "I think they're just protective of me." And after a moment's consideration, I added, "Really protective of me. If Mena doesn't do anything, things will be fine."

Denton grunted, stretching out his leg on the lounger. "Then I have no clue what to do. My sister's asked about you a lot over the years. I know things ended weirdly with you two, but you reached out to her in high school. That's stayed with her. I think over the years you became some kind of hero to her. She wants a friendship with you."

I let out a deep sigh. "I liked Mena. Bryce and Corrigan didn't, but I did. Then she turned crazy and . . ." I had to stop for a moment as the history crashed down on me. The last time I saw her had been at my party. She had screamed at Denton that night, *"You didn't want me to be friends with her because she was yours! You just didn't want to share her."*

"Grace visited her."

Denton looked over to me. He nodded. "She did. Mena always asked how you were doing through Grace."

Another friend turned enemy. No, that's not right either. She apologized. She'd been remorseful, but I refused to accept her apology. I had turned my back on her, then she was murdered. My eyes were becoming itchy so I wiped at them, saying, "Grace didn't deserve what happened to her, whoever did kill her."

"I know Grace got caught up in being accepted at college, but before that and even during that, she kept visiting Mena."

"She did?" I knew she had gone before that. "She kept going? During the year?"

He nodded. "Yeah. Mena's staff told me that they noticed my sister did better after those visits, too."

"That's good. Grace would've been happy hearing that."

"She's here for school." His tone dipped down to a serious undertone. "I told her you were staying here when she asked to live with me, and she was okay with it. I told her about the whole group too, and she never hesitated so I really think she'll be fine this time. She's reassured me that she's here for school and no drama." There was a hesitation in his voice. "I hope that's true."

Remembering how it had hurt him the last time when he needed to send her away, I reached over and squeezed his hand. "She stood up to Bryce and Corrigan. We're not the complete assholes we were in high school, but they were still harsh there. She held her ground. If she could handle them, I have no doubt she'll be just fine at college."

He swallowed, his Adam's apple bobbing up and down, and he gave me a shaky grin. "That's what I'm hoping for. I hope everything will be fine. Our parents are a joke. My dad's always hated her. Our mom's never had the time for her. She's only got me."

Feeling moved by what he was saying I squeezed his hand again. "And me." On second thought. "If she wants me. She might not want me, being that I'm a hated murderer and everything."

Denton chuckled, lifting the wine bottle for a sip. "For some reason, Mena's always unfazed by the media stuff. Even with me, there's a new girl at my side in the magazines every other week, but she'll still ask about my love life like she's got no clue."

"Maybe she doesn't?"

"No." He shook his head. "I pay for her subscriptions. She got all of the magazines. She wanted them. At first, I wasn't sure if I should let her have them. I didn't know if it would add to her stress, but the staff told me she seemed fine. Her psychologist explained it seemed to be an added connection she had to me. Even if she was home with them, and I was across the country, it still made her feel like she saw me every day. So I let her have them, but she's never once mentioned them to me or asked any questions about anything the magazines have said. To her, I'm just Denton as usual."

"You're her brother. She knows you'll never leave her, and you never have."

He whispered, closing his eyes, "But I wanted to once."

I stopped, shocked at his admission. Denton had only been protective, loving toward Mena's stability. That's all I had ever seen from him.

He added, his throat full of choked emotion, "There was a time when I thought about walking, and I feel horrible saying that now. She's my sister. I have to be at her side for the rest of her life."

"Denton." I reached for his leg and rested my hand there. "You're not a brother to her. You're her parent. Wanting a vacation from that responsibility is normal, I think. Hell," I grunted. "I don't think I would've been half as nice as you. With the bitch that I can be, I would've kicked her to the streets and had her learn that lesson to grow up."

Denton laughed. "Something tells me that Mena would've been just as fine out there."

"Yeah." A grin escaped me. "Your sister is tough. That's for sure."

"She is." Then he shook his head and lifted a hand in a helpless gesture. "What am I doing? Worrying about my sister when I know she's tough. She can handle anything. You're right. Even if she goes off the rails a little, she has a spine of steel. She always has, as far back as I can remember."

I nodded. "If you think about it, she must be doing something right. Even if the guys bark loud, I know she's got Bryce and Corrigan scared. That must say something."

He laughed, then tipped his head back and finished the rest of his wine. I assumed he would stop after a few sips. I didn't think there was much left, but as he kept drinking and kept holding that bottle up, my eyebrows lifted. He drank almost half the bottle at once.

I whistled in appreciation. "Where were you when I learned to chug beer for the first time? That would've gotten us in trouble."

He closed his eyes, the corners of his mouth lifted in a slight laugh. "I was here, Sheldon. Always here." One of his eyes opened, and he peeked at me. "Besides, I'm pretty sure you were hardcore with Bryce at that moment."

I barked out a laugh. "You're right. That was in the beginning when we were too scared to be together. We screwed, then fought, and screwed someone else, then fought again before screwing each other. Shit. We were messed up back then."

"No." Denton's eyes were still closed as his head moved from side to side, resting back against the lounger. "You were messed up. I remember it in detail. Bryce loved you and wanted you. You were the scared one."

"Yeah." I couldn't hold back a grimace. "I was really dumb sometimes."

"You were lost," he noted, almost to himself. "Your mom's a piece of shit, and your dad, well..." His arm lifted, gesturing to the house. Then it landed back down with a thud. "He basically abandoned you back then. Kinda nice to have him back, though, huh?"

I shrugged, turning so I was facing forward. My gaze lingered on the pool, being drawn in by the depths of it. "We'll see on that count. The jury's still out for now."

"No, no." He was shaking his head. I caught the movement from the corner of my eye. "No jury. No court talk. None of that. Your dad is here, that's something. Our dad won't have anything to do with us, well, with Mena. He'll talk to me as long as I don't bring her up. How's that for father of the year, huh? Now that's screwed up too. It's no wonder my sister's had some problems. She's had to deal with him as a parent."

"Yeah," I echoed, softly. "You're right." And because I couldn't help myself, the feeling of being watched was too much, I glanced up to the house.

There she was. Standing in her window on the second floor, right above where Denton had me sleeping, stood Mena. Our eyes caught and held for a second, then her hands went to the curtains, and she pulled them shut in front of her.

I had a feeling she still stood there, able to see through them, though.

I waited, holding my breath, and a moment later, a shadow moved away from the window. I'd been right. She had been watching us the whole time, but her window was shut. She couldn't have heard us. I didn't think so.

*

"No way in hell!"

Corrigan's voice woke me the next morning. As I dragged myself out of bed, quickly dressing and brushing my teeth, I continued to hear his raised voice. There were others, but I couldn't make out what was being said. When I got to the kitchen, Corrigan was standing against the wall. He was shaking his head, his jaw was clenched shut, and his arms were folded over his chest. He said again as I stopped in the doorway, "No. No way. I'm not leaving."

"Who said you had to go?" I asked, combing my fingers through my hair. I'd thrown a shirt on and sweats, but I grimaced now as I looked down at what I was really wearing. The shirt was almost see-through so my bra was noticeable, and my pants stuck like glue to me. Then I stopped caring. I was hiding from the public. Who cares what I looked like behind these walls? I shrugged to myself and went to take a seat at the table.

Mena was at one end, eating a piece of toast with a glass of orange juice. Bryce was at the coffee pot and Denton was standing in between. He turned to me. "I did. Mena's going to college today. I asked if Corrigan would take her—"

I sucked in my breath and grimaced. "Do you have a death wish?" I shook my head. We'd talked about Corrigan and Bryce hating Mena last night. He wants to put them in a car with her now? "You're nutso, Denton."

"Thank you." Corrigan threw his hands in the air. "See? I'm not taking her to college. I'm not riding in a car with her. I've covered myself. All my professors know I'm doing online learning this semester. Why would I go back to campus now?"

"Because my sister's going, and I need someone to watch her!" Denton's voice rose to equal Corrigan's. The two were involved in a standoff, both glaring at each other.

I held a hand up. "Wait. Hold on. Why does Mena need someone to watch her?"

"Exactly. Thank you again," Corrigan huffed.

Bryce was keeping quiet, but he was watching the exchange intently.

"I need someone to watch her and make sure everything is fine." Denton rubbed at his forehead. "I need to know everything is okay with her. I just… I can't go. I would've asked Sheldon, but obviously she can't go either and Bryce," he lifted a hand to him, "he doesn't go to college. That leaves you, Corrigan. Please. One day. That's all I'm asking for."

If Corrigan could've killed him with a look, Denton would've been dead three times over by now. Corrigan's eyes were almost bulging out, his lips pressed tight together. Then he muttered, "I can't fucking believe this."

"Maybe it's not such a bad idea."

All eyes went straight to Bryce, who held his hands up in a surrendering motion. "Don't kill me. Just hear me out, but maybe it's not a bad idea." His gaze fell to me, lingering for a moment. "You can ask around to see if there are any new rumors about who killed Grace. I have a hard time imagining her sorority has kept quiet. I bet they might know something."

"Oh my god," Corrigan mumbled to himself. "You were my ally, Bryce."

"I still am, but think about it." Bryce stepped away from the counter. He glanced to me again. "I'm thinking about Sheldon. I mean, that's why we came back to town. We wanted to find something out. After our stint at the hotel, maybe something's come up. We can't find out holed up in this house." His tone was soft, so soft. "You can be our eyes and ears now."

"Do you know how awkward it will be, just showing up on campus? The media's going to be called. The only ones I know who won't betray me are my frat brothers."

"So go to them," I spoke up. I couldn't believe I was agreeing with sending Corrigan along with Mena, but—

"Bryce is right. Go there. Have them ask around for you, that's considering they agree with you and think I've been framed."

"They do. They told me right away when you were taken in. They said if I needed anything, not to hesitate."

"There you go then. Ask them now. Have them scout around campus for you."

"I could just call to do that," Corrigan grumbled, shooting Mena a dark look. "I don't have to drive to campus to get that done."

"Just go."

Corrigan sent Bryce a withering look. "You go."

Bryce sighed, rolling his eyes before he turned back to the coffee pot. Filling his cup, he came over to the table and slid into a chair beside mine. "It doesn't hurt to have eyes and ears on campus. You know we're right."

"Screw all of you," Corrigan burst out.

He was going. We all saw it then, and Bryce relaxed next to me. I said, "Just ask questions. Don't do anything stupid when you're there."

Corrigan rolled his eyes. "I will probably have an hour before someone calls the press. People are going to be taking pictures of me, just to sell them to those tabloids." His gaze locked with mine. "You know I'm going to be harassed like crazy when word gets out I'm on campus."

"So go in disguise."

Corrigan froze. Denton whipped around. Bryce sucked in a breath, and I lifted my own eyes. All four of us turned at the same time to Mena, who had just spoken. She bit her lip at the sudden attention, but shrugged one of her dainty shoulders. She said again, "Go in disguise. Isn't that what you guys did for the hotel? You snuck in just fine. No one knew you were there, at first."

Denton looked around. "You could, you know. I could do a different disguise, or I could call in my makeup girl. She could change your ethnicity if you wanted."

"That is an option," Bryce added. "Even if we already used disguises, that's the thing with them. You can change them, and people won't know."

Corrigan grumbled, knowing he had lost. When he finally agreed, I was still watching Mena. She flushed, ducking her head down as she continued eating her toast, but she was right. Denton had a makeup girl. If she could make Corrigan a different ethnicity, she could do the same to me. Then my ankle monitor suddenly felt like it gained thirty pounds. It was weighing me down.

But if I could get it off, if I needed to for some reason, I could disguise myself. That thought was tucked to the back of my mind.

If I could get it off, if I ever had to get it off.

I didn't want to think about that time, for what reason that could be, and I took Bryce's coffee from his hand and gulped half of it down.

"Sheldon! That's hot."

I didn't feel it and pushed it back over to him. "Thanks." Then I left and went back to my room. Denton was in the hallway on the phone. As I passed him, I heard him say, "Hi, Monica? Yeah, can you come over with your makeup kit? I have a favor to ask."

I shut my bedroom door and leaned against it, closing my eyes. Sliding down to the floor, I sat there. My elbows rested on my knees, and I rested my head in my hands.

I needed a moment, just a moment.

A sense of dread like I had never experienced stirred in me. It was filling me up and somehow, someway, I knew there'd be a time when I would have to get the ankle monitor off.

That was when I knew—the killer was coming to me.

CHAPTER THIRTEEN

THE KILLER

"Sheldon Jeneve, dubbed The Queen Bee Killer, was at the Palloy Hotel earlier today where it looked like she had her own impromptu press conference." The newscaster on the news glanced to her co-anchor. Folding her hands together on the desk, she asked, "Is that what you thought, Derek? It seemed like a spontaneous idea of hers."

Her co-anchor, his hair combed neatly back, wearing a tailored grey suit and purple tie, gave her a polite smile in return. He shrugged, tapping one finger against his chin. "You know, if it was planned or not, it worked. Sheldon Jeneve is all over the news reports today and not in a bad way. She had some interesting points, and if they're true, the police may need to look further into her case."

"That's very true."

No, no, no.

This was all wrong. All wrong. I shook my head, slow at first as I listened to the news report, then faster at the end. I couldn't stop.

"We've kept our viewers up-to-date with any new developments in the murder of Grace Barton. Sheldon Jeneve has been the first and most pivotal suspect for her murder. The police have seemed very confident in their case against her, but she made a plea for the public today, and I have to admit, I think the public heard her."

The female reporter frowned. "You think so, Derek?"

He nodded, organizing his stack of papers in front of him. "I really do, Nancy. She was very passionate, but we only report the news." He held his hand up toward the camera. "Take a look for yourself. If you think Sheldon Jeneve might be wrongly accused, tweet us at #channelyessheldon or #channelnosheldon. Let us know what you think, folks. And on that note, here's a part of her press conference. You can watch the entire video on our website."

They switched to a video of Sheldon at the hotel, but I tuned it out. I had watched it many times already. I could recite it word for word. They were blaming Sheldon. As her beautiful face came to the screen, a scream started to build inside me. I hadn't framed her. Grace's death wasn't meant for this. It was meant for more, so much more. This couldn't happen. I couldn't allow this.

No, no, no.

Then a reporter asked Sheldon, "Who cut your brakes?"

The screaming in my head stopped. My hands were clenched to both sides of my head, pulling at my hair, but the answer was given to me. Right there. Handed to me on a silver platter. I almost laughed. That reporter, whoever it was, just gave me a way to save Sheldon. I moved my hands and looked up, all of my inner turmoil turned off, and I waited with my breath held.

"Guadalupe Ramirez," she answered.

Oh, Sheldon. She was so strong. She turned to look at the reporter. She'd been crying, but she didn't pay her tears any attention. That was my girl. No matter who was coming after her, what was being done to her, she always held strong.

I had to protect her. This is my gift to you, Sheldon. It was not time, not yet, but when it was, I was going to tell her about our connection. She'd be so happy. I knew she would. She had no one. Those two boys were nothing. They didn't deserve to be in the same room as her, much less hold her, be with her, comfort her. But no, I was wrong. They loved her. They protected her. Yes, yes. They were doing what I did. They would protect her, no matter what. I had to remember this.

They were okay. Yes, they were. They didn't deserve her. No one did, but they would protect her.

My hands turned into fists. My fingers started to dig into my skin, and I gritted my teeth, but I didn't feel the pain. The real pain was Sheldon, being with them and not me.

I should be with her, and I will be. I knew that without a doubt. One day. One day, she'll find out about our connection, and she won't be angry with me.

She said the name. Guadalupe Ramirez. That's who had cut her brakes. This person had tried to hurt Sheldon.

It was decided. I knew what to do.

I would hurt Guadalupe Ramirez instead.

No one would dare hurt Sheldon after this. I would make the message loud and clear.

*

SHELDON

Corrigan was disguised to look like an Asian guy.

When Denton's makeup artist heard what we had planned, she was all-in. She grinned at me. "I saw your press conference. Rock on, girlfriend. I say screw whoever killed your friend."

"Thanks."

Corrigan snapped his fingers in the air, pointing to himself. "Right here. I'm the double agent being sent out. I need as much help as possible." He met my gaze in the mirror and winked. "Dim down my good looks. I dare you to try."

The girl laughed, her eyebrow lifted. She drawled, studying his face, "I don't know about that, but I can make you a different ethnicity. That should work."

"Make it happen."

And she did. When Corrigan left, all his golden brown curls were stuffed under a headpiece. His hair was black and combed to the side. He even had on contacts to cover his green eyes. He pressed a kiss to my forehead. I moved back and shook my head. "Doesn't feel right, dude. You're," I waved a hand up and down at him, "not Corrigan, even though I know you are. You know what I mean?"

He laughed, and the sound relaxed me a little. That was all Corrigan right there, in his cocky husky-sounding chuckle. "See ya, Smalls."

"Smalls?"

He didn't respond to my question, but ducked out and headed to the car waiting. Mena was right behind him. She paused in front of me, not looking at me. Tucking some of her hair behind her ear, she let out a soft sigh. "I'll watch him, Sheldon." She looked up now. I was struck speechless at the seriousness in her eyes. She said again, in earnest, "I mean it. He'll be safe."

"Oh-kay." I nodded. "Okay then." I frowned. "Thanks?"

Her petite little chin moved up and down in a firm movement, then she followed behind. Closing the door, there were similar expressions to how I was feeling. Disbelief and just confusion. Denton seemed mystified, with a hand holding the side of his face.

"All right then." Bryce broke the silence. "I say we have our own little pool party." He took off after that, before anyone could agree.

Denton swung around to me. "Okay. My sister was confusing, but that," he indicated where Bryce had gone, "is even more confusing. He and Corrigan seem to switch places every other day now."

I shrugged. "The situation isn't a normal one, you know." A pool party was sounding more and more appealing. "Come on. I can't swim, but I can drink and tan. Let's get in our swimsuits and head out there. I, for one, would like to get wasted. Last night wasn't enough."

Denton grunted, falling in line beside me as we went toward the bedrooms. "Wasted? We weren't wasted. Our conversation was too damn depressing for the alcohol to take effect."

I laughed. He was right. Pausing at my door, I flashed him a grin. "Well, we'll rectify that. See you down there."

He gave me a salute. "I'll get some more wine."

My door was closing, but I yelled through it, "Screw the wine! Let's do margaritas this time." As I started changing clothes, I heard his laugh. "Sounds good."

I was heading back through the kitchen to grab everything when I saw that Beth was in there. She was making sandwiches and she looked up when she heard me in the doorway. A small smile appeared, but the ends looked strained. As she stood at the counter, her head folded back down and her shoulders hunched over.

She seemed sad, beaten down almost.

I pressed my lips together. It wasn't my problem. I moved around her to reach for the martini glasses.

She murmured, cutting some cheese on a plate, "If you're going to drink margaritas, you need the good stuff." She gestured to the pantry with her knife in hand. "There are better glasses in there. I found them yesterday. Much bigger."

"Thanks." I frowned at her, but went and found the margarita glasses she was talking about. She was right. They were huge. Grabbing a whole tray of them, I brought them back out into the kitchen. Then I started looking around for everything I needed.

Again, but without saying a word this time, Beth started grabbing everything I would need. She pulled out the ready-made mix, then grabbed an ice grinder and placed it next to me, along with a pitcher and a big wooden spoon to stir it all.

"Thanks."

She still didn't look at me, but lifted a shoulder. "I might be hoping to have one so I'm not helping out of the goodness of my heart." Now she looked up, sending another small grin at me before she went back to her sandwiches. Pulling out a bag of deli turkey, she began laying slices on the bread, covering the cheese.

"Is that for my dad?"

"Nope." She kept laying meat on the bread. "This is for you guys and your pool party."

Okay. Enough was enough. I stepped back, turned my back so I was leaning against the counter and folded my arms over my chest. "What's the game here?"

She stopped and turned around. "What do you mean?"

"What are you doing?" I pointed behind her. "You told me where the big glasses were, then helped get everything out for me, and now you're feeding us? You're acting like an upper-class mom who's desperate to be friends with her children. For the record, that's not what this is. I'm not your kid. My friends aren't going to look at you like you're suddenly the House Mommy. We're not in high school anymore, hanging out at the house."

"Sheldon," she started, pressing her hands together in front of her.

It was the pity. That's what I was sensing from her and it was grating on my nerves. I didn't need her damn sympathy. I wasn't asking her to be hateful, either, but I'd rather we go back to where she pretended I wasn't around. I shook my head, cutting off whatever she'd been about to say and held a hand up. "Stop."

"What?"

"If you're trying to develop a friendship with me because of my dad, I'm going to clear the record right now. I don't know why my dad stepped in to help me. Maybe he didn't think I could handle it. Maybe he didn't realize I had friends already coming to post my bail. I have no idea. Maybe it really was because he felt guilty over leaving his daughter and now she's up for murder, thinking it was his last chance to mend fences. Again. No clue." I fixed her with a hard look. "But trust me. Once I'm cleared, you and he are heading off again. I have no assumptions that you'll be sticking around, especially if my mother decides to hunt us down and try to swoop in for some money. He's for sure going to take off, but you and me . . ." I gestured around the kitchen, ". . .this whole Suzy Homemaker scene you have going on, it's not going to happen. I will probably never see you again in my life after this thing ends, and it *will* end." I had no doubt about it. "There are three ways this will come to a close. I'll either be free, in prison, or dead. Either way, those are all endings."

"You're so jaded." She looked down, folding her arms over her chest. It was a slight whisper, like she was talking to herself.

"Yeah," I clipped out. "I am. I have been for a long time, but being jaded doesn't mean I'm pessimistic. I'm realistic. That's all. I'm not going to entertain any daydreams about having a father who suddenly remembers he loves me. He broke me years ago. He won't get the chance to do it again, so please." My heart was pounding and my voice had risen. I hadn't realized how loud I was until Bryce came around the corner. He'd been there the whole time. I could tell with one look. There was no surprise, just understanding.

My heart paused, then lunged in my chest.

He was seeing me, the real me, and there was no polished-Bryce between us. The persona he had taken on when he became a soccer player, then became famous, all of it was gone. It was just him, and my god, I had missed him.

I wet my lips, my throat suddenly dry.

He saw my response, and his eyes darkened, but he held himself back, shaking his head in the slightest movement. Beth couldn't see him. He was standing behind her so as she started to say something, he began walking to the pool area.

"—sorry you feel that way. I am."

I swung back to her as Bryce slipped out the door without a noise. "What?"

She finished the sandwiches and set them aside. Washing her hands and then drying them off, she stopped in the middle of the kitchen. Lifting her head, she looked at me, and I felt like she was looking inside of me, seeing me how Bryce just had. An emotion flickered in her gaze, and it was that damn pity again.

I wanted to reach up and grab it from her. She hadn't earned the right to look down on me.

"I'm sorry, Sheldon. I'm sorry you feel this way. I'm sorry that it may even be true. You're right. I'm not your mother, and I may never have the privilege of being your stepmother, not that I would expect you to allow me to fulfill that role, but your insults and this brash exterior aside, don't take the words out of my mouth. When I say it would've been a privilege, I mean it. A privilege. A blessing." A lone tear slipped from her eye, and she brushed it aside with an impatient flick of her hand. "I can't apologize for your mother or your father, but I can only tell you that when I look at you, I don't see whatever you think I see. I see my own child." Her voice trembled. "I lost her four years ago. She was like you, hurt and lost, but she didn't have your fight, and the mother in me is horrified at how jealous I am. I'm horrified too because what kind of a mother am I, to wish that my own daughter had half the fight you do. She chose to end her own life, but if she had fought . .

." Pure agony rose up in her eyes and her head lowered. Her lip started jerking, and I heard the struggle as she tried to control her emotions.

Regret seeped into my pores, but I didn't know what to say. I had never thought about giving up. Even the idea never came to me. Give up? To who? Then some other dumbass would've won. Marcus. The sorority bitches from last year. Even this killer, whoever the hell he was—I'm sure the end for him is me dying.

"I'm sorry." I cleared my throat. Beth wasn't my enemy. I'd been treating her like it. "I didn't know about your daughter."

She nodded, but she didn't look back up.

I had broken her. That thought occurred to me, and I bit my lip, feeling guilty about it. "Look." I shook my head. What the hell was I doing? "I can be a real bitch. I lash out and sometimes, most of the time, I don't even need to lash out. I didn't know you had a daughter, and I don't know what happened to her, but I'm sure she must've been feeling unbearable pain for her to do what she did."

She sniffled and her hand lifted, wiping more tears from her eyes. She still didn't look at me. I realized that she couldn't. Whatever struggle Beth was feeling, it had nothing to do with me. Her daughter was in the room, pressing on her, how Grace pressed on me.

"If it's worth anything, I feel like you were a good mom."

A laugh in disbelief came from her. Still so soft, but it was there. It was a small break from whatever punishment she was feeling at that moment.

"No, I mean it." I tried to think of my own mother, what she would be doing if I had chosen that route. "I don't think my mom would be crying about me in some room with a stranger. She'd be bawling her eyes out at my gravesite, with press scheduled to arrive. I'm sure she'd call them and make sure they timed it just right, catching her breaking down or something."

Beth laughed, still crying. "Your mom's a bitch."

"True that," I grunted.

"Look." She shook her head again and lifted her gaze. Big teardrops were there, hugging the underside of her eyes and filling up to fall down, but she ignored them. "I just wanted to let you know I'm not the enemy. Regardless of what happens with your father, because you're right, I don't know his history with you or what appalling behavior he might choose, if he will leave at the end or not. I just wanted to let you know that I admire your fight. You're a survivor. It's something I wish I had more of in me." She moved forward and grabbed my hands. Pressing them to her chest, she lifted a hand to my cheek. Her hand rested there lightly. A look passed in her eyes, one that I could only conceive as mothering and loving before her hand fell away. She stepped backward and murmured, "You'll come out of this swinging. I have no doubt."

Then she turned and left.

I had no idea what had just happened, but a different sensation had dug inside my chest. No, it wasn't digging. It was filling me up.

"Yo!" Denton popped into the room. A bright pink towel was around his shoulders as he only wore board shorts and sandals. "Oh good. You found the margarita mix. I'd forgotten where that was."

I laughed to myself, shaking my head. I felt loved, and it came from someone who I had been a bitch to. Now I really needed a margarita.

CHAPTER FOURTEEN

I went out to the pool, but restlessness had settled in. Bryce was there, wearing his black swimming trunks, laughing with Denton. Then he posed at the edge of the pool and jumped in, his back muscles rippling from the movement. His dive was smooth, barely a ripple in the pool, and an anchor dropped to my gut.

I had to get out of there.

Had to, or I was going to go crazy.

Denton was about to jump in when Bryce pulled himself up from the side, standing back up on the concrete again. He raked a hand over his face, wiping the excess water off, and he frowned at me. Oh yes, indeed. A vacuuming effect was going on inside me. I felt like he was sucking me in, pulling me to him with just a look.

"What's wrong?"

"I need to go," I croaked. "Somewhere. I have to get out of this house."

Denton started laughing. "You're kidding, right?"

Bryce just frowned. For some reason, I felt like he understood what was going on with me and because he did, he closed his eyes and turned away. I frowned. Maybe he didn't know. Maybe that was in my head and he had no clue what was going on with me— no, that was me. I had no clue what I was doing. I started to wave my hands in the air. "Guys, I have to get out of here. I feel locked up, and we have to go, do something, be somewhere else. I just need," I skimmed the walls of Denton's estate, "outside of this fortress."

"Corrigan and Mena are still at school."

"Good." I snapped my fingers in the air and turned back around for the house. "Let's go there."

"Wait, wait, wait." Denton sprinted so he cut me off at the door. He had his hands up, as if to physically hold me back. "Are you thinking this through?"

I lifted my shoulders up and held them suspended in the air. "I have no idea. I don't care. I'm beyond caring. I just have to get out of this house." A throb started deep inside me. I knew without looking that Bryce had drifted over to us. The closer he got, the deeper that throb burrowed.

Visions of grabbing him and throwing him against the wall were filling my mind up. They were very clear images. I could feel the smoothness of his skin under my hands, how he would be surprised at first, then he would catch on and reverse our positions. I would be the one pressed against the wall and his mouth—I swallowed tightly, dear holy balls—his mouth would settle between my breasts. A lump was in my throat. I was having trouble swallowing around it, but my imagination kept going.

Bryce would slowly lower himself down to his knees, his mouth going with him, trailing kisses in a pathway, all the way down between my—"Let's go!" I burst out, needing to change my thought process.

I pushed past Denton and hurried to my room. After changing, I waited at the front door. Denton and Bryce both showed up not long after that and soon a car pulled up to the front. When the driver got out and opened the back door for us, I almost started laughing.

"What?" Denton paused beside me.

"We can't go in that." I gestured to the car.

"Why not?"

"We need to blend. We can't do that if we have our own driver."

"Oh." His eyebrows bunched together as he mulled over what I said. "What do you suggest?"

Bryce circled around us and started to the side of the house. He called over his shoulder, "Follow me."

"Where's he going?"

I didn't answer. I already knew, and as we followed Bryce heading where I knew he was going, a slow smile spread over my face. I wouldn't be able to wipe it off. He understood, completely. Bryce pulled open the garage door to where Denton kept all his cars. He grabbed a pair of keys and veered toward an SUV.

"Here." He pounded the front of it. "This is blending in."

"For real?" Denton asked under his breath.

"Yes." Bryce grinned at me. "And we're driving it ourselves."

I hurried to the passenger door, but when I got there, Bryce shook his head. "No way, Sheldon." "You're in the backseat. You're the one we really don't want people to see."

I shrugged, getting into the backseat as Denton trailed over. He got into the front seat, as did Bryce, and then he asked, "What are we going to do? We don't want anyone to recognize us."

Bryce flashed him a grin as he started the engine and pulled out from the garage. "Please, Denton. You've worked your magic with our disguises. Now it's my turn."

"Your turn?"

We were waved through the gate, and Bryce pulled out onto the street. He chuckled as he said, "Yep. It's my turn. I have just the thing in mind."

He took us to a costume store and went inside.

Denton looked back at me. "This is for Halloween costumes. What the fuck? I'm not walking around your college campus as a Cookie Monster mascot."

"Oh." I winked at him. "But imagine if you were a shirtless Cookie Monster. You know how many cookies would be thrown at you?" I paused and let him sort that out. "Lots and lots of cookies . . ."

He barked out a laugh. "Not the cookies I want, Sheldon, not at all."

I sobered at that comment. Denton and I talked about Bryce and Corrigan. We had talked about Mena. His love life, his *real* love life, has never been a topic on the table. I asked now, "Whose cookies are you hoping for?"

"Hmm?" He had turned back, tapping his finger against the door as we waited for Bryce. He met my gaze again in the rearview mirror. "What do you mean?"

"Not the cookies you want, so," I scooted to the edge of my seat and leaned forward. Bracing my elbow on the back of his seat, I asked, "You say that like you know whose cookies you want. Who is it?" I frowned. "Not mine. I have to pick between Bryce and Corrigan, and to tell the truth, I want to jump both of them. I can't handle another guy in the mix."

"Sheldon." He pretended to groan, holding his hands over his ears. "No more talk about your sex life. I can't handle hearing your constant rejection."

I grabbed one of his hands and pulled it down. "Cut it out. Whose cookies?" We both knew our friendship was purely platonic, which felt good. "Please, Denton. Trust me. You're doing me a favor. I'd love to hear about someone else's problems. It'll give me a short reprieve from my own."

"It's no one."

"Come on, Denton. You know all of my problems. Spill, buddy. Give me some dirt."

He started to shake his head, but I could tell it was there. He wanted to spill. He wanted to gossip about his love life with me. I opened my mouth, ready to deliver another plea when the door opened again, and an object from my own love life woes popped back inside. A secretive grin lingered over his face as he handed me a bag, then started the car back up.

Bryce said, "Open it up. Let me show you my genius."

I pulled out a masquerade mask. One was black and lacy. A second was pink and glittery. The third was a simple mask that resembled something Zorro would wear. I had no idea what he had planned, but I kept the Zorro one for myself and handed the other two frilly ones forward to Denton.

He took them, and immediately started protesting. "No way. No, man. I'm not wearing this."

Bryce started laughing. "Chill. It's not exactly what you're thinking." As he turned into the right lane, heading for the freeway that would take us to the college campus, he met my eyes in the mirror briefly. "Corrigan texted me when we were changing to leave. He ran into your friend Carolina."

I perked up. "Really?"

He nodded, throwing the left blinker on and merging with traffic. "He said the girls want to do something to help so they're throwing a masquerade ball for you."

"For me? As in I'd be the guest of honor?"

"No. They have no idea we're coming, but the whole thing is to celebrate you or roast you. Corrigan's words, that's how he explained it."

"What's the point of the party?"

"It's all about Sheldon. You might not realize the extent of it," he told me, "but you're both hated and loved on campus. Corrigan said news about the party is already spreading. It's all over social media. The whole point of the party is to get together to talk about Sheldon."

"If she's guilty or not?"

Bryce gave Denton a half-grin. "Yeah, kinda. It's just a big excuse to get together and drink, but I guess the campus is buzzing about Sheldon so it should be a big turnout. Hopefully, we can blend in and overhear something good."

"I bet the real killer will be there."

"Isn't that what you did before? With the other stalker?" Denton was looking between both of us.

I wasn't happy. Another party. Another stalker. Another killer, and a masquerade mask was the only way I could go. I wasn't happy about any of this, but I couldn't do anything else. "Yes," I sighed, frowning to myself. "Another fucking party."

I could feel Bryce watching me in the mirror, but I didn't say anything.

I muttered under my breath, "We need new material. That's it." I announced it, "If I get out of this intact, I know what I'm majoring in."

"What?"

"Criminal justice." It was ironic in a way. "I'm going to be a damn cop, then I can figure out other ways to find my own damn stalkers."

"Well, until then, we keep doing what we know."

"You're right." I clipped my head forward. "Drinking and raising hell. That's all I know. When does this party start?"

"Soon enough. We're heading to pick up Corrigan. We're going to sneak in with his fraternity. They have a plan figured out already."

"So, they know we're going?"

"Corrigan went to his fraternity, and they know who he is. Apparently, they refused to let him into the house until he could prove his identity."

Score one for Denton's makeup artist.

Bryce added, "And Carolina is the only one who knows you might come tonight, outside of Corrigan's fraternity. I doubt the stalker is from his house, Sheldon."

I pressed my lips together. Did I really have to remind him that we had hired Marcus to cater the food for our own party, the one we threw to draw out the stalker? It had worked like a charm, except someone died from that party. I didn't want the same thing to happen with this one. Then again, it wasn't my party, I picked up the Zorro mask, and I'd never used masks like this either.

I guess it was better than nothing, or better than hiding in Denton's house. As I thought that, my eyes fell to Bryce's shoulder and how his shirt moved over his muscles as he drove. I let out a silent sigh. Yes. Staying any longer in that house wouldn't have been good. I would've done something I would've regretted.

Definitely.

I snuck another look at Bryce's arms.

*

"Damn, Sheldon." Michael Reveritt wolf-whistled as he opened the back door for us. He stopped, blocking our entrance, as he looked me up and down. Holding a red cup in one hand and his other arm leaning against the doorframe, Corrigan's fraternity brother smirked down at me. "You've got to be the best-looking serial killer I've ever met."

My eyes went flat, and I shouldered past him, making sure my elbow pressed into his sternum. At his swift intake of breath, I grinned and pressed harder. Then I moved past, smirking back at him, "Oh, Ritt. How I've not missed you. At all."

"Ha-ha." He stepped back as Bryce and Denton followed me inside. Giving both a wary glance, he rubbed at his sternum and let the door close. Jerking a thumb over his shoulder, he said, "Everyone's in rare form. We've been waiting for you, and I have to warn you guys," he lingered on Denton, his smirk appearing once more, "everyone's going as chicks so . . ." He swept an eye up and down both of the guys again before finishing, "guess what you're going as?"

Denton started laughing.

Bryce scowled. "What? No. No way."

As Denton kept laughing, Bryce turned to him. "Why aren't you pissed?"

He got a shrug as a response. "I'm an actor. You do what you have to do." He gestured to Michael and where we could hear everyone in the living room. "If that's what we have to do to blend in." Another shrug. "So be it."

Michael Reveritt looked at me. A speculative gleam in his eye and I shook my head, holding up the Zorro mask. "No way, buddy. They can be chicks. I'm down with that, but I'm chick enough. I'm going as Zorro so give me a sword."

He rolled his eyes. "You're never any fun, Jeneve."

I smirked. "I've got half a country and an entire police department that says otherwise. According to them, I'm too much fun."

"Har-har." He scowled before he finished his drink and went to the counter for a refill. "I've missed that charm. Really."

"Ha-ha." I glanced around. Going to the doorway, I saw that he was right. Most of Corrigan's fraternity brothers were wearing ball gowns, masquerade masks, and wigs. I wrinkled my nose. Half of the wigs were falling off. The other half were in knots. I turned back and surveyed Michael. He looked normal. No dress. No wig. No mask. I asked, "Aren't you joining in with the festivities?"

"Me? Nope." He leaned against the counter with his new drink in hand. "I'm hanging back to be the sober cab."

I gave his drink a pointed look. "Sober cab, huh?"

He flashed me a grin. "Well, you don't need one now, but later," he leaned forward, "I'll be sober then."

Corrigan came into the room then and the conversation halted. We had to take in the magnificence of him. Gone was his earlier disguise. A strapless, glittering green dress with cleavage that dipped low to line the sides of his nipples had taken its place. If he'd been wearing a dark hair wig instead of a platinum blond one, I would've been tempted to call him JLo. As it was, with glitter on his cheeks and his masquerade mask already in place, a silver one with bright and shiny beads, the only thing I could say was, "Well."

I was struggling not to laugh.

He shot me a dark look, but the corner of his mouth lifted.

"Dude." Michael nodded once with his approval. He lifted a hand, throwing it up and around to smack Corrigan on the ass. "If you were a girl, I'd want to doggy pound you."

Denton laughed then, and I glanced over at them. Bryce was trying to hold back his own, too.

"Just wait," Corrigan warned them, smirking. "You think I look hideous? Guess what we have lined up for you two?"

"What?" Denton stopped laughing.

So did Bryce. "Huh?"

In the end, I was the only one who could laugh. Michael Reveritt had said all the guys were dressing in costume and he was right. Every single guy traipsed past me outside the back door in high heels, wigs, formal ball gowns, and their masquerade masks already in position. Each guy gave me a slight smile as they passed by. The only ones left at the end were Michael, Corrigan, Bryce, and we were waiting for Denton.

"Shut it," Corrigan started.

Bryce sent back, "You're the one laughing. You shut up."

Corrigan laughed, then elbowed Bryce.

He returned the favor hitting Corrigan back on the arm.

They were laughing together, jostling each other, and a slow smile was on my face. I didn't think I could wipe it off, but I must've looked like an idiot.

They were really together again. Finally.

"Ta-da!" Denton made his entrance at that moment, but I couldn't tear my eyes away from Corrigan and Bryce. Both straightened, their eyebrows shot up, and they shared another look before laughing.

"What?"

Hearing the irritation from Denton, I pulled my gaze away, then I felt the laughter bubble up myself. His blond wig was swept up into a fancy bun while he was wearing a turquoise dress. It was shimmering with only one sleeve that ended above his elbow. The other side swept underneath the opposite arm. There was no cleavage so it was an A-line dress.

It would've looked stunning, no wait, it did. Denton pulled it off. His high cheekbones, cute red lips, and those beautiful movie star eyes were looking back at us underneath the glittery pink mask.

Then Corrigan burst out laughing. "You look like a mermaid."

Denton scowled, then paused, his eyes narrowed, and he shrugged it off. "I'm a beautiful mermaid then." He raised his head up, looking down his nose. "Don't be jealous, fellas. These high cheekbones have made me millions. Remember that."

BEEP!

Michael snorted, then gestured outside with his cup. "The ladies are waiting. I'd haul ass, if I were you four."

Denton sniffed and marched out first, like he was walking a catwalk. Bryce sighed and went after him. Corrigan lingered behind, his gaze on Michael's cup.

"What?" Michael almost growled.

"You're the sober cab, brother." He gestured to the cup. "Knock that shit off."

Michael narrowed his eyes, but he didn't respond.

The tension in the room suddenly shifted. It'd been there, but I hadn't realized it. I realized it now and it was simmering from Corrigan's fraternity brother. I waited. He looked ready to snap back or throw his drink at Corrigan.

But he only moved his hand to the sink and he turned the cup over, spilling the drink down the drain. Then he placed the empty cup on the side and forced a smile. "Better?"

Corrigan rolled his eyes, reached out for my elbow, and started to guide me outside. As he did, his hand grasped tightly onto me, but I had a feeling it had nothing to do with me. He was holding himself back from saying something in return. Once we were outside and the door shut behind us, I asked, "What was that about?"

Corrigan shook his head, just a small movement to me. "He found out I'm not happy with how he's influencing the other guys, but—"

Bryce shouted from inside the car, "Let's go!"

Corrigan gave me a reassuring grin. "—it's house business. I can't say too much."

Climbing inside and taking my seat between Bryce and Corrigan, I snuck a look at him as he pulled the door shut and pounded on the wall. "We're good to go."

I saw what he hadn't said. He was worried.

And that worried me.

CHAPTER FIFTEEN

When we got to Carolina's sorority house, I saw that I didn't need to worry about being recognized. The three-story house was packed with people spilling out onto the front porch and their entire yard. The house was lit up with white lights strands. As we got out, I could see that inside the house was dark, but those white lights were everywhere. They lit up the porch, wrapped around the posts, trailing down the sidewalk, and I could see more in the backyard.

Again. This party was huge.

Corrigan grunted into my ear, "Well, I can say we're the show I was worried we would be."

"No doubt." There were guys everywhere in ball gowns. So were girls, who were actually trying to look nice and pretty. There were other guys, as well, who were dressed in black tuxedos and black masks, some similar to mine, and some with only the eyepiece on their face.

No one was going to recognize anyone.

"I think that's the point."

"What?" I looked up.

Corrigan was looking down at me. "You said no one's going to recognize anyone. That's the point." His hand came to the small of my back. "They threw this party together last minute so you could come and blend. Carolina did it for you."

A wave of nostalgia crashed over me. Carolina. I missed her. She'd been the only female friend who hadn't fucked me over . . . yet. My jaw firmed. I didn't want to think like that, I couldn't. I gazed at the house and said, "I'm going to find her."

Corrigan pulled his phone out, then showed me the screen.

Tell S I'm upstairs.

When I saw Carolina's name at the top of the text, I nodded again to him. He knew what I had to do, and he stepped back, allowing me to move past him.

Both Bryce and Denton noticed I was leaving, but neither called out to me.

It was just understood among all of us. This party was for me. Like the press conference, I had to do this for myself. Relying on other people, needing them to communicate for me while I sat hiding somewhere else, had me going stir crazy. I had to do something for myself. I had to feel like I was being productive, doing something. Not just sitting. Not just waiting. Not just letting the killer come to me.

Pulling the mask so it completely covered my face, resting on my nose, I shouldered past a group of girls.

"Sheldon!"

I froze. One of them recognized me.

"I hated her. She was such a bitch," that same girl continued.

Relief, then irritation sparked in me. She'd been talking about me, but damn. I rolled my eyes at myself and kept going into the house. People were there because of me. I was going to hear my name more than that, but when I got inside, I was surprised at the almost demureness in the house. Like I saw from outside, the lights were off, but the crystal lights filled the room, giving it a cozy and homey feeling. Soft music streamed from the speakers so as I moved from room to room, people were talking in groups. They weren't drinking from beer bongs or cheering for body shots.

I stopped at the bottom of the stairs and gazed at the kitchen. Bottles of wine lined the counters, along with fruit and cheese trays. People were munching off the table that had bowls of chips, crackers, and more meat and cheese trays.

"What did you think we would throw?"

I recognized that voice and whirled around, already smiling. Carolina stood behind me. Her eyes warm as she said, "My sorority knows how to do classy events. The wild and rowdy parties are reserved for next weekend."

"Hey." I couldn't stop grinning.

"Hey, yourself." Then she stepped in and gave me a hug.

It felt good. This was a friend, another friend. She wasn't looking at me with judgment. She wasn't yelling my name around to get attention. I sighed inwardly. I'd missed her.

"Looking good, Jeneve."

I laughed softly, pulling away. "How'd you know it was me?"

"Raimler texted me, said to look for Zorro. I came down the stairs and here you are." She shook her head, her eyes roaming all over me. "Shit, woman. I've missed you."

"Ha! Aren't you Greek royalty? Are you allowed to curse?"

She gave me the middle finger. "We can do that, too." A group of people entered the kitchen, and Carolina moved around me. Grabbing two bottles of wine, she said, "Come on. Let's go to my room where we can talk freely."

"Perfect." But I grabbed one of the cheese trays before following her up the stairs. When we got there, I didn't waste any time. "Have you heard anything? What about Grace's sorority?" My chest was tight.

Carolina was opening one of the wine bottles, but paused at my question. She shook her head. "What sorority?" She laughed softly to herself. Picking at her fingers, she added, "More than half of them transferred to a different school and different charters. The ones who are still here don't do a thing. It's like the entire sorority died with Grace. With what they did to you, then her murder, no one wanted anything to do with them. Whoever is left just goes to school and that's it. They're not invited to any party in the Greek system. It's like they aren't even here anymore."

"That's . . ." Karma? Ironic? Justified? I ended with, "Sad."

"Yeah, well." Carolina rolled her eyes. "I don't mind."

I looked at her.

She amended, holding her hands up in the air, "I'm sorry about Grace's murder. I am, but I'm not about the house. They vandalized your house, then used her to get to you and made your friend be the one to shove you into that glass table. That's cold. It's karma." She lifted a finger. "Not for Grace. She lost her way and got caught up. I believe that. I feel bad for what happened to her, but I'm not about the sorority. They hurt you, Sheldon. They deserved what happened."

"Yeah, well." Grace was still dead. That was all I cared about. "None of it matters anymore."

"I know." She frowned. "We've been asking questions, and no one knows anything."

"What do you mean?"

"I mean, you didn't kill Grace. We all know that, and we've been asking questions, trying to see if anyone knows anything, but they don't."

"What?"

"I'm sorry." She sat next to me on the bed and looked down at her hands. Folding them together on her lap, she pressed them between her legs. "I know that's why you're here, seeing if we know anything. That's what Corrigan said, but I told him the same thing. There's nothing on campus about you. There are lots of rumors and guesses, but that's it. No one knows a thing."

That was . . . extremely disappointing. I couldn't lie to myself. I bit down on my lip and tried to swallow the disappointment. It was a hard pill to shove down. I murmured, "I see."

"If it's worth anything, people are changing their minds."

"What do you mean?"

"After your impromptu press conference, people are starting to rethink things. More supporters are coming out for you. A lot of people still think you're guilty, but you've got people believing in you."

"Believing in me?"

She nodded. "Yeah."

I blinked a few times. No one believed in me. No one except Corrigan, Bryce, and Denton. Grace had believed in me, once upon a time.

She was gone.

Being with Carolina was harder than I expected. She brought memories back, memories of what she had already talked about. The sorority approaching me, wanting me, but getting Grace instead. She'd been so excited.

'You're wrong, Sheldon. I like these girls. They like me. Is it really that big of a stretch for people to like me?'

She'd been so excited to be accepted, to be liked. That conversation was the first time she covered for them. She had lied to my face, saying she hadn't noticed a thing when she had been the one who shoved me into that glass table, for them, because of them, to protect them.

Oh, Grace. I wish things had been different.

I drew in a breath. Feeling a tear, I could almost imagine her response. I smiled to myself, letting a second tear fall. She would've laughed at me. She would've said something about how things had to happen.

Never regret. Never forget. Only remember, learn, and keep jetting on.

That's something she would've said.

God, Grace. I'm sorry.

"Sheldon?"

Carolina placed a hand on my arm, bringing me out of my thoughts. I jerked back, then smiled to cover myself. "Sorry. Sorry." I shook my head, laughing at myself. "I feel like I'm being haunted by Grace half the time."

Her eyebrows shot up.

I laughed again louder, as I stood up and ran my hands down my pants. "I'm not. I'm not crazy." Seriously. I didn't need to deal with that. "Don't put me in an insane asylum. Jail was enough."

She stood with me, still frowning. Her gaze roamed all over my face, studying me. Then she asked, quietly, "Are you okay? For real?"

I couldn't answer. Not at first.

She asked that like Grace would've. With genuine concern. Without judgment. Like she actually cared.

Carolina had cared. She really did.

The fight left me for a moment. I hugged her, throwing my arms around her. Pulling her in, I squeezed her tightly. "Thank you." There was so much to say, but I only said, "Just thank you."

She hugged me, saying, "Thank you, too." Her hand brushed down my hair to my back. "You're going to be okay, Sheldon. You know that, right?"

I didn't. She didn't. I held her close anyway.

She tightened her hug too. "I mean it, Sheldon. You always survive. You'll survive this. I have no doubts about it."

Good. I blinked back more tears. That would make one of us.

There was a soft tap on the door, and it opened. Corrigan poked his head inside, an apology in his eyes, as he said, "Hey, uh, we were wondering if you ladies would join us downstairs?"

Carolina gripped the wine bottle harder, her eyebrows burrowed together. "Why?"

"Uh." He glanced at me and I saw the stirring in his depths. He was concerned about me. I saw it right away, and I nodded, just a small nod. Instantly, he looked relieved, and his slight grin turned into a typical Corrigan cocky smirk. His head lifted and he stepped more fully into the room. "Well, if you must know, it's because I think Bryce might need some moral support."

"Why?"

I bit back a smile. Carolina was acting like Corrigan was asking us to walk across fire. And judging by the grip she had on that wine bottle, I was guessing she wasn't going to budge for anything.

Corrigan lifted an arm and leaned against the door. "Because we're having a 'Who's Sexier?' contest downstairs among all the guys. Bryce is going to get stomped. I mean, hello . . ." He gestured to himself. "He might be Mr. Big Stud Six Pack Abs Guy, and Denton might be Mr. Beautiful Movie Star, but the playing field's all equal now. We're all chicks tonight, and I don't know if you've checked me out, but I'm some hot stuff tonight."

"Are you?"

He pressed a finger and made a hissing sound. "Hear that? Sizzling, honey."

Carolina's scowl didn't lift.

My mouth dipped down. I hadn't expected that.

Corrigan sent me a pointed look and I read the silent plea for help. I nodded and stood from the bed.

Carolina asked me, "What are you doing?"

"Corrigan's trying to be funny to cover it up, but he's worried. He wants me to go downstairs so he and the rest of the guys can see me. They'll be reassured I'm okay."

"Oh." The scowl vanished and she stood with me, taking both wine bottles with us. "Why didn't you just say that in the first place?"

"Yeah." I beamed up at him as I passed by, following Carolina out of the room. Patting him on the chest, I asked, "Why didn't you just say that?"

Corrigan groaned, shutting the door behind us and bringing up the rear. He muttered under his breath, "Because I was trying to preserve my manhood."

"Ha!" I threw him a grin over my shoulder, descending the stairs. "Your manhood's intact, just not intact while you're wearing that get-up."

He glanced down at himself and stopped on the stair. "You have a point."

"Come on, you two." Carolina was at the end of the stairs. She turned the corner for the kitchen, leaving Corrigan and I still on the stairs. For a brief moment, it was just the two of us. The house was buzzing from conversation, laughter, and now I could hear good-natured shouts, but the stairs were encased between two walls. I got to the bottom and started to go around to the kitchen, but Corrigan grabbed my hand and pulled me back.

"What?"

He stared at me, not saying a word. A beat passed, and he still didn't say a word.

"Corrigan?" I stepped closer to him, angling back so I could get a good view of his face. I saw the cloud of worry. It hadn't disappeared upstairs. He had only masked it. "What's wrong?" My hand started to lift upward to cup the side of his face, but my eyes widened as I realized what I was doing. I clasped my hands together in front of me, but my god, it would've felt so natural to touch him. Placed them on his chest, resting there.

Pushing that need down, my throat was suddenly tight. I rasped out, "Please talk."

"Look." His gaze lifted and traveled above my head. "I know you're here, and you want to rip shit up to find who this guy is, but," he paused, a soft sigh leaving him. "Can you not?"

"What do you mean?"

"I mean—" He cursed under his breath and pressed one of his hands to his forehead. He grimaced as he continued, "I know it's killing you, no pun intended, not to know who this guy is. I get it. I do, but I have a weird feeling. Nothing about this killer, stalker, whatever this asshole is, makes sense. Just . . . can you stay within viewing distance? I need to know you're okay."

"No one can recognize me."

"I could."

My eyes lifted to his, and I held my breath.

They had lowered so his gaze was pinned on me now. He had said those two words so softly and he repeated them again, "I see you, no matter what you're wearing. So," he took a deep breath, "just humor me? Shelve your need to tear ass and ruffle some feathers tonight. I'm not asking you not to do it. I'm asking for you to wait until Bryce or I are there so we can back you up, if you need it."

Corrigan had never told me outright he loved me, but he didn't need to, I felt it then and I couldn't talk, not at first. After clearing my throat, I bobbed my head up and down in a motion I hoped was some form of a nod. Everything felt too much. The sounds from the party doubled in volume, my smell grew more sensitive, my sense of touch too. I was aware of how close he was standing to me, how he was still holding his breath, how he was watching me, waiting, how his green eyes looked so adorable. They were asking me to touch them, to touch him, and my hands lifted before I caught myself.

I touched the side of his face, and he became even more rigid. I felt zapped, but my touch had the same effect on him.

"Hey, guys . . ."

I closed my eyes. That was Bryce.

CHAPTER SIXTEEN

"Oh, sorry." He turned and left quickly.

"Shit." My head fell forward to Corrigan's chest.

His hands touched my hips, holding me for a moment. His fingers curved into my sides, then he murmured into my ear, "I'll tell him what I asked you. He'll understand."

I felt his lips graze my forehead, the slightest touch.

Before he pulled away and left, he said, "Don't worry."

That was easier said than done, but after he went to find Bryce, I waited in the stairway for a minute. I needed to collect myself. I loved them both and I had to laugh at myself. The ordeal of being arrested and framed had pushed that to the side, but no longer. The love triangle had just slammed back into place, front and center.

Killer. I was here to find the fucking killer. That was my main mission.

Love triangle, move aside . . . for the moment.

As I went into the kitchen, I didn't see Carolina or the guys so I moved through the crowd. They were at one side of the living room. A stage had been placed against the far side of the room, and Corrigan was talking to Bryce. Both of them were nodding, and when they were done, Bryce lifted his fist up. Corrigan met it with his, then both turned as one to the announcer.

Just like that, they were fine.

I shook my head. A twinge of envy started in me. I wished I could make things fine, just like that, with a quick fist bump.

Glancing around for Carolina, I couldn't see her, but Mena was at the table, munching on the snacks. She seemed fine and content, but she wasn't. I could tell that right away. As I watched her, she glanced over to the nearest group of girls beside her. A wistful expression appeared on her features and her lips dipped down for a brief moment. Then she would look down at the ground, her shoulders would rise and fall, and she'd grab another chip. It didn't take a genius to know that she was lonely. She had no friends and she was staying at her brother's house, where she wasn't wanted by most of the guests. I felt for her. Mena had never really done anything to me. She just hadn't earned Bryce or Corrigan's trust and she faded away after that. Her mental illness took over, but she was back and the feelings of wanting to protect her were surging back up in me.

I was at the table before I realized I had even moved toward her. When she looked up, we were both shocked.

Her eyebrows lifted and she fell back a step. Her hand flew to her mouth. "Oh."

"Yeah." I frowned and raised a hand to make sure my mask was still in place. Wait—she shouldn't have recognized me. Then I studied her again and saw the slight suspicion forming in her eyes. She hadn't recognized me. I moved closer and said in a quiet tone, "It's me."

"Me?"

Ah, shit. I grinned. "Your favorite serial killer roommate."

Understanding dawned and her eyebrows lifted again as she repeated, "Oh!" She ducked her head down and stepped over so our shoulders were almost touching. "What are you doing here? The guys would freak if they knew."

I gestured to the stage. Denton was announced as the Alpha Mu Mermaid. "You don't recognize your own brother?"

She squinted at him for a moment, then cringed. "Are you kidding me?"

She sounded pissed. I hadn't expected that from her.

"He gets all mad that I'm out and about and look at that. Hypocrite." Cursing, Mena grabbed for another handful of chips. She shoved them in her mouth and continued to glare at the stage.

This really wasn't a side of Mena I had ever seen before. "He's having fun and helping me out."

"Helping you?" Just like that, all her anger melted away and concern replaced it. "Are you okay?" She looked around. "Is the killer here? Is that why you're here?" As she was talking, she grabbed a fork from the table. As her fingers closed around it, I reached forward.

"Okay. Whoa." Taking it out of her hand, I shook my head. "No need for this." After setting it far away, I added, "I don't know, but I doubt whoever he is that he'll do anything. I mean, look around. Plus, I'm not really recognizable."

She seemed to relax, her shoulders drooping slightly. "Still. Stay with me if you're not around the guys. You shouldn't be alone."

I was taken aback again. Mena sounded like she cared, like she was even protective of me. I whistled under my breath. "Let the guys see this side of you, and they'll relax a little. If you're Team Sheldon, that's all they care about."

"I was Team Sheldon before, remember? Bryce hated me."

"Yeah. Well." I shrugged. "Killing Marcus simmered him down. Going through that, it's simmered us all down."

My chest felt tight.

Bryce had said that before, that killing Marcus and going through that whole ordeal hadn't been dealt with. He said I was running from it, and maybe I was. I didn't know. I just knew the thought of remembering that day, as I pulled the trigger, was making my chest feel even tighter. Maybe he was right. Maybe I ran from him because I didn't want a reminder of that time.

Maybe.

I ground my teeth together. Maybe not. I didn't want to analyze it.

"You okay?"

I grew aware of Mena's question. Her concern was still there, but it had multiplied. She was watching me intently.

I forced my head to move up and down. *Nod. Smile. Make a smart-ass comment and move forward. Forget this slight panic attack had ever happened. Okay, go, Sheldon.* I forced another nod, then flashed a grin. I remarked, "So, how does it feel not being the social leper now?" I cringed. The smart-ass comment had been a complete bitch-slap instead. "I'm sorry. That didn't come out right."

She waved me off. "Don't worry about it. I know what you meant."

Cripes. It worked. The small panic attack was forgotten, but man. I said again, "I really am sorry. I'm trying to work on what comes out of here sometimes." Gesturing to my mouth, I added, "And I'm glad I said that comment to you and not the guys. The jokes they would've gotten from that one . . ." I shuddered. "No, thank you. Okay. Back to you. Not being the social leper you used to be. How's the going for you?"

Fuck me.

Mena laughed. "No. I know what you mean. I do." She lifted one shoulder up, pondering the question. "I don't know. It's weird. You guys hate me, well, maybe not you since you're talking to me, but they do." She gestured to the stage. Bryce and Corrigan were both acting like they were on a runway, each with fierce expressions and their chests pushed out. Corrigan pursed his lips together in a pout and struck a pose. His hip jutted out to the side, he rested his hand on it, and then he shoved his other hip to the opposite side. Bryce was at the other end of the stage, twirling around in a circle so his dress flew up around him.

I grunted. "Right now, they look like idiots, but yeah, they're works in progress."

She reached for more chips. "I get why Bryce didn't like me before. I wasn't stable, but I'm better now. I've had years of therapy. I've proven it over and over to Denton. I wanted to come back out here, be with my brother, and try again. Am I dumb? I want to prove myself." Her bottom lip started trembling.

My eyes got big, and I sucked in a breath. She was going to start crying next, but I couldn't blame her. I understood, in a weird way. "Just keep on keeping on. Someone told me one time to keep going, keep fighting, keep surviving. Repeat." I lifted a shoulder. "Sounds like solid advice."

I was doing the same damn thing, every day. I'd keep going. I'd keep fighting, and I'd keep surviving. No killer was going to conquer me. A renewed vow of finding who he was and bringing him to justice surged in me. I was going to win. I had to.

"Uh, Sheldon?"

I glanced seeing Mena was wincing from pain. Crap. I had reached out to her shoulder and my hand was digging into her skin. "Sorry." I released her, then gave her a half-grin. "I got carried away thinking of my own situation."

She rubbed over the spot where I'd been holding her. "Yeah. Listen, I'd like to help."

"Help?"

She nodded, more earnest. "I don't know how. Maybe I can be your eyes and ears on campus. I mean, you guys can't go anywhere without drawing media attention to you, but I can. No one knows me anymore. I won't draw any attention and I can keep my ears open. People don't notice me. I mean, look around." She waved around the table and she was right. There were five different groups, all positioned by the table, but they weren't paying us the slightest bit of attention. They were either watching the pageant, or they were talking with their friends. No one was looking at Mena, or *me*.

I realized that with a start. I hadn't really focused on it before, but it felt good.

No one gave a damn about me, for once. A corner of my mouth was inching upward. I could actually move around, talk, and not fear a video would be sold to a celebrity gossip channel.

"What about it?"

I was pulled from my thoughts again as Mena asked that question. My hand froze in the air; a chip was halfway to my mouth. "Huh?"

"Can I help? Will you let me?"

She looked so hopeful and determined at the same time. For a second, I couldn't register anything. This was Mena, and she was right. She had changed. I could see it in her now. Gone was the creepy, mentally unstable girl. She seemed normal. There was a hint of desperation, but I felt a kick in my gut again. She wanted to prove herself, like she had said.

I swallowed tightly. Who was I to deny this to her when I was trying to prove myself, too. I felt my head nodding, and I rasped out, "Sure. Yes. That would help, a lot."

"Oh, that's awesome."

She let out an excited breath as she said those words, and she was beaming.

It probably wasn't smart of me, but I felt myself melting even more around Mena. All the bullshit from high school had been so long ago. Like she said, she'd been paying her dues for a long time now. Besides, we both remained friends with Grace. Before she went to the dark side of sororities, Grace was a good judge. I used to trust her.

Thinking back on those days, I asked suddenly, "Do you miss her?"

The beaming dimmed. It was a sudden switch, and it happened so fast that I was startled by it. Her face became emotionless, then her head lowered. "Yes." She sounded wistful again.

"Me too."

"She was good to me."

My throat swelled up. "Me too."

We shared a look. Mena wasn't emotionless. I was wrong. She was full of emotion, but she put a mask on. It wasn't a masquerade mask, but a guarded wall. I understood her, and I felt an odd camaraderie with her then.

"I'm sorry if I was bitch to you in high school."

Mena laughed softly. "You weren't, actually. You were one of the few who weren't. Thank you."

"No." I shook my head. "I gave up on you. I shouldn't have done that. I should've fought harder for you, for Bryce and Corrigan to accept you—"

She touched my arm. "Stop. I knew the rules for you guys. I had to earn their respect, and there were opportunities. I knew all I had to do was stand-up to them, and they would accept me, but I didn't. I wasn't strong back then, and that was the other rule to be in your group. You had to have such strength, all three of you did. I didn't. That's the truth. I wasn't ready to fight to be in your group."

"You shouldn't have had to fight."

"But I would've. I saw what happened. Girls tried to use you to get to them. I know why you had such a hard exterior. I do. I get it. I just didn't have the extra skin you did." Her head lifted up. "But I do now. I've worked hard, with therapy and the right meds. I'm strong and stable. I can be your friend now. I know it."

I was starting to grin at her when Denton joined our group. He threw an arm around each of our shoulders and breathed on us. "Hey, sexy ladies." After winking at me, he lifted his arm and wrapped it around his sister. Picking her up, he squeezed her hard. "I love my little sister. Sheldon, have I told you how much I love her?"

Mena gasped and her cheeks reddened. Patting his arm, she said, that beaming expression was coming back, "I love you, too, brother."

He set her back down and ruffled her hair. "Did you guys see that I won? Seems everyone likes the mermaid look." He flicked some of his hair off his shoulder and batted those naturally long eyelashes at me. "Maybe I'll try this role in a movie. Oscar-worthy."

"Hey." Corrigan and Bryce both came over.

Their gazes went to Mena, and as one, kept them there.

Her gaze slowly lowered back to the floor, and I frowned. Enough was enough. I stood in front of her, blocking her from their view. My hand found my hip and I raised my chin. "Stop it. She's in our camp, whether you want her there or not. You're just being mean now."

Both held varying degrees of contempt, but Corrigan was the first to relent. He muttered, "Whatever, but we're going."

"Wait. Now? I haven't found anything out."

"Carolina and the girls are going to keep asking around. My brothers, too. If there's a rumor going around, they'll hear it."

I wasn't sure about that.

Corrigan gentled his tone, "Sheldon, I mean it. You can't force the asshole out of hiding."

"We're thinking we should bait him," Bryce added.

"Bait? Isn't that what this party is for?"

"It's not enough. Everyone thinks you're hiding somewhere or locked up."

"I am."

Bryce said, "Come on. You know what I mean. Let's head back to the house and have a planning session. Figure a way to draw this psycho out of hiding."

"Sounds good to me." Denton still had one arm around Mena's shoulders. He started flicking her ear and she elbowed him in the side. When he did it again, she swatted at his hand instead. He kept going.

He met my gaze then and gave me a tiny grin. I could see he felt bad about what he had said at the pool. I lifted a shoulder in response. They were family.

My gaze went to Corrigan and Bryce.

Families go through hard times. It was unavoidable.

"What about Ritt?"

I frowned, not recognizing the fraternity brother that had come up to our group. He directed that question to Corrigan, and I caught up. Corrigan had signaled to him we were going. He said, "What about him?"

The brother lifted his phone up, a deep frown under his lipstick. "He's not answering his phone."

Corrigan cursed. "Are you serious?"

"Yeah."

He groaned. "I told him to lay off the booze."

Denton waved a hand, getting their attention. "If you need to stay, that's fine. We can wait around. I'm sure," he glanced to me, "Zorro would be A-Okay with that."

I perked up.

"No." Corrigan shook his head, a hard glint in his eyes. "You guys go. Start the planning. I'll take care of this and get back as soon as possible."

"You sure?"

I offered, "We can totally stay." I recognized the girl who had called me a bitch on the front lawn. There was a group that I wouldn't mind messing with, maybe ask why she was so adamant I was a bitch. "I've not ruffled any feathers tonight."

"No." Corrigan shot me a dark look. "Go. I mean it. I want you to stay safe." He spoke over me to Bryce, "I'll be back in a few. Take *her*."

Bryce's hand came to my arm and he pulled me toward him. "I will." He turned, guiding me in front of him, and he said to Denton, "Can you call your driver to come get us?"

Denton nodded. As he pulled his phone out, he was guiding Mena in front of him, weaving through the crowd to the front door. My time was coming to an end. Digging my heels in, Bryce simply adjusted his hold. His arm went around my waist, and he picked me up, carrying me tucked under his arm. My hands flew back, knocking into people, and I tried to keep my feet from doing the same. Clutching to his shoulder, I gasped, "Bryce!"

He apologized to the people I hit, but kept going forward. He was bound and determined. So I pressed my lips shut and let myself be carried out. I was starting to realize whichever one was with me was going to act as a bodyguard from now on—no, a babysitter— but I couldn't blame them. Images of Corrigan bleeding on the floor flashed in my head. The killer could hurt them, too.

"Bryce," I said.

He was ducking around a group of girls, all tipsy and giggling. "Yeah?"

"I'm worried about Corrigan."

He met my gaze. I bit my lip, wondering if there would be jealousy, but he only nodded. "I know. Me too, but he'll be fine for the night. After this, none of us will go out alone again."

"We should wait."

"No, Sheldon."

Denton and Mena were waiting on the curb, and I heard Denton saying, "Okay. Thank you."

Bryce set me down, but I stayed close to him. My hands were on his biceps. I said in a low voice, "We should wait."

His hands lingered on my hips. "I feel weird, too. We need to get you home. I'll come back for him, if you want me to."

Did I?

I was torn at that idea, letting Bryce go off on his own. My eyebrows furrowed forward, and I frowned. Then I sighed. "You stay with Corrigan, and I'll go home with Denton and Mena."

"You sure?"

I nodded. "Yes."

"Okay." He turned to Denton. "You okay with that plan?"

"Yeah. Are you sober?"

Bryce nodded. "I am. I can drive the car home."

"Okay." Denton took a set of keys out of his pocket. "I was just going to have my other driver come back for it, but here. Once you and Corrigan get back to the Alpha Mu house, just drive her home. Be safe."

Bryce took the keys. "Thanks. I will." His eyes met mine and a silent goodbye passed between us. As he left, heading back for the house, I said under my breath, "Be safe."

Corrigan had a weird feeling. Bryce did too, and it must've been infectious. I pressed the palm of my hand to my stomach because I was feeling it, too.

Something was off, something we weren't thinking about.

CHAPTER SEVENTEEN

We were pulling into Denton's house when we saw the flare from the cops' sirens. Two cars were behind us. They parked beside our car, and I was out before anyone else. My heart was in my throat. The drive to Denton's house was thirty minutes. Something could've happened to Bryce or Corrigan.

When Officer Patterson got out of the second squad car, I went over to her. "Sheila?"

There were lines of exhaustion around her mouth and bags under her eyes. Her hair was pulled back into a ponytail. There were strands that had fallen out. I sucked in my breath. Something had happened.

No, no. Not Bryce. Not Corrigan.

She held a hand up. "Before you jump to conclusions, we're here looking for Bryce Scout."

My heart started to pound. "He's missing?"

She frowned. "He's not with you?"

I glanced to the first squad car. The two detectives who had taken over my case were questioning Denton and Mena. The guy was studying Denton's dress with an eyebrow twitch. Then the woman glanced over to us. Catching my gaze, she broke off and headed for us. As she stopped in front of me, her hand pushed back her coat and rested on her hip. Her badge and gun were there.

She looked at Sheila. "Scout?"

Sheila shook her head. "I just asked. Sheldon." She held her hand up to get my attention. "We really need to see Bryce. Where is he?"

This wasn't making sense. I pressed a hand to my forehead, feeling a headache forming. "You're looking for Bryce? Did something happen to him?" Maybe he'd been taken? My anxiety kicked up a notch. "Did the killer take him?" My voice was a hoarse whisper at the end.

I couldn't lose him. I couldn't lose either of them.

She started rubbing between her eyes, the bridge of her nose. "Wait a minute here. So, you're saying Bryce isn't here?"

"Isn't he why you're here?"

The two shared a look, and the other detective raised an eyebrow. "Are you worried about him, Sheldon?"

I gritted my teeth. She hadn't earned the right to use my first name. "It's Jeneve to you." My tone was frosty.

Her other eyebrow matched the other, both raised high now. "Hold on. Putting aside your winning personality, like always, you're saying Scout isn't here?" She leaned closer, growing more serious. "Should we be looking for him?"

"Aren't you right now? And what about Corrigan? They were together." My chest started hurting. I could feel a panic attack coming on. "We just left them. Nothing bad could've happened since then."

Could it?

"Okay." Sheila held both her hands up. "I'm figuring this out. Sheldon, we're looking for Bryce because we have to ask him some questions. To our knowledge, nothing has happened to him. Or are you telling us differently? Should we be searching for them?"

None of this was making sense. "Why are you here if nothing's happened to them?"

"Because—" Sheila started to answer.

The other female de*fec*tive cut in, "We can't say."

Fuck the headache. This officer was a whole new type of headache. I glowered at her. "Well then." I folded my arms over my chest. "I can't say either."

The male detective yelled from the other car, "We got what we needed!" He waved his phone in the air. "Scout was just leaving some fraternity house. Officers have detained him for questioning."

I could feel the female mocking me before she called back, "Is he being cooperative?"

"He is. He's just confused."

"Let's head out then." She whirled her fingers in the air, making a circling motion.

"Wait a minute. Was Corrigan with him? Is he okay, too?"

But they weren't replying to me. As they all started for their cars, I grabbed Sheila's arm. "Wait. He's okay? Nothing happened to him?"

She gave me the slightest of warm smiles. Her tone was gentle. "He's okay, Sheldon." She patted my arm. "I'll inquire about Corrigan, but we weren't here out of any concern for them. We just need Bryce to answer a couple of questions."

"Oh." Then what the hell was happening? "What's happened?"

"I can't say anything, but trust me. In a fucked-up way, this might be good news for you."

Huh? So many questions were racing through me as I stood there and watched both cars pull out of the driveway.

The same helpless feeling that had been plaguing me weighed heavily once again. I felt like an elephant was trying to sit on my chest.

"Sheldon," Denton called from the front steps. He sounded wary. "Come in. The guy told me before they left that Corrigan's going to the station with Bryce, then I'm sure they'll head back when they can."

That *something that is off* was still with me. I couldn't shake it, and I wondered if this was the beginning of an impending doom.

"Sheldon." Denton still waited. I hadn't moved. When I still didn't move, he said, "I'm closing the gate. You can stay out here all you want. I'll wait here."

I glanced back to see that he had settled down on the ground, leaning back against the wall. He rested his head back and closed his eyes. There was no Mena so I assumed she had gone inside, but I didn't care.

Corrigan and Bryce were the only ones I cared about.

As it was, I didn't have to wait that long. Corrigan texted me a few minutes later: **Home soon. B needed to answer some questions the police had. Don't know what's going on, but it was about Guadalupe.**

"Was that Corrigan?" Denton must've heard my phone beep.

"Yeah." I headed back up the stairs now. "They're heading home now."

He yawned, rubbing a hand over his face. His makeup smeared. "That was fast. The cops literally just left."

"Yeah." I frowned, but we'd have answers soon. Offering a hand to him, I helped him up and we went inside. "Where's Mena?"

"She said she was tired. I'm sure she'll be in her room all night now."

He went to the refrigerator, and when he pulled out two bottles of water, I smiled in thanks and took a seat at the table. He sat across from me. "Man," he said. "I'm tired. I need to go back to work. Too much stress trying to find your killer, traipsing around in ball gowns."

I grinned. "I thought this would be second nature to you, Mr. I'm-in-Movies."

He laughed shortly. "Nah. The hours are fine. Even dressing up and pretending to be a fraternity brother who's pretending to be a girl is fine. It's the stress about what could happen to you, now being worried about Bryce and Corrigan, too."

Denton was concerned about them too. I frowned to myself. That thought had never occurred to me, but I didn't know why it hadn't. It wasn't a surprise.

"What?"

He had noticed my look. "You care about them, too."

He nodded. "They're good guys. I do. I'm firmly in the friend-zone, so yeah, I feel like I'm actually friends with all of you guys, not just you."

"Thank you, Denton."

"For what?"

I gestured around the room. "For this, sheltering us." For caring about my family, too. "Thanks for everything."

He gave me a half-grin. "Aw, Sheldon. You're such a softie inside."

I scowled and gave him the middle finger.

"See." He pointed at my hand. "Even that's with love. I can tell."

"Shut up." I laughed.

"Listen, I'm all for staying up and making sure the guys are fine, but," a yawn escaped him, "I don't think I'm going to make it."

"Pussy."

"I'll take it." He grinned. "Come on, Sheldon. Tonight's been a long night. Go to bed. The guys will be fine. They'll be here in the morning." He pointed to my phone. "Corrigan texted you. You know they're fine."

"Yeah, maybe." If I were in bed, I wouldn't be here when they both walked in; I wouldn't feel the urge to wrap my arms around both of them, never wanting to leave them again. Then I shook my head. What the hell was going on with me? I grinned, laughing at myself. I was becoming a sentimental fool. Denton was right. Bed was the right place to go. They'd be there in the morning, no awkward middle-of-the-night hugs to be had.

"Okay." I stood up.

Denton lifted an eyebrow. "That was easier than I thought."

"Yeah, well, you're right. I should get some sleep. Tomorrow . . ." Tomorrow would be another day spent trying to figure out what the hell I could do. "'Night, Denton."

"'Night, Sheldon."

I left for my room alone. He went to the refrigerator for something. If I was going to avoid the late-night awkwardness, I had to go now. If I waited to walk with Denton, I wasn't sure I'd be able to go. I'd wait at that table the whole night, if I needed to, but when I got to my room and after getting ready for bed and crawling under the bed sheets, it didn't matter.

I was still restless.

I still wanted to be up.

I still wanted to hug both of them.

I lay in bed for an hour, tossing and turning, until I heard someone's voice in the hallway. My heart leapt to my chest. Was it—"'Night, Bryce." A door closed, then light flashed under my door. I slid out of my bed without thinking. No, that wasn't true. My internal logic was yelling at me to stay put, but I switched it off. The need to see Corrigan was too much.

I opened the door just as he was closing his.

It opened again, and his head poked out. "Sheldon?"

I sighed. He looked good, so damn good. My fingers curled around the doorframe, and I rested against it, not moving another inch. I could see him. That was good enough. "Hey," I whispered.

His face transformed. The slight concern morphed into a tender grin. "Hey, yourself."

My heart started to pound more, growing stronger with each beat. "You guys are okay?"

"Yeah." He paused, glancing to Bryce's door. "They had questions about Guadalupe for him."

"Oh." I swallowed, a light-headed sensation was filling me up. "Like what?"

He shrugged, the corner of his mouth lifting in a teasing grin as he studied me. He knew what was going on with me. I'd been the one to crawl into bed with him for so many nights. I licked my lips. They were so damn dry.

Corrigan murmured softly, "Like the last time he saw her. What happened? When was the last time he called or texted her? Questions like that."

I frowned. "That's weird."

"Yeah, it is. They asked the last time he saw her assistant, too."

"They did?"

He nodded. "He gave them her phone."

"Oh."

"He said you might be mad since that was a big thing from going to the hotel that day."

"Yeah." I folded my arms over my chest and turned so I was leaning onto the doorframe. I wanted to go to him. It was the next best thing to hold myself back. "I wanted to see what else was on that phone."

He nodded. "I know. Bryce feels bad, handing the phone over, but he thought it would help. He thinks the police are looking into Maria more. Maybe they're taking this case more seriously and looking at other suspects or something."

"Wait." I pressed a hand to my forehead. "You think Maria killed Grace?"

He lifted a shoulder up. "Who knows? Guadalupe's assistant is bat-shit crazy. I wouldn't put it past her—hurt someone that had hurt you, set you up. Bryce showed me some of the messages she sent him. Some were just crazy. She was threatening him, saying that if he didn't go back to Guadalupe, she'd do something to hurt the ones he loved."

"Me?"

"It makes sense. It gives her motive."

"That's insane."

"Yeah. She's insane."

"Oh." I shook my head to clear my thoughts. I had never considered Maria as a suspect. Yes, she hated me and she was nuts about her boss, but killing? "Yeah, maybe. That's crazy, though."

"Newsflash, Sheldon. Whoever killed Grace is crazy."

"I know. I just . . ." A wave of anxiety rolled through me. "I don't really want to think about it now. Tomorrow, we'll figure something out." That was going to be the plan from now on. Every day we had to try something new. We had to.

"Can you sleep?"

My heart lurched back into my chest. That was the problem. "No."

He hesitated, glancing at Bryce's door again.

Corrigan was my best friend. He'd always been there for me. He'd been my shelter and protector. I held out a hand.

He looked at it, but didn't move.

I kept it there, holding it out between us.

He continued to look at it.

My heart was pounding, louder and louder in my eardrums. I wanted him to take it. I needed him to take it.

Then I heard him, his voice hoarse. "You should check on Bryce. He needs you tonight." And his door shut.

His rejection hit me. When his door shut, the sound was like an extra nail to my coffin. I opened my mouth, but there were no words. What the hell was I doing? I glanced at Bryce's door, then I slipped from my room and knocked on it softly.

Looking at the bottom of the door, there was no light shining from inside, and I didn't hear him answer me. I opened the door anyway.

He still didn't call to me, but I could see the silhouette of his body in the bed. He was sitting on the edge with his hands braced on his knees, leaning forward. "Bryce?" I entered the room, calling to him.

"She's missing, Sheldon."

I frowned, feeling a nervousness in my gut. "Maria?" The assistant?

"Guadalupe. She's missing."

Shutting the door, I left the light off and crossed to his bed. I stood in front of him, unsure what to do at that moment. "Do they think something happened to her?"

"Or she's running." He lifted haunted eyes to me. I could see the whites of them from the moonlight streaming in through the windows.

"Running?"

"There were messages on Maria's phone to Guadalupe. They talk about hurting you. There's even one that mentioned hurting someone and making it look like you did it."

My eyes widened. I hadn't actually thought . . . "Are you sure?"

He nodded. "I'm so sorry, Sheldon."

"Sorry?"

"It's because of me. I saw the messages earlier today, and I was going to show them to you, but we got busy with the masquerade ball. You seemed intent on going so I figured tonight or tomorrow, then the cops asked to see me, and they were asking all these questions. I gave them the phone. I showed them the messages. I'm hoping it'll help. I mean, my god, Sheldon. Then there's another suspect. You could get that ankle monitor off."

I didn't know what to say. Guadalupe? Her assistant? I knew they hated me, but to frame me? To kill Grace over it? A surge of anger rose up in me. My fingers curled inward, forming fists. The desire to find them, to hurt them back, was growing stronger and stronger.

"Sheldon?"

"They hurt Grace? So she could be with you?"

"I'm sorry, Sheldon."

I left. I didn't know what to think and finding this out—that was the reason Grace was dead—I couldn't be in the same room as him. Tearing through the door, I stalked into the hallway, but stopped suddenly.

Corrigan was there. He was waiting outside my door.

"Sheldon?" Bryce followed me. He stopped too, seeing Corrigan there. He said, "Let me talk to her."

"No." Corrigan shook his head as a somber look came over his features. "I sent her in there, but she came out." He opened my door and stepped inside. "I'm done with being nice and holding back."

His eyes met mine. I saw the stark hunger in him, and I gasped, feeling it in me, too. I didn't think. I just went to him.

"Sheldon!" Bryce grabbed my arm.

I stopped in my doorway and turned to face him. I saw the agony there, how he wanted to reason with me, but I shook my head.

She was between us. She always would be.

"Sheldon," he murmured again, softening his voice. "Please. I'm just starting to get you back. Please."

There it was. Right there. Pain sliced through me as I said, "Maybe you were right before. Maybe what we did to Marcus put a block between us. Maybe I didn't want to think about killing him and that meant pushing you away because you did it with me. Maybe. I don't know, but I can't undo that. I can't go back. I . . ." I knew. "I choose Corrigan."

"Sheldon!" His eyes widened. Desperation filled them. "Please."

"I shouldn't have to try to force myself to feel a certain way, and right now, I want to be with him."

"Sheldon," he whispered.

"I'm sorry."

CHAPTER EIGHTEEN

It was wrong. I knew the second I shut that door, but I pressed my hand against it, and I stayed there, needing it for strength. Breathe in. Breathe out. Everything was going crazy inside me, but this—choosing and saying the words—this was the craziest thing.

"Sheldon." Corrigan sounded so timid behind me. He was uncertain.

I swung around and shook my head. "I lied to him."

"What?" He went still.

"I lied. I'm sorry, but I did."

"Why did you—"

I thrust an arm out, pointing in the direction of where Bryce had gone. "It's because of him. All of this is because of him. She did it. That Maria person. There's a text saying something about just this thing, about hurting someone and making it look like it was me. They did it." My chest was heaving. "Because of him. So that he would stay with her, and I would go away."

"Are you kidding? That's what he said?"

"It's because of him." But even as I said that, I bit my tongue. That wasn't true either.

Corrigan echoed my sentiments when he bit out, "That reasoning is bullshit. *This* is bullshit. What the fuck, Sheldon? Get your head on right—"

"I'm all screwed up!"

"Then unscrew yourself!" he shouted right back at me. "Yes, there's a psychotic person out there—"

I interrupted, my heart pounding, "Who killed Grace because of him! To hurt me! Because of him, because Guadalupe wanted him. Not because of me. Do you have any idea how Grace's death has been weighing on me?" My voice shook. "She haunts me, Corrigan. I feel her everywhere with me. It's like she's watching me, judging me that I'm not finding out who killed her fast enough."

That could all be over. If it were true, if it had really been Maria . . . would she leave then?

"Sheldon."

I closed my eyes against the pity I heard from him. Gritting my teeth, I wanted to yell at him. I tried to muster up the courage. I wasn't to be pitied. I wasn't weak. I wasn't a victim, but when I opened my mouth to throw some blistering retort back, there was nothing.

I was empty.

Then I felt the tears. The first one welled up and clung to my eye, right on the corner. It held strong. I grinned, even my damn tear was too stubborn to fall.

"Sheldon." Corrigan moved closer behind me.

I held my breath, but whispered, "Don't."

He rested his hand on my shoulder and kept it there. I squeezed my eyes tighter. I wouldn't cry. No more—then they were sliding down, and I couldn't stop them. I was crying. I was falling, and Corrigan caught me under my knees. His other hand circled around my shoulders, and he lifted me, carrying me to the bed.

To be honest, I didn't care where he was taking me. My arms wrapped around him, and I let my forehead rest against his chest. I was back home. I was in his arms, and I felt a small sigh of contentment forming, mixing with all the hollow feelings I had going on.

I had missed him.

He held me during the night. I started to move around, growing restless later, I wasn't sure how long it was. He pulled me back into his arms and smoothed his hand down my face. "Sleep, Sheldon. I know you chose out of anger. I know it wasn't the truth. I'll tell Bryce tomorrow."

I heard the regret in his voice.

Then he added, "But I need to be with you tonight." His arms tightened. "I need to hold you for one last night."

I couldn't sleep after that. Turning to face him squarely, we were both lying on our sides. I lifted a hand and touched the side of his face. We were just holding the other. I remembered the hunger from him earlier, and I felt the same stirrings in me again.

I said, "I don't know who I'm going to choose." Those damn tears were coming back. I felt them. "I can't lie. I haven't chosen because I have no idea. I love both of you. Bryce is passionate, like a thunderstorm." And Corrigan was tender, like a gentle rainfall. Both were loving. Both were my other half. "I'm sorry, Corrigan."

"Sheldon." He sounded uncertain.

"Yes?"

"I've never told you exactly how I feel."

I held my breath. Was he . . .?

"I know you're going to pick, and I know it's going to be him, but." He scooted closer. An inch separated us. I could feel his warm breath on my face. It was warming me, igniting a fire inside me. "Can I—" He bit off, his eyes clouded with doubt.

"What?"

I was staring right into his eyes. I started to plead with him. I didn't say the words, but I was saying it with my eyes. He saw it, and he closed his eyes, a sound of relief coming from him. I felt his entire body relax. Then he inched close, so close, so slowly, until I felt his lips on mine. He held there, waiting for my answer.

I responded. I opened my mouth and moved against him, applying the gentlest of pressure to him. It was what I needed.

Then his hand came to my side, and I gasped. The feeling sent a rush of tingles through me. It was like I hadn't been touched in so long, like this was my first time with a boy. A small dose of adrenaline surged in my blood. I was growing heated from the excitement. I wanted him that night. If this was the only time, I wanted to make it last.

Corrigan cupped the back of my head and rolled so he was above me. I turned to my back and held his face to mine. His lips explored mine. When his tongue slipped inside, it was natural. This was new, but it felt like we'd been kissing like this forever. A surreal emotion was winding around me, dragging me further into a spell.

I needed his touch. I just needed more of him.

"Sheldon," he whispered against my lips.

I kissed him harder. There were words I wanted to say. They wanted to spill out, and I had to hold them back, not until I knew for sure, so I kissed him again, and again, and again. I didn't stop kissing him. Not after his shirt was lifted free, not after I felt his skin against mine, and he was pressing me into the bed. Not after he trailed kisses down my throat, then to the valley between my breasts and over each of them. Not after he continued caressing me, not after his hands circled my breasts, cupping them and rubbing over my nipple. Not after his hand slid inside my shorts, and I felt him rest there, right at my entrance. He circled it with his finger, rubbing over it, and I was panting.

I was silently begging for more, but I still bit down on my lip. If I let those words slip out, I didn't know what else would slip out. Then I felt his fingers move inside me, and he waited, stretching my insides.

I could only pant. I lay there, unable to do anything as overwhelming pleasure was coursing through me. With my eyelids so heavy, I looked down. He looked up. His mouth hovered over me, watching as his fingers continued sliding in and out, building. As our gazes held, his eyes were so damn dark, and then he lowered so his lips were there.

I almost screamed at the touch of them.

I reached out, needing to hold onto something. My hands first went to his shoulders, but he pressed his lips harder. His fingers kept moving, in and out.

"Corrigan," I finally gasped. I could barely talk.

As his tongue swept over me, tasting me, my hand formed a fist on his shoulder. Without looking at me, he grabbed my hand and guided me to hold onto the headboard. My god. I kept panting. My body was overheated. The pleasure kept building and building. I didn't know how much more I could take, but he kept going. His tongue and fingers. He kept stretching me, pushing harder, then he would wait and pause when I was near the edge. A beat would pass. I would come down a little, then he would work me back up.

When he finally allowed me to come, I was spent. I collapsed, and I gasped, drawing in mouthfuls of air and wave after wave rocked my body. I tingled everywhere, where he was still resting on me, where his fingers remained inside me, the slight kiss from his lips on my stomach.

I felt everywhere.

"Corrigan." I wanted to return the favor, and I reached for him.

He shook his head, evading my hands. He grinned at me and said, "Hold on." Then his fingers started again.

My hands clung to the headboard once again.

He never stopped. For the entire night, he would wait until I came. Then he would start again. When I would reach for him, and at one point, I wound my legs around him to hold him still so I could, he'd only grabbed my hands once more. Eventually, I was flipped over, and he started from behind.

I screamed into my bed.

I wanted the feel of him. I wanted the taste of him. But Corrigan held himself away from me. He pleased me until I fell asleep, completely exhausted from our night.

When I awoke, he was gone.

I sat up, seeing that it was morning, but I couldn't move. My body was sore, but it felt satiated. Images of the night flashed in my mind again, coming at me with warp speed. I felt every climax again, every brush of his lips, every thrust of his fingers.

I closed my eyes, savoring the feeling of when he had finally moved up and rested himself against me. He didn't go in. I begged him to, but he didn't. That was when he stretched back over top of me. His hands dug into my hair, and he started to kiss me again. Our mouths fought against each other for control, but it was the delicious type of fight. No one won, not then, but as he grinded into me, I felt his swift intake of breath as he came.

I still wanted him in me. I reached down, but Corrigan caught my hand.

He panted against me, saying, "Not until you choose."

His words should've drenched me in reality, with what we were doing and Bryce in the room next door, but they didn't. I turned to him. My mouth opened. I was ready to choose right then and there, but he shook his head. "No, Sheldon."

"Why?" I was aching inside.

"Because you haven't let him in yet."

"What?"

"You have to drop the wall. You have to let him in. Only then you can really know." He spoke so softly, holding the side of my face as he gazed down at me with such tenderness. "The wall will come down now or later, but it will one day. I don't want to be with you when it does. You need to embrace all those feelings you've locked up."

But I couldn't. I tried to explain it to him. No matter how much I tried, the wall was there . . . except it wasn't. There'd been a time when it was gone between him and me. Bryce had been the old Bryce. And I'd been so scared then. Hell, I had been terrified.

I couldn't argue with what Corrigan was saying so I only sighed and rested my head against his chest. He held me there, his arm stroking up and down my arm for the rest of the night.

I wanted to tell him that Bryce and I had our time. That it hadn't worked, and it probably wouldn't any more, but I couldn't.

"Sheldon?"

Bryce tapped on my door. I braced myself. Guilt, regret. I knew they were coming at the sound of his voice, but they didn't. I felt nothing except gratefulness. I was thankful for the night.—"Sheldon?"

He started to turn the knob.

My eyes bulged out. "Uh . . . wait!" I cursed, needing to lower the panic in my voice. "I mean, let me get dressed."

"Oh. Yeah."

Cursing, I hurried to change. Then sprayed perfume on me at the last moment. Shit. I smelled like sex. I knew I did, but I was already going for the door. Turning the handle, I opened it, and Bryce straightened from where he'd been leaning. His gaze raked over me, then his jaw firmed.

He asked, "Do you want me to leave?"

"What?"

"Leave. Do you want me to leave?" He indicated his room. "You chose, Sheldon."

"Oh." My god. I smacked my forehead. "No, I'm sorry. I—I was mad. I took it out on you. I . . ." my stomach dropped. "I'm so sorry, Bryce. I didn't choose last night. I—"

He waved a hand, cutting me off. "Okay." He nodded to himself. "Okay."

"I . . ." I had no fucking idea what to say. "Corrigan says I have a wall blocking you. He said I won't let you in because I don't want to feel stuff."

He didn't comment. He didn't move either. He didn't do anything.

I pressed my hand to my stomach, then pressed harder. It had started doing flip-flops. "I—" A memory flashed in my mind.

"No," Bryce said firmly, daring me to argue with him. "I said 'make love,' and you said 'have sex.' They're different."

"It's not that different. It's still screwing."

"No," he spelled it out, saddened. "You screw me. I make love to you."

"Um." Mena came up from the stairs and stopped, seeing us. A bewildered expression came over her and she stuffed her hand behind her back, her eyes went wide before skirting to the side. "The cops are here." She bit her lip, but looked at Bryce. "They're asking for you, but I think they want you, too." She directed the last bit to me.

I shared a look with Bryce. Cops coming here was never a good sign.

He ran a hand over his face. "Okay. Uh, okay. Let's go."

The three of us trailed in a single line to the main living room. They weren't in the entrance foyer, and as we passed it, I felt a smart-ass remark on the tip of my tongue. I swallowed it. Not the time. Not the place.

Then we were there, and the cops all sat up from the couch. The female one —I still refused to learn her name— signaled to Bryce. "Can I talk to you privately?"

"No."

"What?"

"No." He gestured to the group. "Unless you're going to arrest me as a suspect, I'm sick of this. Everything you're here about has to do with everyone here. They all deserve to know so whatever you have to ask me, ask me here. In front of everyone."

She pressed her lips together, then let out a short burst of steam. "Fine." She cleared her throat, tugging at the collar of her shirt. "Guadalupe Ramirez is missing." She searched everyone, studying all of our reactions, but there were none.

Corrigan shrugged. "Yeah. So? We already knew that."

"So . . ." Her eyes narrowed, resting on Bryce. "Has she contacted you lately?"

Bryce didn't hesitate. "Yes." He glanced at me, but he was speaking to her. "She'd been texting, emailing, and calling me until two days ago. So was Maria, until we stole her phone. After that, I started getting texts and calls. The voicemails sounded like Maria's voice. I'm assuming she got a new phone."

"Maria?" The male cop frowned, pulling out his phone. "Her assistant Maria?"

"Yes." Bryce kept going, sounding so tired. "Maria is a huge part of Lupe's life. She's obsessed with her. Guadalupe was calling me and asking me to come back to her. At first she was threatening Sheldon, saying she'll sue. When I kept ignoring her, she started pleading. Now all she does is go back and forth between threatening me, saying she'll hurt Sheldon if I don't do what she wants, and begging me to come back."

"What do you say when you respond?"

"I don't." Bryce shot him a questionable look. "I've never responded. To her or Maria. You have Maria's phone. You can check that." He rubbed at his forehead.

"Okay." The two detectives shared a look. "We're going to be very honest with you." She glanced at me. "The phone you got was a goldmine. You were right. There were emails, text messages, the whole nine yards of enough evidence to implicate the assistant in

Grace's murder. They talked about Grace even. They said she was a good subject," she hesitated, "but we're wondering how they even knew about Grace."

"They were there." The words burst out of me before I realized it myself. Oh my god. They were. I couldn't believe it. "The night Grace confessed, they were there. We were at the hospital because of what happened to Corrigan, which—"

The female held up a hand. "We're ahead of you there. We believe they did cut your car's brakes. There's elevator footage of Maria going down to the basement with a backpack and twenty minutes later, coming back up. Her backpack is missing so we don't know what she did with it, but we're guessing she had things in there to do the cutting, and then she got rid of all the evidence."

The male added, "There's a dumpster on the garage level. We're assuming she tossed everything there."

"And they're missing? Both of them?"

The female nodded. "Yes. We're sorry we dropped the ball on this. We really thought it was you, and of course, we can't offer you an official apology—"

"—at least not until we find Guadalupe Ramirez and Maria Ramirez."

"They have the same last name?" I turned to Bryce. "Are they family?"

"We're looking into that, but it might comfort you to know that Maria Ramirez has had psychological assessments done in the past year. She's gone into more than four treatment hospitals. None of them will release information, but if we can prove she's dangerous, they'll break confidentiality." The two detectives grimaced at the same time. "All we have is circumstantial evidence right now, nothing to fully warrant doing a BOLO. However..." The female forced her mouth to grin, though her face was stiff. There were bags under her eyes. "We can do something helpful, at least for you." She gestured to my ankle. "We can remove that today. We have enough so we can take you off the suspect list."

"What?" I couldn't—no—"Really?" But wait. "What about my hair, prints, and you said there was video footage of me?"

As the male officer bent down and started to remove my monitor, the female explained, "We lied about the video footage. There is video footage, but it's more of a shadow. We don't have enough to go on with it. As for the DNA, yours wasn't enough of a match. And we think your hair was there from past visits. We know you two were friends. It won't add up in a court, especially with other evidence being much more explicit."

"Wait. You said my purse was in her car."

"Yeah." They both frowned and didn't answer right away. Then the female confessed, "We lied about the purse. We never had it."

"But . . ." I shook my head, clearing my thoughts. "So, this is done? I'm done?" We knew who had killed Grace? I looked at Corrigan, who was frowning to himself. He was leaning against the wall with his arms crossed over his chest. He didn't look happy. When he saw my look, he turned away.

What the fuck?

I started for him, but the female officer stopped me. She said, "Actually, we're here on another sort of business." She turned until she was looking right at Corrigan. When he realized, he narrowed his eyes. She asked, "How well do you know Michael Reveritt?"

"Ritt?"

I shared a confused look with Corrigan, then saw a speculative expression cross over Bryce's face.

Corrigan shrugged. "He's my fraternity brother. Why?"

"We questioned some of your brothers today. They told us that you and Reveritt haven't been seeing eye to eye lately."

"Yeah. I mean, I'm not the president, but I'm one of their leaders. With Sheldon and what's going on, I took courses online so I could be here with her. The two leaders graduated last year, and the guys who were supposed to step up, just aren't, so it's been Ritt and me. Why? What does this have to do with anything?"

She hesitated a moment, then her partner finished with my monitor and stood up. He nodded to her. "All right. Did your fraternity brother ever talk about Sheldon at all?"

Corrigan cast me another puzzled look.

He wasn't alone. I had no clue.

He scratched behind his ear. "I mean . . . yeah. He was interested last year. He talked about her a lot, but Bryce came back from Europe and I think things stalled on his part. Sheldon was never interested in him. I know he hit on her, but I don't think anything came out of it."

He gestured to me. Everyone's eyes trailed to me, and I shook my head. "No. Yes, Ritt's a creeper. He always was, but nothing unusual to me. He was drinking a ton when we saw him before the party the other night—"

"Party." The female detective straightened abruptly. Her hand fell from where it had been resting on her hip. She asked me, "You went to the party, too?"

"Yeah." I pointed to Denton, Bryce, Corrigan, and Mena. "We were all there. We stopped at the frat house to get Corrigan, but

Ritt was there. He was drinking a lot." I turned to Corrigan. "I just assumed there was a house fight or something."

Corrigan frowned. "There was a disagreement, but it didn't have anything to do with Sheldon. Michael wanted to use some of the house's funds for other things. I said no. I said the house needed to keep doing what we're doing, hosting parties, charity events, stuff like that."

"Other things? You mean like drugs?"

Corrigan grimaced. "Well." He let out a deep breath. "I mean, he might've mentioned something about pot, but I think he was more thinking about anything to do with study enhancers."

The detectives both lingered, staring at him, with speculative looks. It was obvious one of the drugs mentioned wasn't marijuana. I didn't want to know what else Ritt had been about, but I knew Corrigan would never allow that.

"Well." The female sounded disappointed. "I wasn't looking for information where we'd have to do surveillance. Your boy wasn't at the house when you went there, was he? After whatever party all you went to last night?"

"Oh." Corrigan visibly relaxed. "No, he wasn't there. We have no idea where he went."

"And we can answer that." The officer's tone was no-nonsense. "We have him. He was driving recklessly, and one of our squad cars picked him up. Your boy's in the drunk tank, and then after that, he'll be brought up on other charges. He didn't come in willingly." She skimmed a hard eye to me. "Nothing from you? You have nothing to add about this guy?"

I shook my head. "Like I said, he was a creeper, but that was it."

"Well, this creeper had about fifty surveillance photos of you."

Bryce reacted first. He stepped forward. "Wait. What?"

"No way." Corrigan shook his head, but there was doubt there. I saw it, and when he glanced at me, it transferred to me.

Memories of Ritt were coming back to me, but there was nothing that stood out. He was odd at times, and he hit on me when he knew I wasn't interested, but surveillance photos? I shrugged, looking at Corrigan and then Bryce. I didn't remember anything that would've indicated something like this.

"Sheldon?" the female cop asked. "Are you thinking back to anything?"

"Yeah and no. This is a complete shock. I—what? Surveillance of me?"

She nodded, a grave expression on her face. "At your house."

I sucked in my breath. My house?

"At your dad's house."

Oh my god.

"Here. The night you guys came here. He was down the street. He caught the whole thing on camera. There are others too, but basically he's documented almost everything except what's been going on within the walls."

"This doesn't make sense."

"Guys like these usually don't." She sighed. "All right. I think we have what we need. If you guys think of anything else, let us know." She lifted an eyebrow at Corrigan.

His jaw clenched. That was his only reaction.

She added, "I shouldn't have to say this, but I've been warned it would be helpful if I did." She took a breath. "So here goes: If there are any bruises on him because of you, you will only be *helping* his defense and not us. Do not lay a hand on that boy, if and when he's released from our custody. Okay? I repeat, do not lay a hand on him. And besides, there are no pictures of Sheldon before Grace's murder so right now we don't think he had anything to do with it, but still." She held a hand up, following her partner out the door. Then she added, "We'll be having a chat with him once he's awake and sober."

Once the door closed, Corrigan stared at it. His arms were still crossed over his chest, and his shoulders were rigid, bunched forward.

I recognized that stance. It was when he was about to do something bad, something to get himself in trouble.

Bryce moved so he was standing beside him. Neither looked at the other, but I knew, I felt it in my gut, that they were thinking the same thing. Then Corrigan grunted, so softly so only the three of us heard him, "Well, fuck that. Once he's out, we're having our own chat."

He looked up, and Bryce nodded.

Then they turned to me. I lifted my chin in a silent signal. I was in.

CHAPTER NINETEEN

"So, that's it?" Carolina asked me a week later. It was my first venture out in public since the official announcement from the police that I was no longer a suspect. The media had changed. Half still condemned me as the killer, quoting that I was the smartest killer there was. I had killed her, and I was going to get away with it. The other side had raised pitchforks up in my defense. I needed to sue the police force. My good name was ruined. My life was destroyed. I'd never be able to shed this image.

Neither appealed to me.

I wanted the attention to end. That's all I wanted, and that hadn't happened, which meant we all remained in Denton's house. Corrigan and Bryce had started to come around with Mena. She wasn't the hated enemy, and Corrigan told me that his fraternity brothers found Mena in a heated debate, defending my honor on campus last week. They joined the fight, and the students calling for my head on a plate dispersed after that.

Was that it? I came back to Carolina's question and shrugged. "I was a suspect, and now I'm not."

"But—" She stopped running and gaped at me, her mouth hanging open. "Sheldon!"

Spying a bench nearby, I plopped down. I shook my head at her. "How did you talk me into running?" My damn body was aching everywhere, even my cheeks. How could cheeks get sore?

Carolina was jogging in place in front of me, pulling one arm across her chest to stretch. Black running tights, a pink top, her blond hair up into a ponytail—I started to sneer. Sometimes Carolina was too perfect.

But she's a good friend to you so shut it, woman, I chided myself immediately.

"With the evidence they found on Guadalupe's assistant's phone, they're the main suspects." My stomach rumbled, and yes, even that ached a little bit. I started to look around. Maybe I could grab a smoothie or something. "Ritt's supposed to be released on bond today. Corrigan's slipping out to grab him. He wants to have a talk. Bryce, too."

Oh, snap.

I just opened that Pandora's Box, and I could feel Carolina draw upright. Corrigan and Bryce. I had uttered those names, and I readied myself, knowing an onslaught was coming.

"So," she started.

I smirked. She sounded careless and deceptive, but an attack was imminent.

She asked, "Which one was in your bed last night?

Yep. There it was.

I let out a sigh and stood. "I'm good to start running again."

Carolina barked out a laugh, falling in line next to me. "If you think running is going to make me not ask these questions, think again, Jeneve. I run marathons. A one-miler to me is like walking to you."

I gave her the middle finger.

She laughed and only nudged me with her elbow. "Out with it. Just tell me what's going on."

"There's nothing to tell." And there wasn't. I had told her earlier about my night with Corrigan, but she thought it was only messing around. She didn't know that he'd given me an ultimatum. I had to get in touch with my repressed feelings about Bryce first, and then more activities could ensue after that.

It was fucked up. That was my opinion of the whole thing, but I only said to Carolina, "I have no clue what I'm going to do."

"No more evening *activities* with either of them?"

I shook my head. "Nothing."

"Really? Have either of them said a word to you about that night?"

"Nope." That was true, too. Bryce saw Corrigan enter my room. He heard me *choose*, but the next morning I took it back, and there'd been no Corrigan in my room. I had no idea what he was thinking. The only thing I knew was that it was checkmate. I had to drop my wall blocking Bryce, and then everyone could go from there.

"That's so weird."

I kept my mouth shut. If I wasn't ready to deal with my emotions, there was no way I was going to start being a chick and sharing them with another girl. I let out a frustrated groan and put forth a burst of speed. Maybe I could run this shit out of me? That might help.

Carolina laughed, matching my pace again. "You want to sprint the last bit?" She pointed farther down the sidewalk as it weaved out of the park. "There's a coffee shop up above."

I almost fell down from the relief. Thank god for coffee. When we turned the corner, heading out of the park, the coffee shop was two stores down.

We never got there.

"Oh."

Carolina saw them first, then touched my arm, drawing me to a halt.

Then I saw them. Bryce and Corrigan. Both were standing next to a car, wearing baseball caps pulled low and their shoulders hunched forward. They were trying to be inconspicuous.

They were idiots.

I rolled my eyes and strolled over to them. "Really? Are you trying to fulfill the definition of shady?"

"Shut up," Corrigan grumbled, straightening from the car. He nodded at Carolina. "Nice to see you, Royal Princess, but," he opened the back door for me and gave her a polite smile, "this is where your road ends with Sheldon today."

She narrowed her eyes. "Why am I not getting a good feeling about this?"

"Not to be mean." Bryce fielded this one from across the car. His arms stretched over the hood. "But the less you know, maybe the better for you."

I took a quick reevaluation of them now. They were here, waiting for me. How they knew we'd end up at the coffee shop, I didn't want to dissect, but both were grim and serious. Then it clicked—Michael Reveritt got out of jail.

"Oh."

They both nodded, knowing what dots had connected in my head. "Yep," Corrigan murmured. He nodded again to Carolina. "See ya, Smalls."

"For real? You guys are just taking Sheldon and leaving me here? I ran here."

Bryce opened his mouth, but I shot a hand up. Flashing him a grin, I winked. "I got this one." I turned around to my friend. Yes, my friend. She was my female friend, but she wasn't a part of our family. The only person who'd been allowed in was Denton, but since he wasn't in the car waiting, I knew serious damage was going to go down.

Carolina was a friend, but she wasn't my family.

A delicious shiver worked its way up my back and through me as I thought that last statement. Family. I could call Bryce and Corrigan family again. It felt damn good.

But Carolina. She had to be let down in the gentlest of ways so I said, "Uh, Miss-Professional-Marathoner-that-was-just-bragging-how-one-mile-is-a-walk-in-the-park-moments-before," I gave her the sweetest of smiles, "a *walk* back to your house won't put you out."

She stiffened. "Sheldon," she hissed. "Seriously?"

"Okay, seriously." All jokes aside. "Like Bryce said, the less you know the better." I emphasized, "*For your sake.*"

"Oh." She moved back a step, frowning.

Corrigan pounded on the roof of the car, turning for his door. "All right then. We're off. See you at the mixer this weekend." Then he placed his hand on the top of my head and shoved me into the car before he hopped in himself. Bryce got behind the wheel, and all doors shut in an instant.

That was the end of the exchange.

I knew what was going to happen next, and I didn't ask questions. I didn't need to know where they had Ritt, but the farther we drove to the outskirts of the city, the more my adrenaline was kicking up.

I wish I could've gone on that run now. I had a feeling the one mile would've been a cakewalk for me, too. Then Bryce turned into a storage facility and wound the car around a bunch of tall warehouses. He pulled up to one on the end. When we got out, I asked, "Whose is this?"

"Denton's."

"He knows what's going on?"

"He." Bryce shared a look with Corrigan as we headed for the door. Pocketing the keys, he said, "He offered it if we needed privacy."

Corrigan opened the door and said as I passed by him going inside, "He said these warehouses are owned by a few other celebrities, and they hardly ever come out here, if we knew what he meant."

"He said those words?" The inside was dark, but I could feel the emptiness of it. The air was stale, and our voices echoed all around us.

"He did." Then Corrigan came in, shutting the door after Bryce followed me inside. We were in complete darkness for a second, then the light was switched on and my heart dropped.

Michael Reveritt was tied up to a chair in the middle of the warehouse. The only things in the place were a private plane and a car. Storage shelves lined up one end of the warehouse, but that was it.

The plane. The car. The shelves. And Michael Reveritt.

"Guys," I murmured, stepping backward. I just evaded going to jail. I wasn't sure if I wanted to risk it again.

Bryce and Corrigan weren't listening, though. They started forward. Bryce ripped off the duct tape on Michael's mouth.

I cringed, hearing it pulled off and the cry of pain from him. Then he gazed up at them, moved as far as he could to the side so he could see me.

I jerked my gaze away. If Guadalupe and Maria hadn't killed Grace, he was our best shot for answers. This had to be done. I closed my eyes and prayed to myself. We'd figure a way out of this. We had to. I had to trust Corrigan and Bryce. They wouldn't have taken him if they didn't have an *out*.

Then Michael began laughing. "This is hilarious."

Corrigan smirked at him. "Your tone says otherwise."

"Oh, really?"

"Really."

Bryce circled to his side and folded his arms over his chest. "How long have you been stalking Sheldon?"

"What?" A look of panic was settling in his eyes and he swallowed, glancing from Corrigan to Bryce. Then he found me again. A pleading tone entered his voice, along with a slight tremble. "Sheldon, come on."

Corrigan blocked me. "Don't look at her. We're asking the questions."

"Guys," Michael choked out now. "Come on."

Bryce barked at him, "Come on, Ritt. Start talking. We know you have surveillance photos of her."

"You what?"

"The cops told us." Bryce began circling him, talking in a low voice.

If he wasn't going for scary as shit, then he was grossly missing his mark because, damn, I had shivers going up and down my spine, and I wasn't the one in the chair. Ritt's trembling was contagious. I was starting to feel it in my gut, too. Along with it was hesitation. What the hell were we doing?

Then Corrigan added, a dangerous aura coming off him, "You think we'd let you go? Let the cops cut you loose and not do a thing? They told us what they had on you for a reason, Ritt. Over fifty photos of Sheldon. Please." He stopped in front of his chair and leaned down, placing his hands on the arm rests. His face was so close to Ritt's. He was almost breathing on him. "Explain to us how you're not the one stalking her?"

"Did you kill Grace?" Bryce asked from behind him.

Corrigan added next. "Did you frame Sheldon for Grace's murder?"

I watched and realized they were tag teaming. They were both going at him from different angles, different tone of voices, different threat levels. Corrigan was soft and menacing. Bryce was commanding and angry. Both were a threat, and they were both going full-force at Ritt.

They wanted to scare him off-balance. He might crack then.

It wasn't going to work. Ritt was already panicked, but there was also a calmness in him. He wasn't jerking around his chair. He was still perplexed he was even in this situation.

He wasn't going to take it seriously.

He knew Bryce and Corrigan wouldn't really do anything to him, at least, nothing permanent like death or paralysis. They'd kick his ass, but that was it.

It had to be me. I had to do it. I was the wild card. Ritt really had no clue who I really was. My chin lifted.

It was time he met the real me.

As I made the decision, I felt something melting away in me. The old Sheldon was coming out to play, and she was going to have fun. No. She was going to relish this moment. As I stepped forward, the guys sensed the switch in me. Corrigan stiffened with his back to me. Bryce looked up, and his eyes widened. His shoulders jerked back, and he narrowed his eyes next. Ritt saw me as I stood next to Corrigan.

He looked confused.

Poor guy.

Corrigan glanced sideways at me, but he didn't say anything. Neither did Bryce. They were waiting.

Our old dynamic really was back.

Then I spied the knife in Corrigan's back pocket. As I took it out, he frowned at me. He still didn't say anything.

Ritt sucked in his breath. His eyes got even bigger. "Uh, what? What are you going to do with that, Sheldon?" His wrists were taped to the chair, and his hands curled into the armrests. His feet were planted against the floor, and he tried to scoot the chair back.

It scooted right into Bryce.

Ritt looked up, saw that Bryce wasn't moving, and groaned. "Oh no."

I held the knife in front of me and looked at it. It was so small, so sleek, but so lethal at the same time. It was perfect. I murmured, "You know, Ritt, these guys grabbed you to ask a few questions." I looked up and met his gaze over the knife's blade. "But I have a feeling you're not inclined to answer them." I brandished the knife, waving it back and forth. It was almost pretty as the light reflected off it. "So I'm going to give you an incentive."

"W-w-what are you talking about?" He swallowed again. "What kind of incentive?"

I grinned at him.

He sucked in his breath, knowing his question had been the wrong question to ask.

I said, "I'm glad you asked."

Then I flipped the knife in the air, flicked my hand around, caught the handle, and slammed it into his leg.

He went lax for a second, then he let loose with a scream, tipping his head back.

I murmured softly while he kept screaming, "How about every time you don't answer a question, I'll start slicing?"

Michael wasn't listening. He kept screaming, trying to scoot his chair away from us, but it didn't matter. He couldn't go anywhere. I still had a firm grasp on that knife, and it was still embedded in his thigh.

I was holding him anchored in one place.

Then I looked up and met Bryce's gaze. He was startled, and he ran a hand over his face. He wasn't the angry and commanding one anymore. He was hesitant, but that didn't bother me. What bothered me was the new look he was giving me.

He was looking at me like I was stranger.

I drew upright, yanking the knife out as I did.

This brought on another burst of screams, but I dulled them out. I continued to stare at Bryce. Then I asked, quietly, "Isn't this why you brought him here?"

He cursed under his breath. "Sheldon."

I didn't look at Corrigan. Somehow I knew that he wasn't looking at me the same way. Somehow I knew he was right there with me. He understood.

I was tired. I was tired of being stalked. I was tired of being hunted. I was tired of losing friends. I was tired of it all so now it was my turn. I was done with being nice.

I shook my head at Bryce. If he couldn't handle it, he needed to go. He understood the message and moved back a step, but his hands went into his pockets, and he stayed there. Fine. He wasn't leaving, but he wasn't joining in. I got it. So I looked up at Corrigan now, and I'd been right.

There was no hesitation, no shock, no questioning. He was ready, so I told him, "Ask your next question."

CHAPTER TWENTY

Corrigan only had to ask a few. I did a couple more jabs, but I went for shallow cuts. I hadn't completely checked out. I was still sane. Really hurting him wouldn't help us get any information, but he needed to think I would do it. So I let a part of myself out that would've hurt him, the old me. I had hurt people when I was younger. I'd been dumb, but it happened. That Sheldon got locked up after Marcus. I'd been scared of letting her out, but as I did just now, it felt good. It felt right.

Enough of her had to come out so that it was real. Michael had to sense it, that the threat was real, and a part of it was.

Michael denied stalking me. He denied killing Grace. He denied framing me, but when Corrigan demanded to know why he had those photos of me, Michael perked up. He was exhausted as he said, "That's what this is about? Those photographs?"

Bryce made an exasperated sound behind him. "Are you kidding me?"

"Yeah." Corrigan shook his head. "We already told you that."

Michael frowned, looking from Corrigan to me. "For real? It's just about those pictures?"

"What else do they have on you?"

"Uh . . ."

I started forward with the knife, my hand raised.

He cried out, "Okay, okay. I'll tell you everything. I swear. Just—stop with the knife. Stop it."

I lowered it, but raised my eyebrows. "We're waiting."

"Okay. Yes. I'm trying not to pee my pants, anymore." He let out a deep breath, blinking his eyes a few times, and took a second breath to calm his nerves. "All right. This is what I thought you guys had on me, but I couldn't figure out why you were so mad." He looked from Corrigan to me and tried to turn around to see Bryce, but couldn't. He ended up staring upward at Corrigan, a defeated expression already on his face before he started. Then he began, "You know that I wanted to sell study enhancers to college students, right?"

Corrigan nodded, his eyes lidded. "Yeah."

"Well, I know it's stupid. A business owner shouldn't partake in what they're selling, but that's why I wanted to sell it. Because I wanted it. I have a prescription pill problem. I'll take almost anything you give me, but I like Xanax and Ambien the most."

"What?"

He looked to me. "I'm a pill popper. That's my secret."

"You're a what whatter?" I scratched at my ear.

"I'm addicted to pills, and I'm running out. I've been trying to figure out ways to make money so that was why I've been pushing the house to get into the drug business."

Corrigan walked away from me, scratching his head, too. "What?"

Ditto. A pill popper had set me up?

Michael skirted back and forth between us. Every now and then, he'd try to look at Bryce, but he couldn't so he went back to shifting between the two of us. He must've noticed my confusion because he paled, "Oh no. No, no, no. I'm telling you I was taking those pictures. I'm not your stalker. Well, I guess I kinda am, but not in the way you think."

Corrigan's hand dropped back to his side with a thud. He strode forward, his jaw clenched. He growled, "You better start making sense or I swear I'm taking that knife from Sheldon, and I'm not a hundred percent certain what I'm going to do with it. Start explaining everything."

"Okay, okay, okay. Listen," he implored us. "Yes, I took those photographs of Sheldon, but I was just like the paparazzi. That's why they're in the tabloids."

He waited, glancing at us.

There was no reaction.

"Have you guys not seen the magazines? Well, I can't blame you. All three of you guys are all over them, and Denton Steele. I wouldn't want to read some of the stuff they're saying about you guys either, if I were you."

"Michael." A warning growl from Corrigan.

"Yeah. Okay. Anyway, that's it. Since Sheldon was arrested, she's been the number one way for money. I figured a few pictures wouldn't hurt, but I sold those and then realized how much money I could make. Sorry, Sheldon." He lifted up one side of his mouth. "Nothing personal, and for what it's worth, I never noticed anyone watching you. If I had, I would've told Corrigan. For sure."

"But," Bryce walked around to stand beside us. He folded his arms over his chest. "You have pics of her at places that no other paparazzi have. If you're not her stalker, how do you explain knowing where she's been when the others haven't?"

"Oh."

"Yes?" I asked.

"Uh." He bit down on his lip. "Well."

"Fucking tell us, Mike!" Corrigan burst out.

"Okay. Okay. Crap. Don't kill me," he said that last sentence to Corrigan. "I downloaded an app on your phone."

Uh . . . my eyebrows bunched together. "You did what?"

He nodded at Corrigan. "There's a GPS application on your phone. It sends me coordinates of where you are."

"Are you kidding me?"

That came from me. Corrigan still hadn't spoken. The longer he was quiet, the more I started thinking that I needed to take that knife away.

"No. Look. Pull your phone out."

Corrigan didn't move. He was still staring at his fraternity brother. No reaction. No emotion. I shared an alarmed look with Bryce and he nodded. He said quietly, "Where's your phone, Cor? I'll look."

Corrigan never looked away from Michael, who had now tuned into the new danger he was in. Not from me. My urge to knife him left after that first time, but Corrigan had the knife. Michael started looking from Corrigan's face, still an emotionless mask, to the knife. He wet his lips. "Um, Sheldon or Bryce. Can you guys—"

Corrigan burst forward and shoved him over. The chair fell backward. I cringed as Michael went down. His head was going to hit the floor, but it didn't. I didn't hear a thud. I moved over, just an inch so I could see what happened.

Corrigan was cradling the back of Michael's head, but he had a knee pressing down on his chest. The knife was at his throat, and he growled, "You took my phone?"

"Yes," Michael whispered. He let out a quaking breath.

My nose wrinkled. I wouldn't be surprised if he had soiled himself.

"I'm sorry. I'm sorry. I know I violated your privacy, but . . ." He shook his head from side to side, then again. "I really am sorry. She's your woman. When I downloaded it, I knew you'd be going to her. I did it quick, right when the news broke that she was arrested. You were downstairs watching the news. I knew you had left your phone in your room so I did it then. You never knew. I was worried. I thought you'd find it, but you never did."

He had betrayed Corrigan. That was why he was mad, not about the phone. Michael saw a way to make money, and he used him. It was plain and simple. It was also the worst way to violate another brother's trust.

Michael was going to be shunned from the fraternity. I knew it then, and as it occurred to me, Michael's eyes got even wider. "No. Please don't, Corrigan. I love those guys. They're my brothers."

It had occurred to him, too.

Corrigan was silent.

Michael started babbling, begging him not to exile him from the house. All of it landed on deaf ears.

Bryce moved forward, reached down, and pulled Corrigan's phone from his pocket. A moment later, he asked, "It's not called Stalker's GPS, is it?"

"Um." Michael was still staring up at Corrigan. Agony and desperation filtered in. He cleared his throat and croaked out, "It is. I'm sorry."

"Oh my god," I muttered, shaking my head. "Are you serious?"

Bryce handed me the phone as he strode forward. I watched, pocketing Corrigan's phone. He was still immobile, sitting on Michael's chest with the knife to his throat. Bryce stopped next to him and murmured, "Corrigan. Let him up."

He didn't move.

Michael was trembling underneath him, his eyes imploring him, but he didn't dare talk. Corrigan's hold was firm on the knife—that's when I got it. Corrigan was like me. I wasn't nervous. He hadn't been nervous with me either. Because we each knew the other's limits. Corrigan wasn't really going to slice his throat open, but he had no qualm about making him think that. He wasn't going to let him go without a scratch either. The threat of violence from Corrigan was real. He had it in him to do something horrible, like me, like how I had embedded the knife into Michael's thigh. It wasn't lethal, but it wasn't a paper cut. It would be felt for a long time, reminding him of what he'd done, who he'd hurt.

I didn't know what Corrigan would've done to Michael. I knew he wouldn't have killed him, but that was the beauty of him. He wouldn't have done something like I had. A part of me wondered what it would've been, but Bryce cleared his throat again and Michael started crying.

The moment was gone.

Corrigan had to let him up. When Bryce touched his shoulder, he did just that, standing up and turning toward me. His gaze was hooded; he was even keeping me out and that hurt. I swallowed the pang, though.

He stopped in front of me. "Where's my phone?"

I dug it out of my pocket and held it out to him.

He took it without a word and brushed past me for the door.

I turned around. "Don't delete it."

He stopped at the door, his back to me.

I added, "There might be some way of using it somehow. Don't delete it yet."

He nodded and left.

I turned back around. Bryce had helped Michael back up and untied him. I went over to him and tilted my head to the side. Both guys looked up, but Bryce went back to letting Ritt loose.

"Tit for tat, Ritt," I said. "You narc on us, we'll narc on you. And trust me, we'll make it sound worse than anything you can cook up in that fried mind. Got it?"

He nodded wearily. "He's going to kick me out of the fraternity."

"You used him."

Bryce paused and lifted his head. His eyes rested on me, and I felt like he was hearing something in my voice, seeing something through my wall I didn't realize was coming out. I flushed, but then hardened my jaw. I didn't care at that moment. All I cared about was Corrigan.

I added, "You used him, and you betrayed his trust. You abused your friendship, your brotherhood. You should be thankful that's *all* that's happening to you."

We left him there with the instructions to leave the warehouse and lock it behind him. He was instructed to sit and wait. Bryce called a cab for him as we left the parking lot. After he hung up, he glanced at Corrigan. "He's got some major injuries. You don't think he'll say anything?"

Corrigan's eyes were narrowed. "No, I don't think he'll say a word, not if he's smart, not if he wants something worse done to him."

Bryce met my gaze in the reflective mirror. Corrigan had been outside when I said those words. The fact they were almost the same, word for word, wasn't lost on me. Like I realized, Corrigan and I were alike.

We understood each other.

I turned away and felt a slice of pain through my chest. Something else had happened in that warehouse. I had realized how Bryce and I were not alike anymore, and the distance between us felt like an ocean now.

It was almost too wide to overcome.

"Okay," Bryce announced, turning the car to the right on the highway.

Denton's house was to the left.

Before we could ask where we were going, Bryce held a hand up. "Ritt was a dead end, but we need to celebrate."

"Celebrate?" Celebrate what?

He said to me, "Ritt's not your stalker. That's one celebration, and the other is that you're no longer a suspect. We should've celebrated last week, but we didn't. We're doing it now. I don't care what happens. We're drinking. We're laughing. We're taking a fucking break from this world right now."

There was a moment of silence, then I said, "Thank god. I need a break."

Corrigan grinned, and some of my tension eased at that.

Bryce was a genius, although this time away presented some problems of its own. Like the fact that it was only Bryce, Corrigan, and me. I pressed a hand to my stomach, feeling somersaults.

The love triangle just got real.

*

Bryce took us to a biker dive bar on the edge of the city. A line of motorcycles littered the front of it, and when we got inside, it was mostly bikers.

Corrigan said it perfectly, "Well. Being recognized isn't a worry I have for us here."

Bryce laughed and clapped him on the shoulder. "Come on." He wound his way through the room to a table in the back section. When we went past the pool tables, I saw there were others there. They weren't wearing the leather jackets like the rest of the bikers and were wearing jeans and sweatshirts like us. Sliding onto my chair, I could only stare at those people.

"What's up?" Corrigan noticed my reaction.

"I'm not a biker." I gestured around the bar. "I should be worried being in a place like this, but I'm not." I paused, wondering if that was true. "Yep. Nothing. I don't feel a thing. We have the best weapon in the world."

Both Bryce and Corrigan were grinning. They knew what I was going to say.

I said it anyway. "The media. One call and thirty news stations will swarm this place. Nothing's scarier than a camera light in your face and a nosy reporter sticking her mic where it's not welcomed."

"Hey, folks." A waitress came over. She was tiny, her blond hair pulled into two side braids, and she was a burst of fresh air. Her face was heavily made up with blue eye shadow, black lipstick, and glitter on her cheeks. She wore a black tank top with the cleavage area ripped to show more boobage. Her eyes caught and held on Bryce.

I waited for the recognition, then a look of horror would come to me.

Nothing happened. She gave him a slow seductive smile instead.

Corrigan started laughing.

I was grinning, too.

"Shut up, you guys." Bryce ducked his head down, but he was grinning, too.

"Oh-kay." The waitress glanced around the table. "Can I get you three a drink?"

Corrigan slammed down a fifty-dollar bill. "Bring as many pitchers of beer that will pay for."

"All right, indeedy."

He snapped his fingers and pointed at her. "And keep ten of it for a tip."

She winked at him, her voice growing warmer. "I can see who my favorite customers are going to be tonight." Tucking the money between her fingers, she winked back at him. "Be back soon, freshlings."

When she was gone, I smirked. "Freshlings?"

"Watch it. That's the best come-on line I've heard in a while."

Bryce shook his head, listening to my exchange with Corrigan. He groaned. "You guys, no matter what happens, I love you guys."

I sighed. "Well, there went the light-heartedness."

"Yeah." Corrigan glared at Bryce, but there was no heat to it. "Thanks for bringing us back to the depths of hell."

Bryce rolled his eyes. "I love you, guys. I wanted to state it. No matter what happens." His gaze lingered on me. I felt a different message hidden there, something he meant only for me to understand. But I didn't. I didn't even want to try to dissect it. It was then when the waitress came back with two pitchers and three cups.

She never asked for our ID, and before she left, she said, "I've got three more pitchers coming for you guys."

"Five pitchers?"

She smiled sweetly at Bryce. "It would've been six, but your boy gave me the extra for a tip. Lucky for you guys, or maybe not so lucky, it's happy hour in here."

Well. In that case. I slapped down another fifty. "Bring us the entire appetizer list."

"Will do." She seemed to reassess us. "Are you guys celebrating something? You didn't just get out of prison, did you?" She glanced around. "Not that would be a problem. Most these guys have spent time inside. You know what? Forget I asked. I'll be back in a few with that food, sweetums."

Corrigan and Bryce were both grinning widely. I shook my head. "Shut up."

"You're sweetums." Corrigan pointed between Bryce and himself. "We're the freshlings. I think we have our new code names."

"Okay." After the beer was poured, Bryce lifted his cup in the air. "Come on." Corrigan and I mirrored him, our cups right alongside his and then he started, his voice rough, "This is before all the bullshit. Erase what happened to Grace. Erase Sheldon getting arrested. Erase Corrigan in the hospital. Erase Sheldon being pushed into that glass table. Erase her house vandalism. Erase everything. Marcus. Bailey's and Leisha's deaths. Erase all that glorious sex we had." He flashed me a wicked grin. I felt myself grinning back. "Erase Guadalupe. Erase the distance that happened between us in Europe." His eyes lingered on Corrigan. "Erase that we both fell in love with the same woman."

Corrigan opened his mouth.

Bryce shook his head. "I know you've not technically said it, but you do. We all know it. But erase that. Strip all the bullshit away. Let's go back to the beginning. When I was a silent badass."

Just then the door opened again, and Bryce Scout strolled in to take a seat at my table. The quintessential gorgeous bad boy: black Mohawk, sea blue eyes, and cheekbones that couldn't compare to how the rest of his body was chiseled. Corrigan talked, and Bryce listened.

The memory had me smiling, then I remembered another time.

I felt Bryce move around the corner. No sound. No reaction. Nothing, but I just felt him. I looked over my shoulder and stared into his cold eyes.

Denton didn't notice him right away and murmured, "I was wondering if I could offer my condolences right now? Maybe in a bed this time?"

Bryce jerked awake and strode to us.

Denton looked up, startled, and was quickly pushed out the door. Bryce slammed the door shut and locked it.

He stood and breathed. His chest jerked up and down with each raging breath and then he hauled me against him and slammed his mouth down on mine. He ground into me, and I whimpered once as pain and lust slammed full force into me.

"When Corrigan only cared about getting laid."

"I was hoping you'd go."

"Why? Want to get laid?"

I laughed to myself. He was always hitting on me, even though I had been Bryce's girl. So much had changed since then. A second memory came to me.

"He's got a super-fine sister coming to town. I want Shel, since she's hot and heavy with Mr. Sexiest Man Alive to seduce his sister around to our social crowd."

"Seduce?" I grinned. "I don't do girl-on-girl."

Bryce chuckled as a bright smile lit Corrigan's face.

"That'd be perfect! You can do that, too." Like it hadn't already been his secret hope.

"When Sheldon was telling me to sleep with other girls because she couldn't handle being in an exclusive relationship with me."

I groaned. "I liked this speech until that part."

"You've got this cool arrogance that makes them flock to you. It's interesting, though, because everyone in this room knows that the one girl you love, you can't get." Miss Connors had said those words to Bryce about me. It hadn't been true. He had me; I just had been too scared to let him know back then.

"But go back there. It was simple then." The slight humor was gone. I was remembering *back then* a bit differently, but Bryce had done what he said. Everything was stripped away. It was just the three of us. Again. Like always. Feeling the threat of tears, I swallowed that emotion and cleared my throat.

"Bryce." I wiped at my eye. "I thought this was *break* time. Where's the break?"

"I know." His own emotion was there. We all heard it as his voice grew thick. "But I wanted to take us back there when the three of us were strong. No one messed with us. We had each other's backs. I mean, shit, do you guys remember how many people tried to mess with us? We just cut them off. We didn't even put up with their drama. That was us. You guys were my family back then."

"He's so pale," I murmured.

"He'll pull through. He woke up a little while ago."

"He did?"

"He's fighting." Bryce bent and kissed my forehead. "That's what we do."

I closed my eyes as the memory ripped through me. Corrigan had been stabbed, and we were in the hospital. It was right after we had killed Marcus. A wave of nostalgia crushed me, and I couldn't breathe for a moment, my chest was being squeezed closed.

"Why are you saying this stuff, Bryce?"

I looked over at Corrigan. His hand was gripping his cup tightly. His face was an unreadable mask, but I had a feeling he was going through the same torment as I was.

Bryce sighed. It was so soft. "I want to get back there. When I start training again, I'm going to go and do that world, but I'll miss you guys. Corrigan, you'll go back to your fraternity and you'll kick ass. Sheldon, you'll," he quieted, seeing my tears. He choked out hoarsely, "I didn't mean to make you cry."

I ignored the tears and reached for my cup. "What tears? There are no tears." One dripped off my chin to my hand. I ignored it and raised an eyebrow. "I say we put off the future and just be here tonight. Let's get rip-roaring drunk, but let's all promise each other one thing about tonight."

I held my cup in the middle of the air again. I was calling for one more salute, and then the emotional talk was done. I couldn't handle any more.

Corrigan and Bryce held theirs up, touching mine. They were waiting. I was going to say something meaningful, deeply profound.

Then I grinned. "Can we all promise that none of us ends up marrying a biker from in here?"

Relieved grins appeared, and they saluted me with their drinks.

"Will do."

Bryce laughed. "No bikers allowed."

"And on that note, here are your appetizers, sweetums." The waitress arrived with a tray. Another girl was with her. After they put all the plates on the table and collected the empty pitcher, we heard from behind us, "Well. Hell. My boys told me some rich pricks were here. They ordered all this booze and food right away. I was coming over to either warn you off or hustle you myself, but damn."

We turned around and saw a blast from our past. Hoodum stood grinning, shaking his head, as he took us all in. Wearing a black leather jacket and pants that rode low on his hips, Hoodum was grinning from ear to ear.

He'd always been Corrigan's local criminal friend. He had helped us a couple times; the last time was when he installed my security system. Even though that had only been months ago, there was something different about him.

No.

I got it then as he clasped Corrigan in a hug, then patted Bryce's shoulder. He even gave me a hug before he pulled up a stool and signaled for a couple of his friends to come over, introducing them to Corrigan and Bryce.

As everyone was shaking hands, I knew this was the right place to be. Hoodum hadn't changed. We had. Bryce, Corrigan, and I. Somehow, through everything, the three of us had evolved. I had no idea into what, but it felt right. It had gotten us over our slump, whatever it had been, and it was like old times. Bryce, Corrigan, and I were the old trio. We were the same idiots who had been handcuffed together as part of an assignment from our school counselor.

We were that again.

I met Bryce's gaze, and I nodded, trying to say thank you. He nodded back, and then I shut it off—all the seriousness, the bittersweet memories flooding in, the fear that I'd lose this family again. It was all shut off. As Corrigan and Hoodum started telling us a story, where Corrigan tried stealing one of his cars before he realized it was Hoodum's, I grabbed my beer and reached for a wing.

I had no idea how it happened, what exactly had happened, but I wasn't so scared.

We were going to be fine.

I felt it in my gut.

CHAPTER TWENTY-ONE

We were drunk.

We had moved our party outside of the bar. I didn't know what we were waiting for, but we were waiting for something. Then Corrigan laughed and tripped over his own feet. He stumbled down, and would've face-planted if his newfound friend hadn't grabbed him and pulled him back to his feet. "Whoa man, Rick." Corrigan squinted up at his friend. "You look like Rick Schroder. Has anyone ever told you that? Are you related at all?"

The guy had a long black beard with a mustache covering half of his face. What hair he had on top of his head was covered by a dark stocking hat, and his eyes were brown. The biker was over six feet and probably around three hundred pounds.

I would've burst out laughing, but my stomach had been doing somersaults for the last hour. Bryce leaned next to me and breathed on me, "I think Corrigan has beer goggles on, don't you?"

I wrinkled my nose. A wave of cheesy fries emanated from him, and it was making the ones resting in my stomach unhappy. I felt a gurgling sensation in there and groaned. Not good. I was going to hurl.

"Sheldon?"

I held up a hand. "Hold on."

Wait for it. My stomach had moved from somersaults to the Cirque de Soleil.

"Hey." He poked me on the shoulder.

"Hold on."

I turned from him and bent over. Just get ready. I knew it was coming. Then I opened my mouth and assumed the throwing-up stance. Feet apart. Knees bent. Hands on hips and . . . nothing.

"No. Rick Schroder." Corrigan's voice rose. "You don't know who Rick Schroder is? *NYPD Blue. Silver Spoons.* He was on *24,* too. Nothing? For real?"

I groaned and tried to drown out their conversation. It wasn't helping.

"Corrigan."

Bryce decided to join in.

"—baby blue eyes. Blond hair. He's a good-looking guy." Such disbelief. "Still nothing? Wow, man. You have the same name and everything. Rick. You're both Rick."

"My last name's Bellarke." The guy didn't seem too happy to be having that conversation.

"Corrigan."

I grimaced and braced a hand against the wall beside me. It was drumming up, ready to spout out of me—then a deep and sober voice said by my head, "Raimler, your girl's going to hurl."

Bryce exclaimed, "Thank you. I was trying for the last hour."

"Huh?"

His shoes moved closer to me, and I recognized those boots. It was Hoodum, Corrigan's other best friend. He said again, "Jeneve. She's going to hurl."

"Oh, man," Rick Schroder said. "Candy's going to be pissed. She can't hurl on the pavement. She won't let us in tomorrow."

Hoodum said, "Raimler, you need to call a cab."

Corrigan made an exasperated sound. "I would, but I can't find my phone."

"It's in your hand."

"Oh."

I waved a hand, trying to get their attention. We didn't need a cab. We needed Denton. He'd send a car. All those thoughts were flashing through my mind, but I couldn't get them out. The puke was blocking my passages.

I groaned again, even drunk, I knew that made no sense.

Suddenly, instead of the parking lot posts above us, there was a burst of flashing blue, red, and white lights.

"Shit, man."

Hoodum grunted, moving away from my head. "They could be here for anyone."

"You guys are fun, but we're out of here." That was Rick Schroder. He was abandoning us.

Corrigan said, "You and me, Rick. Shake and bake. Shake . . ."

The guy was gone.

Bryce said, "I'll bake with you any day."

A new grumbling started at the idea of baking.

Then Officer Patterson's voice drifted over my head. "You guys are wasted."

I could just imagine her disapproving stance. Hands on her hips and her eyebrows lowered, her mouth turned down from disappointment.

Corrigan snorted. "Nothing illegal about that. We're all twenty-one. And we're not driving."

Another cop joined the conversation. I still couldn't look. If I moved an inch, I'd be spewing. That second person asked, "Why are you guys at this bar?"

"Didn't want to deal with people recognizing us."

"Well. I guess. Anyone at this bar really wouldn't give a flying fuck who you are."

"Come on, Sheldon." Officer Patterson, Sheila, tapped my arm. "Look up. It'll come when it's going to come. We need you guys down at the police station."

Crap. They were there for us. My one thought was, *damn, Ritt.* He had told on us and now we were being arrested for whatever we did to him. Interrogation. Torture. I had stabbed him. No, assault. I was going back to the slammer.

But then Sheila tilted my head up and said, "We found Guadalupe."

"What?" Bryce sounded sober, all of a sudden. "You found her?"

Regret flashed in Sheila's eyes, but she masked it before turning to him. "We need you guys to come to the station. We have some more questions, and then we'll fill you in on everything."

"Oh."

"This way, Mr. Scout." Another cop indicated the second squad car—whoa, there were three cop cars here—and he followed to sit in the backseat. Corrigan went with him.

"Sheldon." Sheila indicated her car.

She started to move away, but I grabbed her arm.

She looked back.

"She's dead, isn't she?"

The regret came back, but she didn't answer. She didn't need to. I saw it and I glanced to where Bryce was waiting, staring at me from his seat with a confused expression. Corrigan had his eyes closed, like he was trying to sleep.

I grunted. He probably was.

"Come on, Sheldon." Sheila softened her voice. "We can go over everything at the station. We came to get you for your safety right now. You can get your car tomorrow, when you're sober."

"What?"

"At the station. Come on." She walked over and opened the back door. Tapping it, she added, "I promise. You'll be told everything, but . . . it's over."

It was over.

I stood there, rooted to the spot. She couldn't mean . . .

She said it again, "It's over, Sheldon. We know who killed Grace."

My body moved on automatic pilot. They did? But Guadalupe was dead? When I got into the car, and she shut the door, I did what Corrigan had done. I closed my eyes, and I waited out the car ride. She said they knew who killed Grace—I'd wait. I wanted to sober up and be clear-headed to hear everything.

I had to.

For her.

When we got to the station, all three of us were taken into the same interview room, and we were given coffee, lots and lots of coffee. Bryce asked if we knew anything, but I didn't answer. Corrigan didn't know anything, and he seemed to be the only one undisturbed. Even before the first wave of coffee, he laid his head down on the table, and his deep breathing told us he'd fallen asleep seconds later.

I was jealous.

Watching him, sleeping now so soundly, I wanted to evade my tension, but I couldn't. Once Sheila had said Grace's name, I felt her with me. She was haunting me again, hovering all around me. My chest felt tight. I wanted to believe they had found her killer. I wanted to, so badly, but until I heard everything, only then could I let her go.

After the fourth cup of black coffee, Officer Sheila came in with the other two de*fect*ives who had arrested me. At my quizzical look, Sheila explained, "They brought me in. You tend to be more cooperative if I'm in the fold, so here I am." Then she folded her arms over her chest and leaned against the far wall. To the female de*fect*ive, she said, "I gave my two bits. It's your show now."

"Thanks for that."

"Any time." Sheila lifted her chin in a defiant gesture.

I was skirting back and forth. There was a power struggle somewhere or a disagreement between the two, but I held my tongue. I'd demand to know later, if I wasn't satisfied with what they were going to say.

Bryce leaned forward. "Is Guadalupe okay?"

I cast a sideways look at him.

He noticed and sighed. "I didn't love her, but I did care about her at one time."

I was too tired, still too inebriated, and too beyond the point of caring to care. I grinned to myself. That made no sense either, but I said, "I know, but if she killed Grace, I'm going to be happy she's dead."

Sheila coughed.

I amended, "If she's dead. *If.*"

He narrowed his eyes. "Do you already know?"

"She doesn't." The female de*fec*tive took a seat across from us. The male sat beside her, and both shared a look. I didn't know what passed between them, and I was beyond caring about that, too.

I said, "Just fucking tell us."

The female took a breath, then started, so damn gently, "I'll start with the good news because, to be honest with you, there's not a whole lot of it. I have good news, then bad news, and even worse news after that, but yes, the good news is that Guadalupe did not kill Grace."

"Oh, thank god." Bryce slumped down in his seat.

I waited, still tense, and I closed my eyes, knowing what was coming next.

"But the bad news is that Guadalupe is dead."

She waited.

I waited.

And there was complete silence.

She had been with Bryce. She had manipulated him, tried to control him, and she had tried to destroy me, but she'd been a person that he cared about once upon a time. And she was dead now.

There was still no sound from Bryce, and I looked up. He was staring at the table, his shoulders hunched forward, his hands spread out so his palms were flat, and the only word I could use to describe him was defeated.

Then he turned to me, and I saw it—one more death. Another person had died. He asked, so simply, "When is it going to end?"

I reached out for him, and soon he was in my arms. He didn't cry. I didn't feel it in his body, but he wrapped his arms tightly around me, and he buried his head into my shoulder. The defeat wasn't just about Guadalupe. It was about Bailey. Leisha. Grace. Now Guadalupe. Feeling tears at the corner of my eyes, I blinked to push them away. If I cried, I wasn't the strong one, and that was my job for Bryce now.

He was hurting. I would be here for him.

Then I felt a hand on my other side and looked over. Corrigan had heard. A deep sorrow was in his eyes, but he didn't say a word. He only touched me to show he was there. I nodded, thankful, then continued to hold Bryce.

The female de*fec*tive murmured, breaking the silence, "Maria Ramirez killed her. She's the one we think killed Grace as well."

"What?" Bryce pulled back, his voice gruff, there was so much emotion being suppressed there. "Maria?"

Sheila stepped closer to the table now. "Yes, Maria. We brought in your old counselor, Miss Connors, if you'd like more explanation, but we believe Maria was Guadalupe's stalker."

"Stalker? I'm not following."

Sheila nudged the male detective on the shoulder and gestured for him to stand. As he did, she slid into his seat and was across from us now. Leaning forward, she placed her hands on the table. They were open, her palms pointing toward us.

I don't know why that movement was important, but it was. She wasn't closed off to us. She was there. She was present with us. She was open to us. She was trying to help us.

She said further, and Bryce pulled away to sit back up, "Maria was obsessed with Guadalupe. You know this. Everyone does. It was very well documented the lengths she would go for her and like the text messages that you found on her phone, she's the one who killed Grace Barton. We now have further proof. They were at the hospital. They overheard that Grace was confessing about being the one who had shoved Sheldon into the glass table. That gave them information and also a motive. They decided together to frame Sheldon, and they did it, because they thought she would go away, and you, Bryce, would return to Guadalupe. That's her motive for the first death."

I flinched at that term. 'First death.' It was said so coldly and . . . like a cop would say. Detached. But I knew that wasn't true. Sheila was bracing him for the rest of it. Grace was dead. We all knew that, now onto the next death and the next blow.

"The night you guys went to Guadalupe's hotel room, she called the police to her room. She pressed charges against Maria. She wanted a restraining order against her."

"Why?"

That one word from him sounded so bleak.

"She said they fought after Sheldon's press conference. And there was a red mark on her cheek, so we arrested Maria, and a restraining order was set into place. However, we don't think that was the real reason she wanted charges brought up against her assistant. We think it was her first step in distancing herself from Maria. We think Guadalupe knew there was going to be blowback toward her. Sheldon's press conference worked like magic. People were becoming more sympathetic to her, but people were going to analyze us more and she knew that eventually we'd start asking more questions. We would get to them, eventually. That's what we think happened; why she called, but all we know for certain is that there had been a fight. The hotel staff confirmed that. They were called with complaints about yelling and what sounded like a physical altercation."

"Shit," Corrigan breathed out. He shook his head. "This is unreal, being told this." He glanced to me.

I didn't say anything. I couldn't. I was holding onto Bryce's hand, but I was clinging to my chair with the other. Was it actually real? Was it really done?

I was scared to hope.

"We think when Maria realized the object of her obsession was turning on her, she felt rejected, and this sent her into a tailspin of panic and rage. Like I said, Miss Connors is here. She can explain it so much better, but like a lot of stalkers do with their objects of obsession, Maria turned on Guadalupe. If she couldn't have her, no one could. Many stalkers end up killing, or attempting to kill, the person they were obsessed with. We found her body this morning in a warehouse."

Another warehouse. The irony wasn't lost on us, considering what we'd been doing hours earlier.

Bryce lowered his head. Again, like this whole time, he didn't say anything, but he was taking shallow breaths, and I knew he was trying to calm himself. Either that or he was just trying to breathe.

Breathe in. Breathe out. Keep repeating and maybe something would make sense at the end? Sometimes that happened. Once I calmed down, I understood things, but that wasn't going to happen here.

Guadalupe was dead, and he couldn't tune out, then come back in and hope it was a nightmare. She was gone.

I pressed my hand to his arm again. This wasn't a nightmare. It was real life.

Everyone was waiting for us to say something, Bryce or myself. Corrigan was waiting, too. As we locked eyes, a look passed between us. I had to be with Bryce that night. He was grieving, and in a weird way, so was I. They had found Grace's murderer.

I needed Bryce that night, and I tried to send Corrigan an apology, but he shook his head. He understood. I got the message he sent me back, and the corner of my mouth lifted up, but I couldn't smile. Like Bryce, I was defeated, too.

I wanted it all to end.

Then Corrigan asked, "Where is Maria? Do you have her in custody?"

They didn't reply.

I looked at Sheila, alarm filtering inside me.

This was the 'worse' part. None of the cops looked at each other. There was no question. This was what they were bracing themselves for and, feeling my stiffening, Bryce looked up, too.

"Do you?" he asked, his voice hoarse.

Sheila looked right at me and said, "No."

Chills went down my back. "What do you mean 'no'?"

"We found Guadalupe's body, but not Maria. She's on the run."

"But." Corrigan jerked forward. His hand rested on the table, curling into a fist. "Again. What does that mean for us?"

"We have reason to believe that Maria is going to *honor* Guadalupe's death with one last act."

Oh god.

My mouth went dry.

Sheila sighed. "She's going to try to kill Sheldon."

CHAPTER TWENTY-TWO

And we were back to the very beginning.

Sheila dropped that bomb, and the song from *The Sound of Music* started playing in my head. Of course. Made total sense. I was going to die one of these days anyway.

Corrigan shoved back his chair and demanded, "What? Where is she?"

Bryce stood too, but slower and he was still holding my hand. Me? I did nothing. I sat and kept quiet because I already knew what was going to happen. As I thought it, Sheila said it, "She's going to have to go back into protective custody."

Which I already was, sort of. Kinda. I was hiding anyway.

"No."

Corrigan agreed with Bryce. "No way."

"We stay at Denton's. He lives in a gated community, and he has his own gate. We have security there already. Sheldon's dad is still there. Have your officers stay there. Put some outside the first gate and some outside Denton's gate. Hell," Bryce bit out. "Put a car on the inside, too. She doesn't leave. She stays where it's safe."

"You don't know where Maria is at all?" That question came from me. I remembered staring her in the eye. I remembered seeing how crazy she was, but she hadn't been intent on killing me then. No. A sick laugh sounded in my head. She only wanted me to go to prison. She killed my friend to do that. My friend.

I am so sorry, Grace.

Grief like I hadn't experienced rolled in. I felt it coming, bubbling up to the surface, and I squeezed my eyelids shut. I couldn't break down, not there, not in front of them. Later. When I was alone, when it was only Grace and me.

I am so sorry, I thought again.

Then I felt a calming touch and I looked up, but no one was there. Sheila was shaking her head. She didn't agree with Bryce and Corrigan. They didn't care. They wanted me at Denton's house. The news of Guadalupe's death was already pushed aside. They didn't want another death. They didn't want my death. I should've been outraged or panicked. I should've been something, but I was nothing. All I could feel was Grace.

She was there. That calming touch must've been her. And it was the dam breaking. Tears for her started sliding down my face. They kept coming; I couldn't hold them in.

I sat there crying as everyone bickered.

I don't know how long it went on. I didn't make a scene. The tears were silent, and I wasn't wheezing or sniffling. I didn't even wipe them away. They formed from my eyes and fell down, sliding all the way down to fall off my chin and onto my arm. It was just Grace and me. That's all I felt in that moment.

She stayed with me, even after some decision had been made, as someone wiped Kleenex over my face, and when I was led out to a back alley. It was quiet. We had gone somewhere tucked away from everyone else. Well, that wasn't true. Bryce and Corrigan were with me. I could hear the murmur of voices behind us and knew those were cops.

Then a car slid to a halt in front of us. I registered that it was one of Denton's cars, but he wasn't in it. *"They called him, and he sent a car, but you're safe, Sheldon."*

Pain stabbed me. It was like she was there and she was the one reassuring me. I swear I heard her voice.

Then we were moving. We were leaving the police station, but they had cars following us. Bryce and Corrigan were talking to me, to each other; I could hear their concern. I didn't want to talk to them. I just wanted to talk to Grace. I wanted to tell her, *"I'm sorry, Grace."* I mouthed the words as I said them to her.

I imagined her sitting next to me and chuckling. *"Only you, Sheldon. You're told you're in danger and you're thinking about me. It wasn't your fault."*

It was. It was all my fault.

"No, Sheldon." I imagined that her voice would've grown stronger. Firmer. *"You listen to me. This was not your fault. This was her fault. She killed me. You did not. Not your fault. Her fault. You got that?"* Then she would've reached over and squeezed my hand.

I looked down, and my hand fell back on my lap. My fingers lifted and I had my palm upward, like Sheila had done before. She was there for us, and I was here for Grace. I could see her hand fitting into mine. After squeezing it, she would've patted it again and said, *"It's not your fault, Sheldon. It's not your fault."*

I kept hearing her voice. She kept repeating those words even after we got to Denton's and I walked inside. There was a different feel to the house. I saw my dad there, Beth, Mena, Denton. They were all there and all watching, but this was my time with Grace. I didn't want any interruptions.

Corrigan asked me, his voice muffled for some reason, "Sheldon, do you need help?"

I shook my head. I wasn't paralyzed or in shock. I was just . . . protective, of Grace and me. Mostly her. If they came in and demanded me to talk to them, then she would go away. I didn't want her to go away.

My answer was enough for him. They stayed back, and I walked past everyone. I went to my room and shut the door. Then it really was just Grace and me.

I went to the bed and perched on the edge, then closed my eyes.

I dropped to the floor. It wasn't a graceful slide or a slow descent. I was on the bed, then on the floor the next second.

"Oh, Sheldon."

Grace dropped down next to me, and she pressed her hands to mine, leaning forward. I could hear her voice crooning in my ear. The tears had come back, and they progressed to sobbing. I couldn't do anything to hold them back, and I started to rock back and forth.

"I'm so sorry, Grace. I'm so sorry."

"Sheldon." She adjusted her position so she was sitting cross-legged right in front of me. She scooted even closer, moving my hands so they were in her lap. "Why won't you believe me?"

"Because it is my fault."

"It is not. I've said it before. You refuse to listen, so snap out of it." Her voice rose, and I jerked my head up.

She was watching me back, a storm forming in her blue eyes. Then she said, softly, but with authority, "I made my own decisions. I opened the door and let her in. Me. That's on me. I offered her wine. I wanted to cry on her shoulder. I wanted to talk to someone, and she was there. I knew it wasn't right. It was in her eye. She wasn't there, not in the right way, but I didn't care. It was me. I didn't want to die, but I am. I'm dead now. You're not."

I started to shake my head. This wasn't about me. I didn't need a pep talk. I wanted to mourn my friend. I hadn't mourned her yet.

"You've said your goodbyes." Grace kept going. "I've heard them, in your heart. I know how torn up you are. I know how much pain you hold in. I understand more now than ever. You've been hurt so much so you lash out first to protect yourself. I get it. I do. And this is my time to apologize to you."

I shook my head. She didn't have to apologize. She already had. She had done nothing wrong.

She spoke anyway, "I abandoned you. You warned me about those girls. That they were only using me to get to you, and I chose them over you. Then I hurt you. I did what they wanted me to do, and it wasn't worth it. Hurting another person is never worth it. For that," her own tears were falling free, "I am so sorry. I was going to make it right between us. I was going make everything right and I was going to win back your trust. That was my plan. I missed you. I missed our friendship. I'm sorry, Sheldon. I'm the one who should be apologizing to you. I'm the one who is apologizing to you. Please forgive me, Sheldon. Please—"

A high-pitched voice, one edging close to the line of hysteria, laughed above my head.

I looked up, anger stirring. She had sent Grace away. A snarl formed on my lips. I didn't care who this person was. Grace was gone. She'd been there, but vanished at the interruption. "Go awa—"

I stopped.

It was Maria.

Her hair was messy, standing up all over, with clumps of dried blood in it. She had a coat on, but underneath I could see that her clothes were ripped and streaked with dirt. Her entire neck was scraped and red. Dried and new blood coated it. And as she stood there, holding a knife, she wavered on her feet.

I stood slowly, and as I did, I could see her struggling. She blinked rapidly and shook her head, as if she couldn't quite see me. She kept blinking and shaking her head, then clenched the knife tighter. She took one faltering step toward me, but paused, and waved back and forth.

"How'd you get in here?"

She smirked. A hoarse laugh came from her. "Sheer force of will. That's how."

I frowned.

"I sucked a dick, got a ride to the gate. That's how I got here. Enough information for you?"

"Oh."

"Oh?" She sneered at me. "Oh? That's all you have to say to me."

Did I? I shrugged. "I've been prepared for this scene since high school. It seems like people everywhere are trying to kill me, so yeah, I guess. You don't scare me." Was that what she wanted? "Did you want me to cower? Cry? Beg? Get on my knees and suck your dick? What? All of them? Which one? What exactly do you want from me?"

I moved forward, and she backed up.

Well.

That was different.

I moved again, and she backed up once more. Tilting my head to the side, I really took in the sight of her. Take away the knife, and she was weak. My nostrils flared as I identified that. She was on drugs, and she was the one who hadn't prepared for this confrontation.

"What happened to you?"

She lifted the knife. A determined gleam entered her eyes, making her more focused and clearer. "I'm the one who asks the questions. Not you. Never you." She looked around and lifted her nose in the air. "You're here, hiding, in another man's home when you have three men downstairs. They're all concerned about you. Saying you're in shock, but you don't look shocked to me." She gestured to the bed with the knife. "You're the crazy one. You look calm, and when I snuck in here, you were talking to yourself. You were having a full conversation with yourself, even lifted your own hand like someone was there. You're nuts. I'm not the crazy one. You are."

She had a point, but it didn't change the fact I was sober, and she was on something. She had the weapon, though. I started to look around. I needed a weapon. I needed something, at least.

"Oh no." Her gleam kicked up a notch and the side of her mouth curved up. "Look at you." She waved her knife in the air. "Remembered that I have the weapon, huh? You bitch."

I kept quiet.

Maybe I was in shock. I should've been scared, but I wasn't. She wasn't even making my blood boil. Then I saw Grace behind her, and I let out a relieved sigh. She was back. She hadn't left me.

Okay, yes. I was crazy. I was thankful a ghost had come to help me out. We both needed to head to the mental hospital.

I remembered Sheila's words, *"We think when Maria realized the object of her obsession was turning on her, she felt rejected and this sent her into a tailspin of panic and rage."*

I murmured, "They said you're obsessed with Guadalupe."

"Shut up," she hissed.

"That you felt rejected by her."

"I said SHUT UP!" She jumped forward, but jumped right back. She still held the knife up between us, but her hold on it had switched. She wasn't holding it like she was going to use it on me. Her hand moved to the side, and she was holding it up, as if to ward me off.

My words. She didn't want to hear what I was saying.

I kept going. "She called to press charges on you that night, didn't she? The cops said they think it was a manipulation tactic. She was distancing herself from you."

"I said to SHUT UP! SHUT UP!"

In a quiet voice, I kept going. Anything to derail her. She needed to feel like I was attacking her. I didn't know what I was doing, but I needed the upper hand. That was all I was looking for. I added, moving to the side, circling around her, "She was going to set you up for killing Grace. That's what she was doing, wasn't it?"

"No, that's not the truth." Her voice cracked. A ring of desperation was coming out.

I moved again, still in my circle.

She countered me and slowly, one step at a time, we were starting to switch positions.

I was half way there. She was directly across from me, her back to my closet now. "You were the fall guy, and Guadalupe was going to get away with it, but you love her, don't you?" Oh yes. This is like Marcus and me. He loved me. He wanted to be with me, but I turned on him. "She didn't want you."

"Shut up."

"You were trying to get her lover back for her. That's all you were doing. I go away, she gets Bryce again, and then she's happy. You wanted to give her happiness."

"Wha—shut up!" she hissed out. Her hand switched back so she was holding the knife, ready to lunge for me. She had regained control. "You don't know what you're talking about. The cops don't know either."

"They said you went to a mental hospital. You went in four times. Are you sure they have it wrong? Maybe you're wrong? What you're seeing isn't real?"

"No," she croaked, blinking her eyes again. "GOD! Why can't I see? I was drugged. They drugged me."

I nodded. "I'm sure they did. They do that to help you."

"No—no! Shut UP! I was drugged against my will. I didn't want that. It messes with your head, what they put in there, and what she did. What she said." Her voice dipped and her lip started to tremble. "Guadalupe. Lupe. My love. She's dead."

I nodded. "Because you killed her."

Her eyes narrowed to slits, and she hissed at me. An image of a rattlesnake came to mind. She was getting ready to strike, and I had nothing to defend myself. Control, Sheldon. Take control again. My heart rate started to pick up. Great timing. The shock was wearing off, and yes, here came my own terror. Crap. I was in the room with a killer, and she was there to kill me, too. I looked at the door. I could lunge for it? But no.

I played it out in my head.

I would reach for the door, and she would stab me in the back. She could get to me. I had to knock her out, or knock her back.

Scream, Sheldon!

I frowned. Where had that come from? I wasn't in my crazy/shocked state anymore. No more Grace talking to me, but damn, that sounded like her. No, I couldn't scream. I didn't want anyone coming in. She could swipe at them too, or my god, they would step in front of me. She would kill them instead. Bryce. Corrigan. I couldn't risk them. It was her and me.

"Look at you," she murmured in a soft soothing tone.

I gritted my teeth. I was scared, and she sounded in complete control now. This bitch was going to win. I knew it then. My mind was scrambling, but I was going to lose. I had nothing to unbalance her. My card was Guadalupe, and I used it.

Physical force?

Did I dare?

That damn knife. If I missed, I was dead.

I glanced at the door again. It was my only shot.

"Lupe's gone."

I looked up. Maria was gazing away from me, lost in her thoughts now. Okay, I just got lucky. She continued, sounding sad, "She killed her. I didn't. I never wanted anything to harm Lupe. She was my light. If she wanted something, I got it for her. I made her happy. That was my job. You wouldn't understand. Your job is to kill. You bring darkness everywhere. You brought darkness to us, to me. I'm full of it now. Only dark. Only death. Lupe's eyes, they were so lifeless."

Her voice started to slur, and I realized the drugs had kicked in again. I started for the door again and this time, she didn't notice. She stood still, looking at the knife like it was a new invention, suddenly placed in her hand. She turned it upside down, looking at the handle, then the tip, and then she leaned forward and smelled it.

She murmured to it next, "You're my last. I have to kill one more, and then I'm done. Then I can join her."

I was almost to the door. Her voice turned chilling, and I stopped. My hand was about to reach for the doorknob. I turned and she was right behind me. Gasping, I jumped to the side. She hadn't stabbed me, but Maria wasn't Maria anymore.

She was gone. All sanity had left her.

She pointed the knife at me. "You killed her. It's because of you that she's gone. We were both taken. We were drugged, that's how we were taken. I woke up from the poison, but Lupe didn't. She was beside me. She was gone, but she wasn't. I saw her beside me and she talked to me. She told me things. That she loved me. That she wanted to be with me too. I should've told her. I lost my chance, but I have one more to do, and then I can be with her. Lupe and I will be together again, forever this time. Just one."

Her eyes were roaming over me and paused on my throat.

It was coming.

I felt it in my gut—FIGHT, SHELDON!

I stopped thinking and my elbow rammed up, hitting underneath her chin. She was stunned from the hit, but she twisted to the side. Her hand started to swing around. I saw the knife poised, ready to slice into me, but I grabbed ahold and tried to kick at her arm. My foot hit the underside. It was a clumsy hit, I got lucky, then I heard her grunt right next to my ear, and I looked again.

BAM!

I was hit across the cheek. A blast of pain blinded me, and I couldn't move for a second, then I felt her coming and she was on me. I was pushed down to the floor, and her knee hit me in the chest. Oomph.

I couldn't lie there. I heard yelling, and I looked around, trying to see who it was coming from, but it was me. I was the one yelling, and she was dead silent. Her elbow rammed into my head again, and this time the pain more than blinded me. It knocked the breath of out me. I looked up—here it was—it was coming.

Maria was half sprawled over me, but she tightened her hold on the knife, and her arm started coming toward me. The edge of it was going to slice open my throat.

I closed my eyes.

I love you, Corrigan.

BANG!

Maria stopped. The knife dropped. Her arm dropped, and a gurgling sound came from her. She looked up to the doorway then her eyes widened, and she started to point. "She—"

BANG!

BANG!

She was shot two more times. This time I watched as the bullets tore into her. The first one got her in the throat. The second one hit her in the chest, and the third was right in her forehead. She dropped after that one.

Then I looked up—Mena stood in the doorway holding a handgun.

Then everything went dark.

CHAPTER TWENTY-THREE

I awoke in a hospital bed, and my hands were interlaced with Corrigan's. He was sleeping in the chair beside mine with his head resting on my bed. I became aware of two things right away. One, my body felt like it was being burned alive and two, I was damn thirsty. I looked around, but the movement had me gritting my teeth. Pain sliced through me. I was afraid to even think about moving, and I sighed in frustration. What the fuck? The room was dark. The door was open, and I heard soft conversation from down the hallway somewhere.

Call lights.

I was in the hospital. They had those magical buttons.

"You're awake."

I glanced back to the door. Bryce was there now. He ran a hand over his face, then let it drop to his side with a heavy thud. In his hand was a coffee.

My nose twitched. "If you wanted to torture me awake, you're spot-on. Coffee's the way to go. And you look like death."

He grunted, moving around my bed and perching on the window frame. "Speak for yourself. You got stabbed by a crazy woman."

"Hey." I tried to smirk. It hurt too much so I grunted instead. "I took that bitch down."

He laughed softly. "Uh, Mena took that bitch down." The grin fled, and he grew somber. "Of which I'm always going to be grateful to her and I," he cringed, "can't believe I just said those two words in the same sentence. Mena. Grateful."

"Hey. She turned out okay."

He nodded, lifting his coffee for a sip, but he stopped. Then he put it on the nightstand between us. "She did." He gestured to the door. "Do you need me to get a nurse or something?"

"No." I glanced around, saw that I was hooked up to an IV pole and knew this was going to be a new form of torture, but I peeled back my bed sheets and started to push myself to the edge. "But I've gotta pee. Badly."

Yep. I gritted my teeth again. Pain. Agony. I was being stabbed all over again. Then the cold air blasted my back, and I wanted to groan. First things first: pee, then complain. That's what I did. When I came back from the bathroom, Corrigan was gone. I frowned. "Where'd he go?"

Bryce's shoulders lifted in a silent breath.

I knew, but I didn't want to know. I didn't want to do this now, not yet. "The door is shut. The door was open a few seconds ago." An anchor dropped to the bottom of my stomach.

"It's time." He didn't sound happy about it.

I knew what had happened. Replaying everything in my head, I knew what I had thought and waking up with my hand in Corrigan's—I grimaced as I asked, "Did I say something?"

He nodded, looking down at the floor for a moment. Then he spoke, his voice gruff, "You called out for him a bunch."

"I didn't—"

He confirmed my fear. "You told him you loved him."

Oh. Fuck. Horror filled my limbs, paralyzing them for a moment. I hadn't wanted that. Not ever. My throat swelled from emotion and I whispered, "I'm so sorry, Bryce."

He lifted a shoulder, but he couldn't hide the agony. "Yeah, well . . ." He couldn't finish the sentence. Then he cleared his throat and said, raspy, "What can I say? I mean . . ." He let out a loud sigh and turned away. I saw his jaw trembling; he was fighting to control his emotions. "I get it, Sheldon. I do. I—fuck. There's no easy way to do this, right?"

"Yeah," I bit out. "If a crazy person hadn't attacked me, then I wouldn't have been high on drugs or whatever, and I wouldn't have blurted that out." I grew quiet. I hadn't known. Not really. I didn't know until I thought I was going to die. That was when I knew. Corrigan was the one.

I felt tears on my cheeks. Goddamn. I was crying again.

"I'm sorry, Sheldon."

"For what?"

"For not being the guy you wanted."

Another wave of sadness rolled over me. "Bryce," I started to say.

He shook his head, stopping me. "We went wrong. I don't know where, exactly, but maybe I should've pushed harder for you. I don't know. I lost you when I left for soccer. I keep trying to blame Marcus and what we did. Because that means it's not my fault. That I didn't do anything wrong. You know, the whole thing about what we did and how you didn't want to deal with it so all those emotions you have about that moment got swept up with us, you and me. All of it got locked away in you, but it's not true."

I was crying. I wasn't even going to try to stop. So I just let the tears fall.

"I lost you when I left, didn't I? When I went to Europe for soccer. That's when it happened. I left you then."

I whispered, "I followed you."

He shook his head. The pain was radiating off him. I felt it. It was choking me at the same time, and my god, I didn't want this to be said. I didn't want to choose. It wasn't—how could I love two men? How . . . I couldn't push past the pain. It was suffocating me.

"I'm so sorry, Bryce." That was all I could say. "I'm so sorry."

"I should've waited a year." He spoke as if he were speaking to himself. "I shouldn't have gone right after high school. Gone to college. Played there. I could've kept you. Kept my friendship with Corrigan the same. Everything would've been the same. And I wouldn't have . . . lost you."

I closed my eyes. It was hurting to see his regret. Hearing it was enough. I felt like I was continuously being stabbed again.

"Can you say something? Please?"

I looked back up. The anguish in his eyes broke me, and the words started to spill. "I don't have anything to say that will make it better. I didn't want to choose. I didn't. I kept putting it off, and I don't know if I ever would've if Maria hadn't—" An image of her holding the knife flashed in my mind. It rattled me. "I—if she hadn't done that, I wouldn't have known."

"You did know. Don't give me that bullshit. I know you knew. He was in your room the other night."

"I was angry with you. I wanted someone to blame. I didn't want to think Grace's death was my fault, and you offered me an excuse to blame someone else." I gentled my voice. "I knew as soon as I shut the door that it was wrong. I told Corrigan that right away. He knew."

"He still slept with you."

"He . . ." I hesitated. "It was in case it was our only night, and we didn't have sex." A voice laughed in my head at me, *But you made love*. I held my tongue. "I'm sorry, Bryce. I'm so sorry."

"Yeah." He hung his head. "You've said that already."

"I—just." I bit down on my lip. My mind was racing and two things kept blaring at me, but did I dare? Would that help him? I shook my head. I couldn't hold anything back anymore. Honesty was what he needed. This had to be done the right way, and that's what I would've wanted. So I started, "Corrigan was adamant that I have had a wall blocking you this whole time. He wanted me to chip at it and break it down. I think he thought that when I did that, my old feelings for you would come back, and I didn't know what would happen then." I glanced down at my lap. The blanket was tangled up in a ball around my hands and I began picking at a thread. "Maybe there's a wall. I don't know, but I've tried. I've tried breaking it down. I can't. I just can't and every time I do, it always comes back to me." I looked back up. My throat was raw. "We had our time."

His head folded back down to his chest.

God. I struggled to breathe. I continued, hoarse now, "We didn't work and sometime in there, I fell in love with Corrigan. The only thing—" I broke off. Did I add this? Would this help him?

Be honest, Sheldon. It's what he needs.

Grace's voice drifted back to me. That's what she would've said. So I whispered, "I'm like both you and Corrigan in different ways, but you and me, we're fucked-up.."

I felt him looking at me again, but this time I was the one who looked away. This was the most honest I've ever been and I felt stripped and exposed. I continued, "We're fuck-ups. We fucked up all the time. In high school. Afterwards. The only thing we did right was saving his life and killing Marcus. I loved you so much back then. I did. You and me, we were an indestructible team. No one was more powerful, but with loving each other, we failed."

That was the truth.

So was this. "You failed me, and I failed you. And during that time, Corrigan became my rock. He'd do a lot of dark shit, but he's never fucked-up when it came to being there for me. He was my shelter. Going back there, going through the same pain, it would happen again. If you and I tried again, it would never work. I'm not in love with you anymore."

He let out a hissing sound.

I bit down on my lip, pausing for a moment.

Keep going, Sheldon. You owe him this moment of complete truth. Do not hold back, Grace's voice whispered to me again. *You wouldn't want it held back either.*

I grinned to myself. Even dead, she was a pain in the ass. She was right, though. I pulled even more at that thread. I kept winding it around my hand. "I think the thing that's been holding me back is that Corrigan is better than us. I don't know if I'm the woman for him. I'm sure there's someone better for him, and that's the truth about him. I don't deserve him, but if he'll have me, I'll be a better person because of him."

"Sheldon," Bryce choked out, shaking his head. "He's not better than you. Don't talk about yourself like that. I don't like hearing that. You're a pain in the ass, but you're the fiercest and most loyal person there is. If someone is loved by you, they are goddamn lucky."

"Yeah." I pulled harder at the thread. "Maybe. I'm supposed to be letting you down. Stop making me feel better about myself."

He bit out an anguished laugh. "Yeah. So sorry. Go on breaking my heart."

I grinned ruefully at him. He mirrored my look, right back at me. I murmured, "I do love you, Bryce. I always will."

His head jerked up and down in an awkward motion. "I know. You're just not *in love* with me." He sighed. "That's so fucking cliché."

But it was true, and tears were rolling down my face again.

"There was no easy way to do this." He was still half whispering and he gestured for the door. "We decided to get this over with. If we didn't, it would just gut the other guy. That's why Corrigan left, to give us this moment. Sheldon, I—" he choked off his words. "I can't. I can't do this right now. I—" He shoved upright from the window frame. "I love you. I love him. I love the three of us, and we'll make it work, somehow. Just . . . give me time."

"Bryce?" He was going. I didn't want him to go, not yet. "Don't—"

It didn't matter. He crossed the room, cupped both sides of my face in his hands and gazed down at me. He was shattered. That's all I could think, and then he leaned down and pressed his lips to my forehead. He whispered against it, "I will always love you, but you're right, our time was then. Your time with Corrigan is now." He turned and pressed his cheek to my forehead, resting there a moment. "Make it work with him."

My hand reached up, and I grabbed ahold of his arm. My fingers clamped down. I didn't want him to go, but he pulled away. Moving out of my hold, he lifted the corner of his mouth in a small half-grin, but it looked like it was breaking him at the same time.

A sob erupted from me.

He was going.

The moment was here that I had been fighting for so long.

I closed my eyes. I didn't want to see him go.

"Bye, Sheldon."

I felt him leave.

I curled over, pressing my face into my lap. No matter how much time would pass, I knew a part of me went with him. The part of me that had loved him in high school, that had been scared of being with him, been scared of losing him, the part of me that loved getting in trouble with him, that loved everything about *the us* we had been together.

That part went with him, and I would never get that part back.

I sat there and cried.

*

They told me things later.

The police. Officer Sheila. Even Miss Connors came. Everyone was there, everyone except Bryce, and they told me a lot of stuff, but I wasn't listening. I heard words about how Maria had snuck into the community and somehow intercepted Denton's car. She was in the trunk. That was how she got through and snuck into the house. There was mention about a stop that the driver did. They think that's when she got into the trunk.

I didn't care, but Maria's words floated back to me. *"I sucked a dick, got a ride to the gate."*

More explanations were thrown at me then. How Mena got Denton's gun. She had snuck one out of Denton's locked gun cabinet. Then she had heard my screams and came. I was the one who opened the door, when I was trying to escape. It was then, when I fell down and Maria was about to stab me again. That was when she shot her.

Mena killed her.

Mena saved me.

I didn't care about that either.

As they kept explaining more and more, how they didn't understand whose warehouse Maria had kept Guadalupe in. They were still figuring out who owned it. There was more. Neil was there. Then Beth. Then Denton and Mena. My dad was professing how happy he was that his daughter was alive. Then Mena was hugging me too, wrapping her skinny little arms around me. She told me to get better, then she looked at my dad. An odd look was in her eye and she reached out for my dad. He took her hand, squeezed it with a tear in his eye, and she professed, her other arm still holding me strong, "I will take care of her."

He frowned briefly, then squeezed her hand again and smiled. "Thank you. Just thank you so much." On the last day he came to visit, he said I was always welcomed to visit. They were going home. It was time, and he loved me. He would keep in touch. When he left, I could see that he was thankful to be done with this nightmare.

He never said the words, but I saw the relief on his face.

I wasn't sure if I wanted to visit my dad or not, but Beth, she glanced back and gave me a little wave. Beth hadn't been that bad.

I might visit her.

Then Carolina came.

She was more fun than the rest. Instead of asking how I was, she took one look at my face and plopped down in the chair beside me. I was told the Greek gossip instead. She talked. I listened, but I still wasn't really listening. Half of me was in that room for the following days while they monitored me. The other half was gone. It was with Bryce, wherever he was.

He never came back.

Corrigan was there and he was the one I chose, but I was broken. Half of me was gone. I didn't know how to explain that to him, but Corrigan did what Corrigan always did.

He never asked.

He never pressed.

He was my friend.

He wasn't more, and that's what I needed.

There were more visitors, but it was the same thing. I half listened, I half didn't care they were there until the day I was released from the hospital.

Corrigan took me to a hotel. It was decided before we left the hospital. I didn't want to go back to Denton's. Too many memories. I didn't want to go back to my dad's either. Too many annoyances and my old home was out—way too many memories there. So a hotel was chosen, and my dad paid for the penthouse. It was his last parting gift. Mena had sighed then when she heard Corrigan talking to Neil over the phone. I heard the envy from her. In that moment, I saw her for the real her. Remembering how

Denton shared his concerns about her, how her own father had never loved her, and their mother didn't want to deal with her—I saw the real Mena. Her body was of a twenty-one year old, but she was a six year old. She was a little girl, one who wanted a family.

She wanted a father like mine.

She swung her gaze to mine, and she blinked, startled. Then she grinned, running a hand over her face. "Sorry. Did you say something?"

I shook my head. "You're lucky."

"I am?"

"To have a brother like Denton." She did have good family. I wanted her to know. "He's one of the best."

She nodded. "I know." She beamed at me, her cheeks growing pink. "I'm very lucky."

Then it was time. Mena and Denton went their way. There were hugs between everyone. We acted like we wouldn't see each other in years when Denton and Mena were coming over the next night for dinner. Mena was going to spend the day with me at the hotel pool. I couldn't swim, but I was going to tan, or at least have a few cocktails. She suggested I invite Carolina, so that was the plan. We were going to have a girls' day and, even though they never said a word, I knew the guys were going to check on Bryce. Corrigan, Denton, and Bryce were going to have a guys' day.

It hurt.

I wasn't allowed to go, but I chose. I had to get used to it.

Then they went their way, and Corrigan and I went ours. When we got to the hotel and after Corrigan checked us in, he held my hand in the elevator. My dad had paid for six months. This was going to be my next home, at least for a while.

When we got there and went inside, I didn't see the extravagance. I didn't care. Corrigan took my hand and led me to the room, then, as he cupped my face in his hands, I crumbled.

I whispered to him, "He's gone."

"I know," he whispered back.

"I can't—I can—,"

"Sshh." He kissed my forehead and murmured, "You can mourn him, say goodbye to that relationship. He's coming back. I mean, we're going to still be friends, but—"

It wasn't going to be the same.

My eyes searched his. Was this really okay? For me to cry for another man in his arms, but Corrigan understood. He nodded, breathing out, "Yes, Sheldon. You loved him. You can take all the time you want to let him go." Then he pulled me to his chest and smoothed a hand down the side of my face, tucking my hair behind my ear. He sheltered me there and said, "You have to do this. You can't love me completely until you let him go. Then, when it happens, then we can be whatever we're going to be." He tightened his hold on me, a sense of possession to it, "And I, for one, cannot wait for that to happen."

Me too. I held onto his arm, trying to relay my words, but I couldn't. Me too, but first, I did as he said.

I started to let Bryce go.

CHAPTER TWENTY-FOUR

Corrigan held me that night. I slept half the night and the other half was spent just lying there in his arms. It felt nice. It felt healing, but when morning came, I knew it would take a while. He knew it too. When he got up and made coffee right away, I could feel his concern, but he kept quiet. When I wasn't looking, I could feel his eyes on me. The fact that he was biting his tongue spoke volumes. At one point, I let out a haggard sigh and leaned against the wall, bending over with my head over my knees. Then I just breathed in and out. I closed my eyes and stopped everything for a moment.

He moved into the room from the bedroom. In a gentle voice, he asked, "Sheldon?"

I didn't open my eyes. "I'm good. I just . . ." I just need this hole in my chest to close back up, "a minute. I need a minute." Mena would be coming soon. She had texted thirty minutes ago that they were on their way to the hotel. Carolina had messaged a few minutes later that she'd be coming in an hour. She had a sorority meeting first.

Outsiders were coming. I had to put on a game face. No one saw me vulnerable except Corrigan and Br— just Corrigan now.

A deep sense of mourning rolled through me like one giant riptide.

"Hey." Corrigan came to stand right next to me.

I tensed. He was going to touch me, try to comfort me, and the injustice of that tore at me. It wasn't fair. The man I loved shouldn't have to console the woman he loves over the previous guy. And with that thought, I stuffed it down and I looked up. Straightening my back, I nodded at him. "I'm good."

He gave me a half-grin. He had bags under his eyes, too. "Liar."

"Let me pretend." I grinned back, but like him, I could only form a half one. It wasn't in me to force a full smile.

His hand lifted and touched the side of my face, his finger resting near the corner of my eye. He murmured, studying me, "You don't have to. Not with me."

I started to say something, but paused. We hadn't talked about him and me, our new relationship status. I bit down on my lip. Was I ready for that conversation now? Right before Mena got here and Corrigan went to check on Bryce with Denton?

"Sheldon." He moved to stand in front of me, and he held both sides of my face. "Stop worrying. I get it. I do. Your job is to grieve and then heal. Grieve Grace. Grieve what happened to you. Grieve Bryce. I'm not a douche bag. I get what happened. You chose. I do. I'm the guy. I got the girl, but you lost a family member. It won't be the same. You have to mourn him. I will be here. I'll always be here, waiting for you, picking you up, carrying you, holding you. I'm here. No matter how long it takes."

My hands lifted and rested on top of his, holding him as he held me. I wanted to melt down and curse at the same time. "Goddamn. Why do you have to be this guy?"

He laughed, his lip lifting upward. "What guy?"

"The guy." I gestured to him, from top to bottom. "You're understanding. You're considerate. You're strong. You're a fucking badass, too. You're that guy."

He pretended to groan, still grinning. "The annoying guy."

I smirked. "Hell yes. The annoying guy because he's so perfect. That guy."

Laughing softly again, he leaned forward and rested his forehead on mine. Then he whispered, taking both my hands in his and holding them between us. He whispered to me then, "Don't you know?"

"Know what?"

"I have to be that guy." A cocky smirk came over him. "What other type of guy could handle you?"

"Oh." I grinned and pretended to punch him in the chest. "Now you're the smart-ass guy, huh?"

"I've always been the smart-ass guy," he softened his tone and pressed his lips to mine, achingly tender. "But I'm the other guy too, the guy that loves you back."

There it was.

We hadn't talked about it, not really.

"That's not fair," I said.

"What's not?" He lifted his head and leaned back an inch.

"That. What I said whenever I said it."

He chuckled. "You said it quite a few times and you said it first when you woke up in the ambulance."

"I was in an ambulance?"

He nodded. "You were. I was with you."

"And Bryce?"

"He was, too."

Oh . . . my chest tightened. "I wish I hadn't said it."

A frown flickered over his face.

"Not because I don't mean it. I wished I hadn't said it then, when he was there and when I can't remember it." Okay. Cue my girly moment. Three. Two. One . . . "I wanted to say it when all of this was dealt with. I wanted to hear it back from you. And, I know it's really dumb of me, but I wanted to say it so I could see your face. You know, the face someone makes right after they hear those words." I shrugged, feeling an uncomfortable lump forming in my throat. "It would've been the *first* time we said it to each other. You know?"

He let out a ragged laugh, and pressed his forehead against mine again. He was breathing hard. "Yeah. I know. I know."

Then we heard the door's buzzer.

The best timing in the world.

Mena's voice called through the door, "Guys? Sheldon? It's me."

I couldn't hold the disappointment in and must've made a sound because as I started toward the door, Corrigan grabbed my arm and swung me back to the wall. He caught my face in his hands before I could ask what he was doing and he pressed me back. His hips were against mine. His stomach rubbed against mine and his lips came down on mine.

Holy— He kissed in a rough manner. Possessive. Hot. Primal. And it took only one second before my body went up in flames.

Mena knocked on the door again, but the sound was distant.

Only Corrigan. His lips opened over mine, taking me over, and I answered his command back. He wanted me. I felt his need and, my god, my body wasn't holding anything back. I couldn't, even if I wanted to. I had no control over my body. Since that night, since he held himself back from me, I'd been starving for him. He was here. He was giving himself to me and—the phone was ringing.

Loud thuds came next from the door.

Mena shouted from the other side, "SHELDON! CORRIGAN! ARE YOU GUYS OKAY?" She paused for a moment, taking a breath and she yelled once more, "DO YOU NEED ME TO CALL THE POLICE? I WILL!"

Corrigan ripped his lips from mine, stalked to the door, opened it, and barked out, "One fucking second while I say goodbye to my girlfriend!"

Girlfriend.

Mena's eyes blinked, and her mouth opened an inch. "Oh—"

He had called me his girlfriend.

Then he slammed the door in her face and came right back to me. My eyes ate him up. His hair was tussled, his eyes fierce, and he had a scowl on his face.

He was gorgeous.

Then he was in front of me, and he wasted no time. His lips found mine, and he lifted me up against the wall. Stepping between my legs, he continued to kiss me, taking control and I loved it, and him. I arched my back off the wall, kissing him back as hard, as hungrily, as demanding as he was and I knew—this was the right man.

I had chosen right.

He swept a hand up my back, resting against my skin, and I drew in a gasping breath. Tingles shot through me, all the way to my toes, and he paused, lessening his hold on me. My legs wrapped around his waist, and I took over the kiss.

We weren't done.

Mena could wait.

*

Mena did wait. We continued and lost track of time. When Corrigan finally called a stop, we were both half in our clothes and half out. Panting, he gave me a rakish smile and ran a hand through his hair. "Shit."

Shit, indeed. I laughed hoarsely, shaking my head. "Well. If I didn't have stitches down my side, I know what we'd be doing all day today."

"Yeah." His gaze was raking me up and down as I buttoned my shorts and straightened my top, pulling my bra straps back over my shoulders. "There's more we can do tonight."

Tonight. That felt right, too.

"What?"

I looked up. "What?"

"You sighed."

My eyes widened. "I did?"

He nodded, a fondness settling over his features. "You okay?"

"I am." And I was. I meant it. Corrigan narrowed his eyes, studying me again, but he saw that I did mean it and he nodded. "Okay then." Moving forward, he pressed his lips to my forehead, that same loving gesture like always, and he whispered, "I love you, Sheldon." A second kiss. "I'll see you later."

Feeling off balance from all the love and niceness, I swatted his ass as he turned for the door. He glanced back, and I gave him the middle finger. He frowned. "What's that for?"

I lifted a shoulder up, dropping my hand at the same time. "Just . . . doing my normal thing. We're being too nice to each other. It makes me uncomfortable."

Before he opened the door, he flashed me a grin. "In that case, have fun today, bitch."

"You too, dickwad."

Barking out a laugh, he opened the door and breezed past Mena.

She started inside, but turned back to call after him, "Goodbye to you, too."

"Yeah, yeah," his voice faded as he went to the elevators.

Shutting the door, she rolled her eyes. "I guess saving your life didn't change everything. He's still a dick to me."

I didn't say a word. I had a feeling there was an idiotic-looking grin on my face as I thought, *Yeah, but he's my dick now*. Then I said to her, "Let's go get our cocktails on. I haven't been able to drink for a while, and I'm going to rectify that today."

"Aren't you on meds?"

"Yes, and it's called tequila. Let's go. Poolside, here we come."

Mena laughed, but followed me out ten minutes later. It was after we had gotten comfortable, after we ordered our first round of drinks, that she said the words that would change everything.

Nothing could've prepared me for what was going to happen next.

*

MENA

I wasn't sure if Sheldon was ready to hear the truth. I wanted to tell her. It was time. She deserved to know everything that I had done for her, for us. I wanted to, but . . . as I followed her from the elevator and to the pool, I wasn't sure. She had a brave face, but I caught the grimaces of pain.

She looked so tired.

My heart ached for her. She had been through so much. I didn't know. Did I tell her? Or should I just keep watching over her?

An overweight woman stepped in front of her and Sheldon had to brake suddenly. As a curse spilled from her lips, she sneered at the woman before going around her, zeroing in on our chairs.

That was good. There was some of the old Sheldon. She was a fighter. That's what Marcus always told me. Man, thinking of him now, I couldn't help but reminisce. I missed him. We had a good friendship in school. No one knew about us. We kept it secret, but he understood. He loved Sheldon as much as I did. The only thing we didn't agree on was Bryce and Corrigan. They were so horrible to him, like they were to me, but I understood their heart.

They loved Sheldon. They were protecting her. Anyone who went against them had to earn their place beside her. She was their Queen. The name fitted her, what the media had dubbed her—The Queen Bee Killer.

She had ruled over school, and she would rule everywhere else in life. I had no doubt.

Sheldon was going places. She was special.

"Move it along," she snapped at two teenage girls. They were giggling together, and Sheldon groaned in the next instant. She said to me, "They're ogling the lifeguard. Go figure." The girls hadn't heard Sheldon so she placed a hand on both their shoulders and barked, "Move. Now. Or be trampled to death."

One girl gasped. She was all bones with a red bikini on, and I knew instantly she was the popular girl at her school. Her friend glanced nervously at her, waiting to follow whatever the first one would do.

A fond smile graced my face.

The old Sheldon would've been these girls' worst nightmare. She would've eaten them up. That's what she did. Anyone who tried to manipulate her, use her, control her, and Sheldon snapped back—with teeth. She had a bite to follow her bark.

"You don't have a shot with him, honey." Sheldon pointed at the girl's chest. "Those are A cups, if even. Stuffing them will fool 'em for one night. Once that top goes off, poof, there they go. Yep. See." She pointed across the pool. "That girl's got a good C cup." Moving past them, she threw over her shoulder before heading to a lounger, "And a couple years of experience, if you get my drift. Find a guy in your grade. They're more worth it. Trust me."

Both girls had moved past their shocked pretentious ways. They were glancing at the guy, considering what she had said as I moved past them.

Yes, she still had that bite.

It was something I loved about her. I was proud she had that fighting spirit in her. I wished so many times I had inherited that from my father. I hadn't. I had inherited a different way of fighting. I did the unthinkable. I did what people feared, but secretly wished they could do. I was the stalker in the night. Sheldon would give out orders, commanding people to do what she wanted, but I was the type who pulled the strings.

People were like chess pieces. I lined them up until I knew how to strike them down. Not Sheldon, though. I never would have to strike her down. That's why I protected her. That was my job, even if I had been doing it in secret for so long. Like last year, when I snuck in to her house. Denton's makeup artist had helped me, even though she never realized I hadn't been going to a costume party.

I had gone to Sheldon's house wearing Marcus' face. I wanted to check on her and make sure she was fine. I remembered her scream. I hadn't expected her to see me. No one usually did. I was always in the shadows, but in hindsight, I should've known. Of course, Sheldon would be the one to see me.

Dressing as Marcus had been my homage to him. I never thought about how it would've frightened her, and I was angry with myself. I should've thought ahead.

I hadn't.

I needed to make it up to her, then I heard what Grace had done. She turned her back on Sheldon. She hurt her. She betrayed her.

She had earned her place in Sheldon's inner circle and she performed the worst sin. She abandoned Sheldon.

When I heard everything, I knew how I could make things right for Sheldon again.

So I did what I had to do. Grace thought I had come to comfort her. She called me earlier that night and told me what she confessed. She was going to make things right with Sheldon, but it was too late.

She had stabbed her in the back. I wasn't going to allow her to do it again so I poisoned her wine that night. When she started gasping for breath, she reached out for me. She wanted me to help, but I stood there and waited.

That's when she realized what I had done, and she knew I was the protector.

That look in her eye, when she realized who I was, it had given me an adrenaline rush. I was important. I was necessary. I wouldn't let her get close to Sheldon any more. Then there was peace.

Grace was home. I had helped her, too. I knew where she was; she was content. She was probably watching over Sheldon too, just like I was, but on the other side.

Yes.

As Sheldon ordered the first round, I knew it was time. I had to tell her.

"Crap. I gave him the wrong card." She held her room card. "Shit. He has my credit card. I don't want him to use that."

"I'll grab it. Hold on."

See? Protecting her. That's what I was doing.

CHAPTER TWENTY-FIVE

SHELDON

"Marcus and I were friends."

The words were spoken casually. Mena was applying tanning lotion on her arms beside me, at the hotel's pool. No one was paying attention to us. It was nice. For once, I felt normal. For once, I felt like everyone else. For once, I let myself breathe. Things would be fine.

Then Mena spoke, and I frowned. A little girl ran giggling past me. Her mother was fast on her heels and she swept her baby up, saying, "Oh, you. You think you're such a little sprinter, don't you?" There was a mixture of relief and amusement in her voice.

For some reason, that made me smile. I didn't know why, but I would remember this moment, years later, and wonder why that detail stuck out to me.

"What did you say?" I asked Mena, shielded my eyes with my hand to my forehead. I thought she said—no. I laughed. That couldn't be.

"Marcus."

She said his name again.

My heart paused, one solid beat, as his name sunk in. "What?" I felt gutted.

She nodded. "He was my friend." Her voice was carefree, like we were discussing if we should go for coffee or not. Then she paused and looked up, meeting my gaze. "We talked about you a lot."

"Wai—what?" I swallowed. "You mean like Leisha and Bailey? Was he going to do the same thing to you?"

She laughed again. The light-heartedness of it sent chills down my back. "No, Sheldon. Not like that. I wasn't like those girls."

"But," she had to have been. "Mena, we were friends. He targeted those girls because of me. It would make sense if he had . . ." I trailed off. She was so confident, so sure. And a bad feeling took root in my stomach.

A part of me knew before she said the words, but it still didn't temper the shock when I heard, "He didn't pick those girls, Sheldon. You're silly if you think that."

"Wha—who—" I stopped again. Chills were all over my body, I felt them in my spine, wrapping around my feet, even moving up to my teeth. They began to chatter together now. "Mena, w-what are you saying?"

She gave me a smile. It was so sweet, but so menacing at the same time. She said, "When's Carolina coming today?"

"Caro—what?" My heart was racing now, and Mena narrowed her eyes, tilting her head to the side as she studied me. I tried to give her a smile. I failed, but I murmured, as my hand slipped from my leg to the phone beside me. Mena didn't know it was there.

I thought back now. She had been watching me. She saw me put my phone in my bag and then move the bag underneath my chair.

Thoughts were whirling in my head. I had to get help. I had to notify someone.

She had turned away. When the waiter came over to get our drink order, I gave him the wrong card. She went to grab it for me. She had gotten up from the chair to go over to him. That was when I grabbed my phone and laid it beside me, not thinking.

Thank god.

I had put my bag back. It wouldn't look any different. She wouldn't have any idea.

"Sheldon?"

"What?"

Mena was still frowning, her eyes roaming all over my face as she returned to the lounger next to me. "Did you call Carolina? Is she coming today?"

"No." I forced the ends of my mouth up. "I mean, she has a meeting. She can't come today."

"That's too bad." She looked down at her lap.

"Why?"

"Huh?" Her head lifted back up. "What?"

"Why?" I swallowed over a lump. "Why is that too bad?"

"Oh." She shrugged. "No reason. I don't know her that well, but she seemed nice at the hospital. I've heard a lot about her."

"From who?" As I kept asking questions, I dialed the first saved number on my phone, then I remembered it was my mother's and I could've cursed myself. I didn't know why I kept her number the first on the list, but it was there and I started a silent prayer, hoping she'd answer, hoping she'd figure it out.

Please, Mom. Please be a mom for once in your life.

"Grace."

"What?" I jerked upright. *Grace?*

Mena reared back from confusion. "Are you okay, Sheldon?"

"Y-y-yeah." Another smile. Another attempt. "What were you saying before? Grace told you about Carolina?"

"Yeah." A speculative look entered her eyes and her eyebrows moved forward. "Grace kept me informed. She told me everything about you."

I waited, expecting her to go back to flipping through the magazine. She didn't. She set it aside and sat up, turning so she was sitting facing me. She swung her legs off the side of the lounger, and she said, "I have to tell you something, Sheldon, and you can't freak out."

"Mena?"

"Promise me you won't freak out."

She was so earnest. I searched her eyes, studied her how she'd been contemplating me a moment before. There was no maliciousness there. No evilness. She . . . I swallowed tightly. She seemed distressed, about to confess something. My gut clenched. What the hell was she going to confess?

Then she asked, rushed, "We never really talked about it, but did Denton ever tell you about our parents? How they were best friends? You know, before my parents got a divorce."

"What?" This was from left field. "What are you talking about?"

"Just bear with me." She sounded so patient and a maniacal laugh ripped from me. She was calm, and I was ready to launch from my lounger. There was irony there somehow. "Sheldon?"

"Yeah, yeah. Yes, he told me, but I was there. I remember those times. It was fun." And it had been, before something happened. "Your parents got a divorce and stopped being friends with my parents."

"But do you know why?"

"Who cares?" I grimaced. "I mean, you might. I'm sorry."

She laughed, shaking her head. "Same old Sheldon. You're always so funny."

"No." I shook my head. I wasn't funny. Not at all.

"What?"

I hit the volume on my phone, making sure it was the highest it could go, then I turned to her and said, "What did you mean when you said Marcus didn't choose those girls?"

"Because I did."

Oh my god.

I started to fall back, but my fingers curled around the seat and held on. I had to keep going. I had to get all of it from her. "What do you mean by that?"

She laughed, but then it ended on a serious note, a bone-chilling note. "You know why, Sheldon." A gleam entered her eyes. "Why don't we discard the bullshit. You know who I am."

There it was.

I said, "You killed Grace?"

She nodded.

"Why?"

A sad smile flittered across her face, and she let out a soft sigh. "Because she had to go. I always knew. It was hard, though, like I knew it would be." A tear fell from her eye, and she let it trickle all the way to her chin. She never touched it. "I loved her and for a while I thought I wouldn't have to, but that night she confessed. I couldn't put it off any longer. I had to do it."

"You had to kill her? *Why?*" The last question ripped from me.

She frowned. "You really don't get it?"

"Get what?"

"Our parents. They were best friends, Sheldon. My dad, did Denton never talk to you about him? How he hated me? How my parents got a divorce and stopped hanging out with yours?" She frowned, shaking her head. "Do you really not get it?"

"What are you talking about?"

"I have to protect you. It's my job."

"Bu—what? Why?"

She laughed, and I held onto my chair. I knew then I would remember that laugh for the rest of my life. It wound its way down my spine, and a shiver went through my body.

Nothing would be the same. I knew it. Whatever she was going to say next, there would be no undoing it.

Then she said, almost laughing as she did, "I'm your sister, Sheldon."

CHAPTER TWENTY-SIX

I didn't move. I didn't think. I didn't breathe.

Then it all started coming at me at the same time. When Denton told me, *"Our parents are a joke. My dad's always hated her. Our mom's never had the time for her. She's only got me."*

When my dad had snorted. *"He grew up next door. His folks were best friends with Sharon and me."* He shuddered. *"That was a big mistake."*

When Denton had confided in me so long ago, in high school. *"Mena has been . . . awful lately. I don't know what's going on with her. She just is angry and she takes it out on everyone. Dad's called me three times this weekend to come over because he can't handle her anymore."*

I choked out, "What?"

Denton's voice haunted me again. *"Our dad won't have anything to do with us, well, with Mena. He'll talk to me as long as I don't bring her up. How's that for father of the year, huh?"*

"I'm your sister. Neil's my real dad." She let out a breath and rolled her eyes. "My mom and Neil had an affair. That's why my dad has hated me all my life. You're so funny. You never realized that? I mean, we were neighbors. They were best friends. It makes sense in some warped way, but that's why. We're sisters. No one else can threaten our relationship. I'll protect you. I will. Corrigan and I will protect you now. It's both of our jobs." She rolled her eyes. "If he wouldn't be such a dick all the time, he wouldn't be so bad."

My heart kept thudding against my chest. This was a nightmare that I had woken up to. It wouldn't leave. "Our relationship?"

"You and me. Sisters. Friends. That's why Leisha and Bailey had to go."

I couldn't swallow. "And Grace?"

"Duh. Yeah. You and she had that falling out because of the stupid sorority, but she called me that night. I knew you cared about her, but I couldn't let her hurt you again."

"So you went over there?" My tongue felt like lead, weighing me down. I couldn't believe any of this.

"I went over there. We had a glass of wine and then . . ." She stopped, closing her eyes for a moment. "They never told you how she died?"

I couldn't believe I was having this conversation. It was wrong. It was surreal. It shouldn't have ever happened, but I asked, knowing I needed it to be told in case my mother was actually recording it. "No. They never did."

I heard the detective's voice in my head again. *As for the DNA, yours wasn't enough of a match.*

"I poisoned her."

Oh my god. I drew in a shuddering breath. I couldn't talk for a moment.

Mena said further, "I had Marcus kill the others. I told him to do what he pleased. He and I—we bonded over you. I never told him you were my sister. I just said we were close and it was meant to be. He thought the same thing, but, you know, in a very different way. That's why he stabbed Corrigan. You were right, by the way."

Oh. Joy. Was I?

"He was going to kill Corrigan and Bryce no matter what. You were right in killing him, and I overheard you and Bryce. I know the two of you set him up. I don't blame you. He was really sick. He would've killed me too. He was so possessive of you. I recognized it early on. I knew that eventually he would come for me. He wouldn't be willing to share, but I will. I know you love Corrigan, and I'm okay with it. It's a different relationship that you have with him versus me. I've always understood that. Corrigan and Bryce were your fiercest protectors. No one deserves you, but they protected you. For that, I've always been thankful to them, but I'm your sister. It's my job to take care of you too. I won't let anyone hurt you. I promise."

"That's why you killed Grace? And had Bailey and Leisha killed? They were female friends?"

"Well, yeah. They couldn't have that sisterly bond. They would've tried. I mean, come on, Sheldon. I know they would've tried. They were thirsty to be close to you, but they would've done what everyone does."

They weren't. They so weren't. Tears started falling free from my eyes. I couldn't stop. I was afraid to ask. "What does everyone do?"

"Turn on you." She was so calm, so certain of herself. "They would've hurt you. I couldn't let them do that. Like Grace did."

Mena kept spewing more craziness, but I started to tune her out. She wanted to talk. She wanted to spill this from her chest. A fog began to come over me, slowly fading everything away. Mena's voice, so abnormally chipper, grew muffled. A word here and there slipped through the fog, but it was so dense, it was becoming a wall. It was closing around me, and all I could think about was, what the hell was I going to do?

Mena confessed.

Carolina was coming.

Carolina was in danger.

Stay in public. That's what others would tell me. Mena wouldn't hurt Carolina or me if there were around witnesses.

I looked over, and she was still talking. She was even smiling. She looked so happy.

I felt nauseous.

Then I heard myself saying, my voice sounding loud and distorted through my own fogged wall, "Let's go to the room."

She stopped. Concern flashed over her face, her forehead wrinkled together. "Are you okay?"

No. "Yes, wait. No. I feel a little sick. I should lie down."

"Okay. Yes. That's a good idea."

We got up and when we got back to the room, I pressed a hand to my forehead. "You know, Mena, I feel kinda feverish. I think I'm going to lie down. Take a nap."

"Oh."

I saw the suspicion in her depths and reached out, squeezing her hand. "Can you come over tomorrow night? We can do movie night?"

"Oh." The wrinkle in her forehead disappeared, but her mouth was still pointing downward. "You sure?"

I nodded. "Yes. Well, to be honest, I think the whole sister thing is a lot right now. You know?" I smiled, making sure I looked tired, peaked, and genuine. *Smile, bitch. Smile until the psycho killer leaves.*

"Okay." Her head bobbed up and down and her shoulders rolled back. "That sounds good. Tomorrow can be sister movie night."

"Yes. That sounds great."

"Okay. I suppose I should grab my things and . . ."

The buzzer sounded from the door.

Mena's frown appeared again and she glanced at me, finishing her sentence, ". . . go? Who—"

"Sheldon!" Carolina banged on the door again. "You said you'd have a glass of Merlot waiting for me, but guess what? You don't. I checked the pool. There's no you and more importantly, no Merlot for me. I know you're in there." She groaned, laughing at the same time. "Please tell me Corrigan didn't come back for a quickie. You still have stitches. You can't rip those suckers." She snorted then. "Suckers. Oh, that word. Okay, come on." Another bang on the door. "Seriously. Let me in. I need to get classy wasted right now. The damn sorority meeting has driven me to drinking so let me drink, woman."

"You . . ." The betrayal appeared first in Mena's eyes. They darkened, her eyebrows burrowing together. The sides of her mouth pinched downward, and she turned toward the door. As she was turning for the door, hurt replaced the betrayal, and right before she was completely facing to the door, I saw the anger. She sucked in a breath. Her shoulders lifted, becoming rigid, and her hands formed into tiny little fists.

"Mena, don't." I hurried to block her.

She stopped and clipped her head from side to side in a savage movement. "Get out of the way."

"Carolina hasn't done anything."

"You did. You lied to me."

"Mena—" I stopped. I had no idea what to say.

She continued to shake her head and her hand lifted, pinching the skin on her forehead. "Why? Why? WHY?"

I backed up against the door. My throat was dry and I held up my hands. "Mena . . ." I had nothing, though. I had lied to her. She was crazy. What the hell had I done?

Carolina knocked on the door again. Her voice sounded so close now, right behind me. "Sheldon? What's going on in there?" She paused, then asked, "Are you o—oh."

I heard the alarm starting in her voice, and I closed my eyes. That wasn't good. It was the final nail in the coffin. And as I looked again, Mena was gone from in front of me. What? I stepped forward. "Mena?"

I moved four more steps when she reemerged from the hallway. A butcher knife was in her hands. I groaned. "I didn't know they had those in hotel rooms."

She lifted the knife and examined it. "Only in penthouses, I'm sure." Her hands tightened around the handle bar. "Move aside, Sheldon. You know what I have to do."

I backed all the way to the door. "Carolina hasn't betrayed me."

"BUT YOU BETRAYED ME!" she bellowed out, holding the knife with both hands now. She was gripping onto it like it was a lifesaver. "Move," she hissed through closed lips. "You hurt me. I have to hurt you back."

Done. I shot forward and held my arms out, turned upward for her. "Go for it. Hurt me."

She jerked backward, her hand trembling. "No. Never you. Never." Her eyes narrowed. "What is wrong with you? I would never hurt you."

I pressed my lips together. She was already looking toward the door again. I was running out of time so I dropped my arms and straightened to my fullest height. My chin lifted. My eyes narrowed. And my shoulders rolled back. Then I cocked my head to the side. "You're not getting through me."

There was no reaction from her.

"I mean it. It's you and me. There's no way I'm letting you hurt any more of my friends."

"Move, Sheldon."

"No."

Her eyes snapped back to mine, and her top lip curved into a snarl. "I said move."

I stood my ground.

We were at an impasse.

Then she murmured, a cruel grin alighting her face, "I could slice you. You would be weakened from the blood flow, and then I would step over your body, open that door, and plunge this into your friend. That's how easy killing can be."

"I thought you said you wouldn't hurt me."

"If you are standing in my way, I will do what I have to do. Harming you is not the same as killing you. One slice won't kill you, and don't think I won't do it. I've hurt myself at moments when I had to."

A shiver crawled down my spine. I didn't even want to know about those moments. "I won't let you hurt her."

A keen look entered her eyes and she drew closer. I grew wary. Right here, this was the killer in front of me. I could believe everything she had spouted by the pool. She was tiny, but there was an unnatural aura coming from her. She was cold, yet happy. She was calculating and eager at the same time. I had never viewed this Mena before. Crazy, yes. Hurt, yes. A lost little girl not long ago. But this woman? Another shiver wracked through my body, tightening every nerve in my body, making my stomach churn. This woman was a serial killer.

"Move, Sheldon. I'll only say it this last time."

"One slice won't take me down, bitch—"

Her hand darted, and I felt a little nip across my throat. "What?" I frowned in confusion. Her knife had blood, and she stepped back. I saw there was a lot of blood. Then I felt a cold trickle moving over my skin, and I glanced down. Blood, dark red, almost black, had already covered my chest. I touched my neck, then pulled it away. As I saw the blood on my hand, the pain hit me, and everything sagged out of me.

A metallic taste filled my mouth. "Wha—"

Mena stepped closer to me. Her hand went to my arm, and she began to move me aside. It was a gentle touch, but firm and guiding at the same moment.

Then the cold started in. "Mena, what did you do?"

"I told you. One slice to move you out of the way."

My knees began to buckle then and Mena helped me to the floor. She murmured, straightening back up, "Don't worry. I'll take care of Carolina and then call 911. They'll think Carolina attacked us." Resolve settled over her face. "I'll have to cut myself, but I know how to do it. Everything will be fine." She patted my shoulder and moved to the door.

Time slowed then. I checked out of my body and from a distance, I heard myself yelling, "RUN, CAROLINA! RUN! RUUUUUNNNN." No, I wasn't shouting. I was screaming. Mena glared at me, her nostrils flared, and she reached for the door. Then she moved to the side. I saw what she was going to do. Carolina would rush in and she would gut her, take her by surprise, as Carolina would come to me first. Her hand had a firm grip on the knife behind her—but it wasn't Carolina's body that came through the door first.

Bryce rushed in, his eyes wild and his skin pale. He was first to come in. There were others behind him, but I couldn't tear my eyes from him. He was the first victim.

She narrowed her eyes, but as he saw me, her arm started to swing around—she was going for him. I tried to sit up. My hand reached out, but it was happening too fast. I couldn't stop it.

And then someone else shot through the door. A firm hand gripped Mena's wrist, but it happened too fast for her to stop. She was lunging at Bryce with her arm, using the weight of her body to help with her force.

That hand flicked her wrist around so the knife was pointed to her.

Mena impaled herself on the knife. She choked out, and her eyes trailed upward, then widened as she saw Corrigan scowling back down at her. "You," she breathed out. "You love her, too. I know—"

He punched her, and her body crumbled to the floor.

"Down, bitch." Then Corrigan turned to me. "You okay?"

And I passed out, for the umpteenth time.

EPILOGUE

My call to my mother had gone to her voicemail. It was her assistant that heard the alert from her phone and listened to the message. When she heard enough, she made two calls immediately. The first was to *Daughter's bf* in my mom's phone. That call went to Bryce and the other call was to 911.

Bryce was with Corrigan and Denton. All three of them got to the hotel first. I was told later that the guys carried us to the elevator. They were in the lobby when the police arrived. Paramedics weren't far behind them. Corrigan had been carrying me. Denton carried his sister and Bryce helped Carolina, who had gone into shock when she realized what had happened.

Mena survived her own stabbing and charges were brought against her. She was sentenced to life in prison. It never went to jury so some information was never leaked, like that she was my sister. My father never found out, and everyone who did know had sworn to secrecy. It would only hurt him, and he seemed happy with Beth. Even though my own relationship would never be repaired with him, this was one way I was helping him, in my own way.

It was exactly one year ago that I found Grace's killer. This was the first day I would speak to her again.

The visiting area was cold and impersonal.

Sitting in that seat, waiting for the guard to let Mena through, was surreal. Sitting here now, waiting to talk to her through a wall of glass and a phone between us for our conversation, I couldn't help but ask myself why I was there. She took away so many people in my life. During the trial, I listened to every detail and every day, I got sick afterwards.

She had sought Marcus out. They bonded over their love for me and she was the one who molded him into a killer. She insisted they had to protect me. Everything was because of her. Marcus, though he had his own share of crazy, had been swept up in her delusional world.

I killed him, and I couldn't help to think if I ever would've done that if she hadn't entered his life? His blood was on my hands. Thinking about it now, I stared straight ahead and my hands curled into my lap, tugging on my sleeves. I gritted my teeth. It was her fault. All of it.

Then I heard a buzzing sound and a far door opened.

Mena was led inside wearing a bright orange jumper. The guard undid her chains and she walked to me, smiling.

I tugged harder on my sleeves. Damn. Even now, even after I had testified against her and shared everything she told me, everything she had done to me, she didn't hate me. There was love shining back from her eyes.

As she took her seat, she placed a hand to the glass wall and spread her fingers.

The usual response would be to place mine on the other side.

I still didn't even know if I wanted to *talk* to her, much less that response.

Coming to see her had been my only thought process. I wasn't sure how I would react when I actually did see her, but she was here and she was reaching out for me.

My stomach turned over on itself again.

She frowned, pulling her hand away, and indicated to the phone. She picked hers up and waited, still frowning at me, her flawless skin marred from the lines in her forehead.

"What are you going to say to her?" Denton had asked when I told him I was coming here. He was wrecked by everything. Learning all she had done and the trial had been brutal on him. His career had taken a hit. Movies dumped him, but his agent spun it. Denton was urged to do a one-on-one interview with a primetime news channel. It worked. Some people cried out that he knew what she had been doing. They didn't believe his tears. He was playing the sympathy card. But everyone else, like me, had been moved by his interview. He had been one hundred percent honest.

He loved his sister. She had been unloved by one parent and ignored by the other. He tried to protect her, and he knew she had problems, but this—everything—had been unprecedented.

Denton welled up then, and he fought to keep the tears from falling.

The image of one of their A-list actors so raw and so exposed had swept through the nation. There was renewed Denton love, and it created pandemonium. All his old roles came back, and he had offers like he had never had before.

Everyone loved Denton.

Everyone hated Mena.

But the two of us, Denton and myself, we were in the middle.

He asked one time in the courtroom, we had both remained seated as everyone left so the entire room was empty except for us two, "How can I still love her? After the destruction she caused?"

I had no answer. I only said, feeling the same dazed and numb sensation I heard in his voice, "How can I when I just found out?"

"Do you?"

I didn't look at him, but I knew that he had lifted his head, watching me. It was another question I couldn't answer, but I didn't *not* love her. That was all I knew. I only replied, "It's all a mess. That's what I feel. That's all I feel."

Denton still loved his sister even though he hadn't come to visit her yet. And me—looking at her now, holding her phone to her ear and waiting—I still had no idea how I felt.

My hand reached for the phone. That old feeling of being dazed and confused came back to me now. It never left me during the trial. I pressed the phone to my ear, but didn't say anything. My throat didn't work all of a sudden.

"Hi," she breathed into her phone. The relief was so loud.

I almost put the phone back. I didn't want to hear her relieved.

"Uh," she glanced down at the table. Then laughed to herself. "This is so weird. Why is it weird?"

"Because you killed my friends." I stared hard back at her. Anger stirred in me. "Because you hurt me."

She flinched, "Sheldon, I . . ."

You what? YOU WHAT? I yelled at her in my head, but said nothing. I waited as chains started to wind around my body, starting at my feet, then calves, then thighs. It wrapped around my waist, looping around my chair and worked its way around my shoulders, ending around my neck.

I was weighed down. I was trapped and bound.

That was how I was feeling as I waited for her to talk.

"I love you. You're my sister."

I almost started laughing. "That's it? That's what you say?"

"I don't know what you want me to say?"

I didn't either. I shook my head. "Why am I here?"

"I'm glad you are. I didn't think anyone would come, but," she hesitated, "how's Denton?"

Hurt. Angry. Devastated.

I was holding back. I couldn't do that anymore. As I gripped the phone tighter and cleared my throat, Mena raised her head. She knew something was coming and she was ready.

Oh, no, honey. You're not. I sneered at her then. "You want to know how your brother is?"

She opened her mouth to respond. I didn't give her a chance. I kept going, "You *destroyed* him. Acting like the broken man he is might've helped his career, but you ruined him. I have no idea if he'll ever come to see you. Hell," a bitter laugh came from me, "he couldn't believe I was coming here. You manipulated Marcus and turned him into a killer. I don't know if he would've been one without you, that's the sad part. I might not have killed someone if you hadn't been involved. I had friends who would still be alive. *Alive,* Mena. They aren't, and that's at your hand. You're a psychopath. And as I'm staring at you, you don't care. You have no remorse. You're just," I was gutted. Her eyes were beaming back at me. My words weren't making a difference. "A statue with a fucked-up moral compass. You're fucked-up."

I was done.

I started shaking my head and I looked down.

"No." She pressed her hand to the glass again. A whimper left her. "Sheldon."

I couldn't look at her anymore. I stared at her, but I wasn't seeing her. I was seeing Leisha behind her. Bailey. Grace. Guadalupe. Maria. Even Marcus. All their blood was on her, and she had done it because she loved me.

Their blood was on me.

Numb and cold, I hung up my phone. She was crying out through the glass, begging me to stay, but I turned deaf ears on her. Standing, I walked out with my heart ripping in half. Those people died because of me.

She had wrecked her brother, and as I left the prison, I knew she had shattered me as well.

Walking through the parking lot, I heard a wolf whistle and glanced up. Corrigan lifted two fingers in the air. "Yo, hot woman walking." He flashed me a cocky grin. He was standing outside his car, his arms spread out on both sides of him, holding onto his car and his legs were crossed at the ankles. With his green eyes and his golden brown hair that he'd cut recently, he looked like a movie star posing in a blockbuster ad. All thoughts of Mena fled, and I took in the rest of him. He was wearing designer jeans and a shirt that molded to his form, showing off his broad shoulders and his tapered waist. The wind kicked up then, riffling his shirt so it stuck to his form, and I glimpsed the six-pack I already knew was there.

Bryce had always been the athlete. His body was the most cut and was sculpted from his soccer training, but Corrigan was no slouch either. Since Mena's last attack, we'd both started running together. Whereas it made my legs feel like lead, it seemed to have transformed Corrigan into a lean machine. Knowing an answering grin was on my face, I started for him, and the closer I got, the more my mouth watered.

Corrigan was delicious.

As I stopped right in front of him, his eyes were holding mine, watching intently. He dropped his arms from his car to rest on my hips. He didn't pull me into him; he only held me. It was an intimate touch, and I shivered from the memory of this morning, how he had been so gentle as he made love to me. It had brought tears then, and I felt some tears threaten to spill again.

He murmured, "I'm trying to be dashing here to distract you from your sister."

I jerked my head up and down. My hand lifted to rest on his chest and I felt his cement-like strength there. I absorbed it because, to be honest, talking to Mena had taken some of my fight. "Thanks. I need that."

"Should I ask how it went or do you really want to be distracted?"

I lifted a shoulder. My eyes lingered on his lips. One touch from them and all feelings would be wiped away. He could make me forget. Bryce used to be able to do that. He was hot and passionate. He made everything disappear and melt away, but then it came back. It always came back, but it was different with Corrigan. Corrigan transformed the world for me. He lifted me up. He spun me around. He made the world look like a beautiful painting. I was craving that feeling again. He could make everything feel all right. Even Mena. Everything would be all right with her. I could handle it, if Corrigan was at my side.

"Sheldon?" His hand lifted to my cheek and he traced his thumb over my skin, a gentle caress.

I let out a soft sigh. "Have I told you lately how much I love you?"

The corner of his mouth lifted up. "Yes. This morning. I think you told all our neighbors, too."

I laughed and moved into him. Resting my forehead against his, I breathed out, "I do. I love you."

His voice dropped to a husky whisper. He said back, "I love you, too."

"You make me feel like a pansy-ass girl." I wrinkled my nose. "I was way more hardcore with Bryce. What the hell, Raimler? You're making me weak?" My tone was teasing, but my god, I was addicted to him. I think I always had been. A few words from Corrigan had always been needed to make me feel better.

He tightened his hold on my hip and jerked me farther against him, aligning our hips so there wasn't an inch of space between us. He leaned down and nipped at my lips, grinding into me. "If I do, then you do the opposite for me. Trust me, Jeneve, I'm rock hard right now."

I laughed and swept a hand down between us. He sucked in a breath as I slid my hand inside his jeans. I didn't go farther. I held my hand there, my fingers touching underneath his waistband, and I let them linger.

Corrigan laughed hoarsely. "Yep. I'm now like a rocket. Thanks, Jeneve."

Grazing his lips with mine, I teased, "Maybe we should head home and do something about that, huh?"

He groaned and pulled his lips back, but resting his forehead to mine, he looked at me, peering right into my eyes, his green eyes suddenly sober. "We have that dinner premiere thing tonight."

I let out a matching groan and lifted my head back. "For real?"

He nodded. "You promised Steele we'd go."

My hands lifted from him and raked through my hair. I shook my head. Corrigan's hand fell back to my hips. I said, "I totally forgot Denton was opening his restaurant tonight."

"Bryce is bringing his new girlfriend, too."

A litany of curses spewed from me then. "Way to really make me not want to go."

He laughed, his eyes scanning my face, then falling and resting on my lips. "Bryce said he really likes this one so you have to be nice to her."

I snorted. "Nope. No way. Once he finds a girl who can handle me, then maybe I'll give my approval. Until then, sorry, buddy. I'm not holding in my bitchiness so he can keep getting screwed by some weak-ass wannabe."

"Sheldon."

"Not going to happen." My eyes flashed in warning. "I'm protective of him. That'll never change. You know that." Bryce would always hold a special place in my heart. Corrigan knew this and understood this.

He said, "You've consistently started to get meaner and meaner to them since the first one."

I shrugged. I didn't care. Things had been tense and awkward during Mena's trial. There was supposed to have been time apart once my decision had been made known, but it hadn't happened.

Because of the trial and all the legalities since Bryce had been there when Corrigan flipped her wrist so she stabbed herself, the whole idea of giving the other person space from me hadn't happened. Instead, Corrigan and I figured out our new relationship only when Bryce wasn't around. When he was there, things had gone back to normal, how the three of us were all only friends. When the trial ended, Bryce did go away then and six months ago, he resurfaced with a new girl at his side. Corrigan and I ran into him by accident at Denton's newest movie premiere, but we should've known. Of course, Denton would invite Bryce, and of course, he would invite Corrigan and me. But seeing the model attached to Bryce's side had been hard at first.

Bryce was my first love. A new wave of sadness and grief came over me that night. I didn't love Bryce the way I loved Corrigan, but that had been another night when I started to relinquish my hold on him. He would find another girl. I knew this. He wasn't mine anymore, but it still stung at moments. Corrigan had pressed me when I grew quiet that night. I hadn't known how to talk about this with him. I was with him, but mourning another guy? But he understood. Corrigan always understood and he said to me that night, "Bryce is yours. He's mine, too. He's family. You let him go a long time ago, but you still care for him. You still love him. Those feelings, as strong as they were for you, won't disappear overnight. I'm still here, no matter what. I understand, Sheldon. It would be the same thing if you had chosen him. You wouldn't be able to stop loving me in one night. He would've understood that, too."

"It makes me the worst person in the world."

He pulled me to his chest and whispered, cradling my head to his shoulder, "It makes you a person who loved. That's all it does."

And the tears had started, but he was right. I didn't love Bryce the way I loved Corrigan, but releasing him took a while . . . The more girls he brought around us, the more territorial I grew, but I was to the point where I only wanted the right girl for him. If she wasn't worthy of him, she wasn't going to get him. I wouldn't let him have anyone less the best.

Hearing that he had another girl coming, I only gave Corrigan a smile. "We'll see how she handles me."

He shook his head, rolling his eyes, but he couldn't stop a grin. "You need to let him find the girl, not you."

"I just want to make sure she's good enough for him." My throat swelled. "He deserves the best."

Corrigan pulled me back to him, pressing a kiss to my forehead. He held me and whispered, "He'll find her."

Just like we have.

He didn't say the words, but I closed my eyes and thought them. My hand lifted to his arm and I held him back. He was right. Bryce would find his happily ever after, just like I had with Corrigan.

Then I snorted to myself.

Corrigan asked, "What?"

I pulled back, grinning at him. "You're my happily ever after." I snorted again. "Why does that make me want to curse?"

Corrigan rolled his eyes. "Because it's sappy and cheesy. It's all those mushy feelings you hate to acknowledge." His hand lifted and pressed against my chest, resting over my heart. "Because you're happy and you're scared to death to admit it?"

"Yeah." Those damn tears were coming back. I covered his hand with both of mine, my eyes holding his. "Goddamn, I love you."

His lip lifted in a tender smile. "I love you, too."

Always. Forever. Screw it—Corrigan was my fucking fairytale come true. Grabbing his shirt collar, I pressed my lips to his.

We were going to be late for Denton's restaurant opening.

THE END

WWW.TIJANSBOOKS.COM

A LETTER TO THE READER

To the reader,

This is such a hard letter for me to write, but I felt it was necessary and also because Jaded was so near and dear to my heart. One of the reasons this is so difficult is because this is my own goodbye to this series and the other is because I want you, the readers, to know that I feel for those who wanted Sheldon with Bryce. When I write my books, I usually send it off sporadically to get an idea of what people's reactions, but I didn't with this one. I had to keep it quiet because of the love triangle and who Sheldon chose so to be honest, I'm not sure how this book will really be received, but I knew that no matter the outcome, I had to write it from my heart.

I never wanted to write this love triangle. I really didn't. In my heart, Sheldon was with Bryce and that was who she would always end up with, but in the middle of Still Jaded, I realized there was a love triangle there whether I wanted it there or not. I remember the night I realized this. I got up and walked away from my computer. I was upset. I didn't want to do this to readers, but the connection Sheldon had with Corrigan couldn't be denied. I couldn't suppress it or write around it. I felt this would be a huge injustice to the characters in this series and a huge injustice to

Corrigan, who I respect so much as a character so...I wrote it. I wrote what was in my heart.

When I finished Still Jaded, Bryce was still Sheldon's first choice. I think this love triangle was a big reason why I kept putting off finishing Jaden. I wrote Jadeite and abandoned it. I didn't like what I was writing and then the first two chapters of Jaden were produced. I loved it. It was strong. It was Sheldon to the core, but again, I put it off. I think a part of this was because I had no idea who she would choose. I still thought she would be with her first love, Bryce, but I was so conflicted. I really had no idea and then my writing career took off and I was writing other books, but Jaden was always in the back of my mind (like how Davina Comes is too).

So I scheduled a pre-order for a year in advance and I knew I would have time to really mull over how this book was going to go. Well....I was an idiot. I have outlined this book eight different times and with eight different endings. Every time I tried to write Jaden and follow the outline, it wouldn't. Those characters had a mind of themselves so all those outlines were thrown into the trashcan.

The only thing I knew from the beginning was that Mena was the real stalker. That's it. It wasn't until I was half way done with Jaden that I knew who she had to choose. And I couldn't bring her to choose Bryce because I wasn't feeling it. In my heart, her love for Corrigan is a different type of love than what she had with Bryce. Corrigan makes Sheldon a better person. Bryce was her first love and a part of Sheldon will always love him in that way, but it wasn't the deep love she has for Corrigan. Corrigan is her future while Bryce was her past.

The other reason for this letter is because I love the Jaded series so much. This book was a big factor that gave me hope for a writing future. It kept me going. I wrote Jaded, Home Torn, and Sentiment Lost all at the same time in my life. It was when I had to decide if I was going to sacrifice a job with a stable income for a possible future in writing. To me, I felt like a coward. I felt that I was choosing to hide in my stories instead of being the 'adult' and stepping down a career path that would take me away from writing. When I commit, I give my whole heart and if I had chosen the other path, I would've given my whole heart and focus to it, and during that time when I had to make this decision, I remember writing a chapter of Jaded. I posted it to Fictionpress and I drove up to see some friends that evening. I checked my email that evening and saw a flood of comments. That was when I realized people were actually reading and they were invested in this story. I don't know if Jaded was the ultimate reason I chose to purse writing, but seeing that response was a factor that helped.

So with this letter, I just wanted to express that I really do feel for the Bryce shippers. I don't want you to feel that I wrote this and published, not giving a care. I do. I really do and all I can say is that I hope you still loved the story. I wrote this book for you guys and I hope you loved the journey as much as I did. Thank you from the very bottom of my heart!

Love, Tijan

ACKNOWLEDGMENTS

I have to thank my editor, The Word Maid, my proofreaders, Chris and Paige, and the few who read Jaden before I published it. Oh—thank you, Ami, for formatting Jaden for me!!! Thank you so much for your words of encouragement and also helping me so much! I already dedicated this book to Kerri and Lisa (I'll notify them that this is them since I'm only using first names), you two breathed new life into the Jaded Series and helped get my butt rolling on finishing the series. Then to all the Tijanettes in the fan group!!!! You guys have your own community in there. You're there for each other and also gush about all the books you guys read to each other. Thank you for all the support and encouragement everyone in that fan group has given me!

A special thank-you to all the readers who have followed me and loved Jaded from the Fictionpress days! Anyone who messages me and shares that they started following me from then always gives me such a great feeling. Just such a heartfelt thank you for sticking with me and also for loving these guys, even when I know there's a lot who don't understand Sheldon.

Like always, thanks to Jason and my puppy Bailey! Both are so cute and have no idea I thank them in my books!!

9 781951 771256